Praise for
The End of Men

"In 1995, I wrote a short story, *Baster*, inspired by some goings-on in my friend Karen Rinaldi's life. In 2003, that story, significantly altered, became the Jennifer Aniston movie *The Switch*. In 2016, another film, *Maggie's Plan* directed by Rebecca Miller, appeared, this time based partly on Rinaldi's unfinished novel about said events. And now, Rinaldi has finished that novel, creating yet another version, her own version. I knew it was a good idea the first time I heard it, but I had no inkling it would prove quite so fruitful. Given the subject matter, however, how could it be otherwise? Certainly, this is a story that keeps on giving."

—Jeffrey Eugenides

"With humor, bravery, and panache, Karen Rinaldi puts her finger straight on the tender conundrum of the female experience, where work, love, and motherhood intersect."

—Rebecca Miller, director of *Maggie's Plan*

"Karen Rinaldi's *The End of Men* is in every way marvelous. A sharply drawn story—or more accurately, stories—that gets everything right. Warmhearted but painfully close to the bone."

—Anthony Bourdain

"Cool and hot, sweet and sharp, *The End of Men* is a beguiling modern tale of four self-made women who are doing it their way, and the men who're along for the ride. I read it in one sitting, without checking my phone. A novel can't possibly come more highly recommended than that."

—Karen Karbo, author of *The Gospel According to Coco Chanel*

"I love all of the women in Rinaldi's novel—Isabel, Anna, Beth, Maggie. Having grown up in a world of women—women who compete with each other, love each other, mother together, navigate life together—I found it thrilling to read a book that is unapologetically about women and our intertwined lives and essential friendships."

—Elizabeth Lesser, bestselling author of
Broken Open and *Marrow*

"In Karen Rinaldi's coy and sprawling novel, men still matter. Only we see them through the eyes of four brilliant and fierce women for whom having it all is very much a work in progress. Anna, Beth, Isabel, and Maggie collectively are like the phases of the moon: hormonally, emotionally, and romantically attuned. Expertly woven together, their voices become a New York City tableau of marriage, children, life, death, careers, pregnancy tests, love, and, um, men."

—Betsy Lerner, author of *The Bridge Ladies*

THE
END
OF MEN

KAREN RINALDI

HARPER ● PERENNIAL

NEW YORK ● LONDON ● TORONTO ● SYDNEY ● NEW DELHI ● AUCKLAND

This is a work of fiction. Names, characters, places, and incidents are products of the author's imagination or are used fictitiously and are not to be construed as real. Any resemblance to actual events, locales, organizations, or persons, living or dead, is entirely coincidental.

HarperCollins books may be purchased for educational, business, or sales promotional use. For information please e-mail the Special Markets Department at SP-sales@harpercollins.com.

P.S.™ is a trademark of HarperCollins Publishers.

FIRST HARPER PERENNIAL EDITION

Designed by Leydiana Rodriguez

Library of Congress Cataloging-in-Publication Data has been applied for.

ISBN 978-0-06-256899-1 (pbk.)

17 18 19 20 21   LSC   10 9 8 7 6 5 4 3 2 1

For Rocco and Gio—the beginning of everything

Women are always better liked if we sacrifice ourselves for something bigger—and *something bigger* always means including men, even though *something bigger* for men doesn't usually mean including women.

—Gloria Steinem, *My Life on the Road*

Even if we're constantly tempted to lower our guard —out of love, or weariness, or sympathy, or kindness—we women shouldn't do it. We can lose from one moment to the next everything that we have achieved.

—Elena Ferrante, in an interview by Rachel Donadio,
New York Times, December 9, 2014

PART ONE

EARLY SUMMER

CHAPTER ONE

Isabel

NOW THAT ISABEL was pregnant, she knew what it felt like to be an eighteen-year-old boy. All she could think about was sex. Combined with morning sickness that began from the moment she awoke and continued throughout the day, Isabel wasn't sure from moment to moment whether she wanted to vomit or fuck.

She called her best friend, Beth: "I think I have gestational schizophrenia."

"Get used to it," she said. "This is just the beginning."

"This is not what they tell you to expect when you're expecting. Did you go through this?"

"Yes . . ." Isabel suspected she wasn't really listening at all, so Isabel was surprised when she continued. "Remember where I was, Is, when I was pregnant? No, sex wasn't on my mind." She paused. It wasn't unusual for Beth to be doing three things at once. "I gotta go," Beth finally said. "Call me later if you're still feeling like Sybil."

Isabel hung up the phone and checked her e-mail. A long list of blue messages on the screen called out for her attention. She cherry-picked the urgent ones and those from her husband, Sam, who was often away on business. His latest informed her that he was going to be stuck in Chicago for two more days on a case. In her extra-hormonal state, the news made her cry. Did she miss him, she wondered, or just want to get laid?

Her tears stopped when her boss, Larry Pond, the publisher of *Pink*, stuck his balding head around the door into her office.

"Isabel, come by my office at three. I want you to meet the candidate interviewing for the open position . . ."

Isabel tried to blink away her tears, but it was too late. Larry noticed and shifted nervously.

"Is everything all right?" Larry asked in one of the least sincere voices Isabel had ever heard. He looked down at his shoes.

Everyone around the office called Larry "the Turtle," partly because of his last name, but mostly because of the penis-like shape his head and neck formed together. Isabel couldn't decide if he was a wounded soul or just a dickhead. Even as she thought it, she saw Larry's eyes lift from his shoes and land on her breasts, now swollen from pregnancy and proudly displayed by the décolletage of her dress. The Turtle colored, then quickly turned and walked away.

A wave of nausea hit her. Isabel pushed away from her desk and glanced at her calendar, where she saw two meetings on opposite sides of town, one at four o'clock and another at five thirty.

She buzzed her assistant, Tina. "I feel like hell. Cancel my appointments for the rest of the day," she told her. "I'm going out for a smoothie. I'll be back in time for my three o'clock with Larry, but I'm going home afterward. If anyone needs me, I'll have my cell."

As associate publisher of *Pink*, a trendy women's fashion magazine, Isabel spent a lot of time wooing clients. But in the past week, it had been hard for her to find the energy to go on sales calls. Her first trimester was kicking her ass.

The smoothie joint was a favorite haunt of hers and the former publisher of the magazine, Christopher Bello. Isabel hadn't seen him since she'd become pregnant. She walked up Fifth Avenue, dreamily remembering the time, years ago, when she and Christopher had met during a January blizzard to pelt each other with snowballs.

He'd called her at home and commanded, "Corner of Commerce and Bedford. See you there in fifteen minutes," and hung up.

Isabel hadn't questioned why or considered not showing up for one minute. Instead, she had dutifully pulled on her shearling-lined boots, grabbed her goose-down coat, donned a red-and-white woolly pom-pom hat (she'd forgotten her gloves), and trudged through the snowy streets to meet her playmate.

It was late evening in Greenwich Village and the streets were eerily deserted, the constant din of New York City muffled by the blanket of snow that had been falling since morning. Determined to beat him there, Isabel ran as best she could in her cumbersome boots the whole way, only to be ambushed by Christopher from behind the moment she turned onto Commerce Street. He grabbed her around the waist, swung her around, and pulled her down into a six-foot mound of plowed snow. He lay on top of her, smiling his Cheshire cat smile while pinning her arms above her head.

"Hello," he said.

"Hiya, Chris," she said, making a feeble attempt to extricate herself from his hold.

In that moment of respite, she relaxed her body under him, which he took advantage of by shoveling handfuls of snow down the back of her coat.

"You. Mother. Fucker!" Isabel retaliated. She squirmed out of his grip and pushed his face into the still-soft snow. They rolled around like frenzied puppies until, breathless, they stopped to watch the snowfall swirling in the golden streetlamps. When Isabel's frozen hands began to ache, Christopher put each of her fingers into his mouth to warm them.

That was just a few months before she met her husband, Sam.

ISABEL JUMPED WHEN she heard her name spoken, though it was said almost too softly to hear through the noise of the city street. Christopher was sitting on a sidewalk bench, slurping from a large plastic cup.

"Christopher!" she shouted, overcompensating for her bewilderment at seeing him moments after she had been thinking about him.

"I was watching you walk from a block away. You look delicious. How are you?" He swept her into the air, kissing her on the lips. She was far from petite, and that his slight frame could lift her effortlessly made her giddy.

Isabel kissed him back and felt something move in her belly. *It's too soon to feel the baby kicking*, she thought, quickly stopping herself from thinking any further about it. After

Christopher put her down she grabbed his cup and took a long sip and handed it back to him. "Mmm . . . Avocado, pineapple, basil. Am I right?"

"Yep, but you missed the turmeric."

"My favorite! I was just going to get one myself. Come, walk with me, tell me what you've been up to. But first, I have to confess that I was just thinking about you and now here you are. Are you some kind of demon?" Part of her had always believed he was.

Christopher's eyes lit up. "I am just back from a Wicca conference in Maine," he admitted.

"Wicca?" Isabel asked.

"Yeah, you know, witches, sorcery. Not the Wicked Witch of the East stuff. This is the real thing. This weekend I was exploring being in dreaming . . ."

Last year he'd done Carlos Castaneda, now it was bubbling cauldrons. Christopher was always exploring some new discipline—Buddhism, Zoroastrianism—anything to occupy the time he had on his hands and all of it in an effort to rise above the masses. It was one of the least attractive parts of him, this tortured struggle to come to terms with his own humanity. Rocked by nausea and the surprise of seeing him, Isabel couldn't bear the thought of hearing about his latest effort to find himself.

"Please, don't tell me the details. I'm not sure I'll like you anymore if you do."

"Okay," he agreed easily. Christopher did have his charms. "Let's talk about you. So, how far along are you?"

She stopped short on the sidewalk and pushed him away from her. "What are you talking about?"

"I'm a demon, you said it yourself. Besides, I had a minute to watch you walk down the street. I couldn't help but notice your breasts. You've gone up a cup size or two, you haven't gained weight, and I know you didn't get implants."

Christopher's inscrutability often lulled Isabel into thinking that he wasn't paying attention, when in fact nothing went unnoticed with him. It was incredibly annoying—there was nowhere to hide.

"Almost three months and nobody knows yet. I don't want to tell anyone until after I have the amnio," Isabel told him.

Christopher smirked and looked away. The mention of the amnio was clearly one step further than he was willing to go, conjuring prospects of the messiness that life can bring.

"Please keep it to yourself," Isabel added, knowing it was a silly thing to ask. The fact of her pregnancy meant little to him—at least in the sense of how it affected *her* life. How or if he related at all to the prospect of her pending motherhood, she had no way of knowing.

They walked together silently for a few blocks. Isabel held on to his arm, leaning against him. No matter how long it'd been since they'd last seen each other, the pair quickly fell into an old pattern of contentious adoration. Theirs was a slippery connection, perhaps the reason it had continued as it did for so many years. Suddenly, Isabel felt light-headed and thought she was going to vomit.

"Chris, I need to find a bathroom . . . right now," she said. All color drained from her face.

Christopher slipped his arms under Isabel's to support her and led her into a Tibetan clothing store. "Excuse me," he said to the woman behind the counter. "Could my wife please use your bathroom? She's pregnant and not feeling very well."

He held Isabel's hair back as she vomited what was left of her breakfast and the few sips of Christopher's smoothie onto his Belgian loafers and into the sink.

When she stopped, he wiped her forehead and mouth with a handkerchief he'd soaked in cold water.

"You okay?" he asked.

"Fine, now. Thank you. Sorry about the shoes—they were very nice before I threw up on them." She felt weary and at that moment wished Sam was there to take care of her. "I think I'll pass on the smoothie and just get back to the office."

Christopher guided her out of the store and back outside. He raised his arm and signaled a taxi over to the curb. He opened the door for Isabel and then slid in next to her. "I was heading downtown myself; I'll drop you off."

Isabel rested her head on Christopher's shoulder and almost fell asleep in the few minutes' drive back to the office. He helped her out of the car and kissed her forehead good-bye. "Take care of yourself."

Isabel waved good-bye to Christopher as the car continued down Fifth Avenue. "See ya, Chris."

He was already a block away.

Waiting for the elevator to take her to her office on the eleventh floor, Isabel suddenly remembered her three o'clock meeting. She had just a few minutes to brush her teeth and push back against the nausea that remained and the exhaustion taking its place. Her doctor told her that she would feel better once her body finished building the placenta for the baby. But it wasn't the exhaustion that distracted Isabel—she'd worked through plenty of that before and for far less worthy reasons. No, her distraction manifested as a profound desire to retreat into herself, to spend time alone. It seemed counterintuitive to her that she should feel this way. Wasn't she, now that she was pregnant, supposed to need her man more than ever? When did the oxytocin kick in? The fact of the matter was she felt less needy and more self-contained than ever before. Isabel wondered if her shift inward was an instinctive protectiveness over her baby, or if it was in response to the belief that after the baby was born, her life would be in service to another.

At 3:05, Isabel rushed down the hall to the Turtle's corner office, furnished, predictably, in hideous executive chic. The Turtle had no personal style whatsoever and had merely insisted on the costliest collection in the catalog. The editor in chief had tried to give him some tips on how to personalize his office when he came on board, but the Turtle had asserted his authority by not listening in the slightest to anything she said. Hence the oversized cherry-veneer desk, straight-backed armchairs fashioned to force visitors to sit unnaturally, and brown-and-black-striped couch with enormous arm bolsters and hunting-themed matching pillows. The Turtle was sitting behind the needlessly large execu-desk without a piece of paper in sight. Isabel plopped herself down on the couch, not even pretending to feel fine.

The Turtle looked at her with raised eyebrows.

"Didn't you want me to meet the person you were interviewing?" she answered to his unspoken question.

"Oh, right, yes. Well, she arrived a bit early and already left. I didn't think she was right for the job," the Turtle told her as he shifted in his seat.

"Really? It's only a few minutes after three. That's an awfully quick interview," Isabel commented, mildly curious about what would inspire him to dismiss someone so quickly. "What was she like?"

"She was, um, I don't know . . . She didn't seem special," he responded. He laughed before continuing. "Besides, she just got married and I got the feeling she'd be looking to have a baby soon. I think we should hire women who are either too old to have children or too ugly to get knocked up—haha!"

Isabel choked on her own saliva in shock. "You've got to be kidding me, Larry! Did you really just say that?"

"Jesus, Isabel, I was just joking," the Turtle sputtered.

"Ask me my theory on jokes sometime," Isabel said, suddenly finding the energy to pop up off the couch, turn on a heel, and walk out the door.

Dickhead, she thought as she rushed down the hall toward her office. *He is definitely a dickhead.*

Tina waylaid her before she could get the door closed and handed her a dozen phone messages, mostly from accounts, one from her mother, and one from her sister, Anna. The Turtle's remark had given her a shot of adrenaline. Now that her appointments were canceled, she considered staying late to catch up on work, especially since Sam wasn't coming home.

Unable to shake the Turtle's remark, Isabel called Sam's cell, but he didn't pick up. Leaving a message, Isabel made sure she didn't betray any of the panic she was feeling. No point in worrying him. Then she dialed Anna's number at Red Hot Mama. Anna was the CFO of Beth's maternity clothing and lingerie company and they'd been going gangbusters lately.

"Hi, Anna, it's me. Do you think I can get fired because I'm pregnant?" Isabel asked the moment her sister answered.

"No, Issy, you can't. What put that idea in your head?"

"The Turtle just said that he only wanted to hire women who weren't going to be having children. Actually, he used the phrase 'too old or too ugly to get knocked up.' I had to run out of his office before I tossed it all over his couch."

"How is that man able to keep a job?"

"I don't know, but he scares me. Seriously, his comment seemed directed at me, but he can't possibly know I'm pregnant . . . Tell me I'm just hypersensitive right now."

"Don't worry," Anna reassured her. "The feeling that the world will no longer value you because you are going to be a mother will disappear once you realize that you'll get better at your job because the bullshit will become meaningless and will roll off your back. You'll become doubly efficient since your perspective will be clearer and you'll be able to make better decisions. Not having time to waste is an asset employers should value more. If the Turtle knew that, maybe he *would* want to fire you. Don't let him in on the secret; it'll scare the hell out of him."

Two years older than Isabel, Anna had already been where Isabel was heading. Of course, it drove Isabel crazy sometimes that Anna had an answer to everything. Still, while she often thought of Anna in terms of their childhood taunt, Miss Know-It-All, Isabel felt lucky to have her.

Isabel could hear chanting and yelling coming over from Anna's phone. It sounded like a rally. "Are the Hare Krishnas back in the hood? What's all that noise in the background?" Isabel asked.

"It's a hundred women shouting, 'What do we want?' 'Shut down Red Hot Mama!' 'When do we want it?' 'Now!' You can't make this shit up. I mean, it doesn't even have the right number of syllables! And it's all women—I can only see one guy. Anyway, the launch of our new line isn't going over so well with certain groups. It's been crazy here all day. Funny thing is, business has never been so good.

"Listen, I gotta run. I have a meeting with Beth. Come on over if you're feeling blue. We could use your input, especially as a woman in your condition. Love you, bye." Anna hung up.

Dialing her mother, Isabel hesitated, then hung up and decided to call her later. If she recounted the insult from the Turtle, her mother might use it to launch into a common harangue. Mama Ducci didn't fully understand why women today insisted on being and doing everything. She was especially tough on Anna, whose husband was a stay-at-home dad. Isabel didn't have the energy to argue on her sister's or her own behalf.

ISABEL LOOKED AT a few of the account reports for the month, trying to concentrate on work. Her inability to focus just made her more paranoid. "Maybe the Turtle is right," she wondered aloud. She rested her forehead on her folded arms to stem the return of nausea and the tears about to fall.

The hell with it, Isabel thought. She was just grabbing her jacket to leave for RHM when her phone rang. She waited for Tina to pick it up, then pressed the Tom button to privately listen in on who was calling. Isabel had named it the Tom button because she felt voyeuristic every time she used it.

She immediately recognized Christopher's voice, and she momentarily thought to ignore the call but found herself unmuting her end to say, "I'll take it, Tina."

"I just wanted to check up on you," Christopher said when he heard her voice.

"I'm fine now. I was distracted from my nausea when I was in the Turtle's office and he made disparaging comments about having babies."

"That's because evolutionarily speaking, he ought to be prohibited from procreating. His is a gene pool we'd all be better without. The man is not human." Christopher had had plenty of run-ins with the Turtle when he worked at *Pink*. The last laugh was on the Turtle when Christopher left the magazine, sullying the magazine's biggest account and putting the Turtle in a compromised position. It almost cost the Turtle his job, and he had yet to recover from the humiliation.

"Well, bumping into you was the highlight of my day. I'm just about to head over to Red Hot Mama. There's a big to-do about the new line Beth just launched. Apparently there are a lot of people who don't think pregnant women have the right to nice underwear," Isabel said, making a mental note to pick some up for herself while she was over there.

"Why not pick some up and meet me later?" Christopher suggested.

Isabel flinched but couldn't bring herself to acknowledge the coincidental remark aloud. "Be serious, Christopher. Listen, thanks for checking in. I'm going to go . . ."

"I was really calling to see if you wanted to come with me to see a play tonight. We can have dinner afterward."

"I'm not really up for it," she said. She didn't entirely trust herself to be alone with Christopher. Between her unfathom-able sexual agitation and unpredictable nausea, and Christo-pher's uncharacteristic attentiveness, she figured anything could happen—and none of it good.

"Please come. If the play sucks, we can leave. I'll even take you home early if you get too tired. I'll pick you up in front of Red Hot Mama at six."

"Fine," she said, surprising herself at how easily she had capitulated. "Sam's not coming home tonight anyway," she added, regretting it immediately.

"Good. See you soon."

Isabel tried Sam one more time and left him a message say-ing she wouldn't be home until later that evening. She didn't offer any more information on the message. She could tell him about it when he got home—knowing beforehand that she was with Christopher wouldn't make him feel any better about his extended stay.

RHM was located just a few blocks south of Isabel's of-fice. The storefront, framed in aluminum-cased windows, had a simple, modern vibe. The two floors above the store held the office space where Beth and Anna worked. Blue sawhorse police barricades were lined up in front of the building, and abandoned picket signs had been stuffed into the garbage can on the corner. The storefront's plate glass window was cracked and had been temporarily repaired with gaffer tape. The ac-rid smell from the burned lingerie lingered in the air. Inside the store, Beth sat in one of the modern but lush moss-green armchairs. She appeared to be sleeping. It was unusual to catch Beth in a moment of repose. The front door was locked, as a security measure during the protest. Isabel thought twice about disturbing her friend. She tapped lightly on the glass door and was surprised when Beth turned toward her. Seeing Isabel, Beth stood and smiled a welcoming smile as she walked over to open the door.

"Hey, Is. Wow, look how thick and beautiful your hair is." Beth stroked Isabel's long golden-brown hair. "Pregnancy agrees with you."

"Hey, sweetie. Looked like you were dreaming, sitting so still in the chair like you were. Are you upset about all this?" Isabel asked, sweeping her arms toward the debris.

"You mean the protest? Hell no! We'll get more media coverage than we could pay for in a year. No, I was on the phone with Paul earlier. His mother is harassing him again about being sick. He sounded like hell. He actually passed out when I was still talking to him. His sister, Helen, was there to take him to the hospital."

Beth took a deep breath and ran her hand through her short red hair.

"I wanted to meet them there, but Helen said that their mom doesn't want me around, that I'll just make the situation worse by showing up." Beth practically spat these last few words.

Paul Marchand was the father to Beth's daughter, Jessie. He'd been battling AIDS unsuccessfully for years and was often sick, in spite of the available treatments to combat the virus and its opportunistic infections. Beth had confided to Isabel that she was convinced he was trying to commit suicide through personal neglect.

"His mom still doesn't get it?"

"No, she still blames me for his illness, which makes no

sense whatsoever. You'd think she would have a clue between the pneumonia and KS. Anyway, all this mess"—Beth pointed to the store window—"this is very good news for us. Though I think your sister might be a little wigged out by the whole thing. You should talk to her."

"What do you mean?" Isabel asked.

"I'm not sure what's up with her. She seems a bit unhinged. Maybe it's the protests, but I think it might be something else," Beth said.

"Okay, I'll try to catch her upstairs. See you in a bit." Isabel went the back way up to the offices, where she found Anna behind the half-closed door of her office. She was putting her desk in order, getting ready to leave. When Isabel knocked, Anna was startled and let out a cry. Her hair was unkempt and there were dark circles under her eyes.

"Rough day, sis? You don't look so great," Isabel said affectionately as she fell into one of the purple Eames chairs across from Anna's desk.

"Yeah, it's been a crazy day. I'm just really beat. No news there. How're you feeling?" Anna asked.

"Sam's not coming home until Friday. I'm going to have dinner with Christopher." What would be a non sequitur in another exchange was logical progression in conversation between the sisters. "I bumped into him today and threw up all over his shoes. He guessed I was pregnant before that, though. My breasts gave it away. Then he calls this afternoon and asks me to a play. I'll never understand the man."

"He is adorable, though." Anna vocalized the completion to Isabel's thoughts. She was the only one who seemed to understand the pull between her sister and Christopher.

Anna's brow furrowed again, her mouth tightened. "I've got to get away from today's madness. I need to see my kids."

"Weren't you going to meet to strategize about the undie-haters?" Isabel asked.

"Yes, but Maggie just called and said she's got to take care of some crisis with her stepson, so we're going to meet early tomorrow morning instead."

A formidable triumvirate ran RHM: Beth Mack, Anna Ducci-Schwartz, and Maggie Harding, its publicity director and strategic consultant.

"Okay, little sis, see ya. Have fun tonight. And behave yourself."

"Oxymoronic, that," Isabel said as Anna kissed her on the nose, grabbed her purse, and left.

Isabel stuck around her sister's office for a few minutes. She sat in the desk chair and tried to see what Anna saw every day. There were photos of each of her boys as infants and a recent one of the two together, sitting inside a colorful Hoberman sphere, looking otherworldly and beautiful. Isabel wondered if having children made life more difficult or lent clarity to what was important. Isabel guessed the latter, but she still had some doubt.

She shook off the uncertainty and turned her focus to the wall outside Anna's office. Hung side by side were the two ads causing the protests earlier. The one featuring tennis star Agnes Seymour holding her newborn child was a stunner. Over her lactating breasts, she wore a sheer black nursing bra with black polka dots and silk lavender trim. The right breast flap lay open, suggesting a glimpse of an extended wet nipple just suckled by the baby. She had on matching thong underwear. She looked strong and sexy and ripe. The copy line read, WANT SILK?

The ad next to it featured film star Milly Ling, about six months along, wearing a teddy and shorts in sheer mauve with black Xs sewn into the fabric and black satin trim. The copy line read, DO YOU WANT YOUR MAMA?

Isabel laughed out loud. She had to admit that the ads were gutsy, though hardly raunchy. The collection was tasteful and elegant—hard to find, pregnant or not. *What a stroke of inspiration*, thought Isabel. *Leave it to Beth.*

Isabel had tried to bring in RHM ads to *Pink* at its inception. Discounted rates for new product launches provided incentive for retailers, and it made sense for the hottest women's magazine to have the exclusive first run. *Pink* presented itself as a progressive fashion magazine, but when the Turtle saw the ads he rejected them, saying the campaign would offend the other advertisers. Isabel took copies of the RHM ads along to her accounts to ask what they thought. Across the board, her clients went wild for them. Isabel tried to convince the Turtle that he was wrong to assume that they would lose advertisers if they went ahead, using her private research as proof. But the Turtle considered her action insubordinate and refused to discuss it any further. When Isabel told Beth, Anna, and Maggie about the Turtle's position on the ads, Maggie suggested taking it to the gossip pages. But in the end, Maggie thought better of it and told Isabel it would be too easy to trace back to her.

. . .

ISABEL RETURNED DOWNSTAIRS to find Beth now standing outside smoking a cigarette. She absentmindedly offered a drag to Isabel.

"I'll faint or vomit or both if I do," Isabel said, disappointed. "Can't wait to see what the Turtle has to say when he hears about all this on the news." Isabel pointed to the break in the storefront window and the barricades. "He'll be a self-satisfied prick for sure."

"We can always turn it back around on him by putting in a story about how *Pink* is aligned with these freaks against underwear by refusing to take our money to advertise in the magazine. Couldn't be good for the profile of the magazine. Just say the word. I won't have Maggie do it unless you feel okay about it, though." Beth's opportunism took a backseat only to her closest friends and her family. Anyone else was fair game.

Beth headed upstairs to her office, much to Isabel's relief. She wouldn't have to explain to her friend exactly where she was going and with whom. Moments later, Beth returned.

"What are you still doing here? I thought you left. Headed home now, do you . . ." Beth trailed off as she saw Christopher pull up in a taxi.

Beth looked at Isabel with a *what the fuck is he doing here?* look. Isabel knew that if she acknowledged Beth's silent question she might reveal more about what she was doing to Beth than Isabel knew herself. Beth was harder to fool than her own mother or shrink. Avoiding Beth's inquisitive stare, Isabel grabbed Christopher's hand and waved good-bye.

CHAPTER TWO

Anna

ANNA WAS STARTLED awake by a shooting pain in her right arm. She tried to move her left arm, but it had gone completely numb. It took a few seconds to assess the situation: her two young sons were attached to either side of her like Velcro. She reached over Henry, who was sleeping in the middle of the bed, for her husband, Jason.

"Baby," she whispered into the dark. "You there?"

Her hand fell onto a bunched-up pillow, used as a barrier to prevent Henry from falling over the edge of the bed should he squirm from Anna's grip in Jason's absence.

Anna tried to disentangle from her sons without waking them. "Oh, guys," Anna muttered. "We've got to stop sleeping like this."

Jostled awake by his mother's movements, Henry pushed himself up on his knees and held his face just an inch above his mother's. Anna inhaled his sweet, moist breath.

"Ba-ba," he articulated forcefully—he was hungry—before giving her his version of a good-morning kiss. He bumped his forehead against hers and smiled a wet baby smile, drooling onto his mother's cheek. He then pointed to his big brother, Oscar, still asleep on the other side of his mother with one small arm flung across her body. "Oh, oh."

"Shh, don't wake Oscar," Anna said without effect. "Let your brother sleep." As if a one-year-old would listen to reason. Henry proceeded to hit Oscar in the head with his warm palm, getting the desired response.

"Henry, I'm sleeping, don't do that," Oscar scolded. Then, "Mama, are you here?" A common rhetorical question from her three-year-old: he asked it only when he was wrapped around her.

"Yes, Oscar, I'm here."

"Are you staying home with me today?"

"No, sweetheart, I have to go to work, but I'll play with you this morning until I have to leave, okay?"

"I want Papa," Oscar responded, a tremble in his voice. He was going to start crying in a second.

Henry, growing impatient with the conversation, tried to throw himself off the bed. He couldn't quite navigate the three-foot drop, and Anna had to grab him by the back of his pajamas to help him down without landing on his head.

It was only five thirty in the morning and the entire family was already wide-awake.

Just then, Jason came in with milk for the boys and a steaming cup of coffee for his wife.

"When did you get up?" Anna asked, yawning. "I didn't even hear you."

"About an hour ago. I couldn't get back to sleep once Oscar came into bed."

Anna and Jason had given up on trying to discipline the boys about sleeping in their own beds. Each evening started out with the best intentions, but by morning either they were all asleep in the same bed, or Anna was with Oscar in his bed or in Henry's with him, or Jason was with either or neither, in which case Anna was with both in their bed. Sometimes the configuration changed several times in the course of a night. The first thing Anna did every morning when she woke up was to take inventory of who was where. This morning, they all stayed cuddled on the bed together and read books until Anna had to get up to take a shower.

"Okay, boys, I've got to get going." She kissed Henry's belly and Oscar's head and gave Jason a lingering one on the lips before crawling out from the messy bed and heading for the bathroom. It was one of the most difficult parts of her day, the moment when she had to physically pull away from her sons and husband.

Anna hurried through her shower to give herself a few more minutes with the boys. She was dressed in what Oscar called her "work clothes"—Anna was certain it was the first time Jil Sander was ever referred to as "work clothes." This morning she had on a sleeveless, formfitting dress in gunmetal gray with bright yellow piping. Her chestnut hair was held back with a sheer yellow scarf and her long legs were bare. Already sun-kissed from weekends outside with the boys, she put on some pale lipstick, a bit of mascara, and was ready to go, with an extra twenty minutes to spare. She found Jason and the boys blowing bubbles in the tiny backyard off the ground floor of their Brooklyn brownstone duplex.

"What're you guys doing?" Anna asked cheerily, hiding how glum she felt on this beautiful June morning. What she wouldn't give to put on her "play clothes" and hang out with her family all day.

"We're blowing bubbles with Papa," Oscar answered. "You go to work, Mama. Leave now."

"Okay, Oscar, Mama's going." Anna looked to Jason, who gave her a sympathetic smile. She hesitated before turning to leave.

"Go, now," Oscar repeated.

Henry was climbing onto his father's back and singing in an angelic high voice a monosyllabic version of "Twinkle, Twinkle, Little Star": "Ma-ma, ma-ma, ma ma ma . . ."

"Fine. Good-bye, boys, have a fun day!" Anna said, trying to hide how hurt she was. Waving to Jason, she turned toward the door, but returned to kiss each one of her boys before leaving. Oscar pushed her away. He wasn't making it easy this morning.

Anna took a deep breath as she walked away. Some mornings Anna had to use all her resolve just to leave the house.

When she got out of the subway in Manhattan, a voice mail from her husband pinged. She called him back.

"Are you okay?" Jason asked.

"Oh, yeah, you know . . ." Anna sighed to stop from crying, not so much from what had transpired this morning as from the call from her husband, who understood her so deeply. "I know what it's about. It's just uncanny how a three-year-old can cut to the heart like that. He's brutal."

"He doesn't know what he's saying, Anna. He certainly doesn't mean it. He loves you like crazy, you know that, right?"

Jason stating the obvious was comforting to Anna but made her want to cry even more.

"I'm fine, baby, really. Thanks for calling. I'll check in with you guys later." Anna clicked off.

She wondered what it was that made it impossible for her to get over leaving her family every morning. She knew plenty of mothers who couldn't wait to get out of the house for a break. It caused nothing but heartache for Anna every day when she left. And the strain was emotionally depleting her.

Blue barricades along the sidewalk in front of RHM blocked easy access to the store and the offices above. Anna pushed one aside and squeezed through. When she got to the door, she thought twice about it and she returned the barricade to its intended secure position.

Upstairs, a female police officer in riot gear examined a roster of all the employees at RHM as Beth's assistant handed the officer a cup of coffee.

"Good morning, Officer," Anna greeted her. "Do you expect the crowd to be violent?" Her attempt to sound casual failed as "violent" caught in her throat, making it come out as "violet."

"*Violet?* Not sure what you mean . . ." the officer said.

"No, sorry, Officer . . . I meant to say vio*lent* . . ."

"Ah . . . Well, there's no way to know for sure, but we need to be ready in case it does," she replied. Anna had expected more assurance than that.

Not ready to speak with anyone else yet, Anna retreated to her office with a cup of her favorite genmaicha tea. The day had barely started and she was ready for it to end. She couldn't wait to get back to the safe haven of her houseful of boys.

Before wallowing too long, Anna turned on her computer and flipped through her pile of phone messages. Beth would pop in soon, and she didn't want to seem depressed. Anna knew she was causing concern lately with those closest to her, and she couldn't bear to answer another question with an "Oh, I'm fine . . ." She didn't feel fine, far from it, but she didn't know how to ask for help either. It mortified her to complain about a life she had established for herself. She had resigned herself instead to figuring it out without burdening others. When she was honest with herself about it, Anna knew she couldn't bear to be anything less than in control. But lately she felt the opposite of in control.

Once she turned her attention to the first task of the day, tracking sales, she became distracted from that untethered feeling she'd been having lately. Work could always pull her out of herself. Now that she had made it to the office, the tasks in front of her were welcome distractions.

Anna was proud of her contribution to the success of RHM. As the company CFO, she helped Beth breakeven after year two and make a profit after year three while growing the business. Taking a risk to come on board as the fledging company's financial officer five years ago proved to be both lucrative and personally satisfying. She'd left the comforts and bureaucracy of a big corporate job where she was the US financial director for a large clothing manufacturer. She joined RHM as a start-up knowing she would be involved with almost every aspect of the business. Her role included chief operating officer, having learned the job on the ground out of sheer necessity.

Every company culture is a palimpsest of those at the

top, and RHM was no exception. Almost everyone who had started with the company and joined over the past five years was still there. Each employee received stock options and four weeks of paid vacation after year one. Supportive and flexible, RHM attracted a bright and creative staff of young people, mostly women. The only two people who left the company hadn't been able to function under pressure and within a certain level of chaos. The flip side of RHM's flexible and tolerant workplace was an expectation for the entrepreneurial spirit. With more work to do than people to do it all, when someone was not pulling their weight, Beth wasn't afraid to send them packing.

To build on RHM's early success, Anna was now exploring various opportunities for growth outside of RHM's line of lingerie. She had a meeting set up for ten o'clock with a start-up that developed toys by mothers for preschool children. Usually optimistic about her job, Anna wished she felt more ambitious on this particular morning. She checked her watch. "Damn, it's too late to cancel the appointment now," she muttered. "Oh, well . . ." Anna was sure she could fake her way to enthusiasm; it just took a bit more of the energy she felt wasn't there to spare.

At ten on the dot, Anna was buzzed for her meeting. A tall, attractive woman, midforties, with close-cropped salt-and-pepper hair and stylish reading glasses perched on her nose, strode into Anna's office wheeling a large red leather case. She held out her hand and introduced herself as Sharon Morgan. Anna took her hand and smiled: "Anna Ducci-Schwartz." She took a liking to Sharon immediately and relaxed into a productive discussion about approaches to toy development.

In keeping with the practical but provocative approach of RHM, Sharon presented progressive toys for newborns and toddlers meant to satisfy from a tactile point of view as well as to educate. Sharon noticed the picture of Henry and Oscar sitting inside the Hoberman sphere.

"Now that is the perfect toy! So beautiful, and a genius work of engineering! Have you ever seen the enormous one hanging at the Smithsonian?"

"Yes, I have . . . it's mind-blowing!" Anna smiled as she looked at the photo of her boys. "My husband is an architect, and I think he bought it more for himself than for the boys. They all play with it. Nothing makes my boys giggle more than when Jason closes the sphere around his head and pretends he can't get it off . . ."

Just then, Anna's personal cell phone rang, which meant Jason was calling. Anna kept two phones, reserving one for family calls in an attempt to draw some line between her home life and work life. She excused herself and walked out of her office to answer the call.

"Hey," Jason said, sounding excited. "We're calling from the park. Henry just said his first word. Hold on . . ."

Anna heard fumbling in the background as Jason tried to get Henry to repeat the word. She could hear him saying, "Tell Mama what you just saw in the sky, go ahead, say it, Henry, what flies in the sky?"

"Aa-plaa," Henry whispered.

"Airplane? Honey, did you see an airplane in the sky?" Anna encouraged him, but she heard the phone fall and figured Henry had thrown it on the ground.

Jason recovered it. "Did you get that? He said 'airplane.' A two-syllable first word—not bad, huh?" He was clearly excited, and Anna grinned from ear to ear, picturing her three boys palling around together.

Before Anna could answer, Beth walked by and pointed thumb and pinkie toward her ear and mouth, making the *call me* gesture before disappearing again.

Anna nodded and then heard, "Anna, are you there? Can you hear us?" It sounded like there was quite a bit of commotion at the playground.

"Yes, I hear you. Listen, I gotta go. I'm in the middle of a meeting. Kiss the boys for me. I'll call you later. Bye."

Anna returned to her office, where the woman from the toy company was packing her samples.

"I am so sorry for the interruption . . ." Anna told her.

"Not at all. I understand completely." She smiled, warm and knowing. "How old are your children?"

"Three and one."

"Oh, two little ones! Busy, huh?"

"There's no word for what I am." Anna sounded harsher than she intended. She smiled apologetically to make up for it.

"Ain't that the truth."

"You?"

"Fourteen, eleven, and nine. It gets easier. Well, sort of . . ." They both laughed.

"That's a relief," Anna said, not really believing it.

Anna didn't want to engage in one of those conversations about children, working mothers, exhaustion. Under normal circumstances she welcomed the camaraderie, but today she was afraid she might burst into tears or betray her ambivalence about working at all. She showed Sharon out of the office, and they parted with plans to continue discussions about a future partnership. When Anna returned to her desk she sat down heavily and heaved a big sigh, releasing the overwhelming urge to cry.

Distracted by the noise building outside her window, Anna stood up from her desk to look at the crowd of protestors gathered on the street below. Their chants were incoherent but vehement, shouted with fists punching the air for emphasis. Anna felt an irrational hatred for them.

"Go home, go home, go home," Anna whispered through the window, her forehead pressed against the slightly cool glass. Was she talking to herself or to those screaming on the sidewalk? It was what she wanted to do more than anything in the world. She simply wanted to go home.

"Damn, I forgot to call Beth," Anna said aloud as Beth appeared like magic, standing on the threshold of Anna's office. She was clearly excited by the commotion below.

"The fire department should be here any moment. Lucky us . . ." Beth was practically dancing in the doorway.

"Don't these people have anything better to do with their day?" Anna wondered aloud.

"Thank them, Anna. They will make our year, I promise!"

"Aren't you scared some nutjob is going to go postal? How can you not be worried?" Anna sounded a bit unhinged, even to herself.

"No, Anna, I really am not worried about it. And all the press about this is more promotion than we can afford to buy. I love these freaks out there doing our jobs for us."

Clearly exasperated by Anna's lack of enthusiasm, Beth

turned to leave. "Listen, Maggie is on her way here for a meeting in a bit. Stick around if you can so we can strategize. I'm going to watch the firemen do their thing . . ." she huffed before disappearing.

Anna felt sick to her stomach. She needed to get away from the chaos building around RHM. With Beth gone, Anna slipped out the side of the building through the delivery entrance. She headed toward a church a block away from the office that she visited whenever she needed a few minutes of solitude. She had been raised Catholic and attended Mass every Sunday as a child. She still found churches comforting and meditative, even if she no longer bought into the dogma that came with them.

The shouts of the protestors seemed to follow her—was there a wind carrying the voices in the direction she walked? As she stopped to track the sound, she spotted a rider getting out of a taxi right in front of her. Anna jumped in without a destination in mind, just to get away from the noise. It took a moment before she knew where she wanted to go.

"Please take me to the Metropolitan Museum of Art, Eighty-First and Fifth," she told the driver.

When Anna had first come to Manhattan, she'd lived in a cramped studio apartment and the Met had become an extension of her home. She'd found solace in its grandeur, where she could wander alone for hours through the galleries. Getting lost in the museum helped her to get lost in her thoughts. She'd worked out many conflicts over the years surrounded by the great art and artifacts of the museum. The sheer size of the collections and the histories they held helped Anna to put her conflicts in perspective. She always left the museum with a renewed sense of scale about whatever it was that ailed her.

The fine early-summer weather kept visitors away, and Anna enjoyed the relative vacancy of the museum. She roamed the galleries, looking for the quietest parts of the building, and found herself wandering among the collections of Greek and Roman art. As Anna slowly strolled past a sculpture of the Hellenistic period, her attention was captured by a bronze of sleeping Eros. Depicted as a plump baby of twelve months or so, Eros had his right arm resting across his body. So tender and lifelike in his repose, the sculpture made Anna smile at the thought of Oscar and Henry, likely home now and napping after their playtime in the park.

The feeling didn't last. When she calculated the cost of her impulsive trip to the Met, it was time away from her boys. An hour spent seeking solace meant fewer moments with them, squandering the precious little time that she had. Ann's mood darkened again. Suddenly she saw in Eros not a sleeping child but something that turned her cold with fear. In that moment, Eros seemed in permanent repose. His eyes would never open.

Anna inhaled quickly and her breath caught in her throat, then turned to find her way out of the museum. She wanted to get back to the office, where she could complete the work of the day and return home to her boys.

Anna stood on the sidewalk outside the museum for a few moments to regain her composure, feeling slightly dizzy. She scolded herself for succumbing to terrifying thoughts: "What is wrong with me? Am I going mad? Maybe I need some lunch before heading back to the office." She said all this aloud to herself, suddenly feeling self-conscious and a bit kooky. She grabbed a spinach knish from the street vendor outside the museum and hailed a taxi back to the office.

When she got back to RHM, there were three voice mails from Beth of escalating intensity. In the last, Beth sounded furious: *"Where the fuck are you, Anna? I need to talk to you now! Call me back as soon as you get this."*

Beth's tone startled Anna back into work mode. When Anna dialed Beth's number, she was relieved to hear from Sacha that she wasn't at her desk. Anna didn't want to talk to Beth—or anyone at the moment—and for some reason, this made Anna start to cry.

Previous to Oscar's birth, Anna had considered herself emotionally even-keeled, at least relatively speaking. But the moment Oscar emerged from her body, a dam of feelings burst open. She'd never felt the kind of paralyzing fear she now struggled to push out of her dark fantasies. Oscar's birth pierced her heart in such a way that she understood dread for the first time. She'd called her mother the day after Oscar was born when it dawned on her that her life had changed irrevocably. She wasn't sure she was so happy about it.

"Mom, this is terrible. You didn't tell me it was going to be like this."

"What, Anna?" her mother asked. "Going to be like what?"

"That loving him like this would be a kind of terror. I love him so much, I'm going to spend the rest of my life worrying about him."

"Welcome to motherhood, honey. Do you think your father and I ever stop worrying about you and Isabel and Bobby? Never." She could barely hide the satisfaction in her voice. "You'll get used to it. Strange to say, but true."

"I don't want to live this way," Anna protested.

"Too late, honey. Anyway, it's worth it, you're worth it. Oscar is worth it."

IN THE PREDAWN hours of the day following her visit to the Met, Anna awoke to an odd sensation. She'd slept fitfully throughout the night between Henry's cries from teething pain. At first she thought, incomprehensibly, that she'd wet the bed, until she touched between her legs and felt the unmistakable stickiness of blood. *That's odd*, she thought. She wasn't due for her period. The boys were, miraculously, still in their bedroom. She pulled herself out of bed and into the bathroom. Sitting on the toilet, drops of blood fell into the bowl.

She'd been gone from bed for a while when Jason tapped on the door. "Hey, baby," he whispered. "Are you okay? Can I come in?"

"Yes," she whispered back.

"What's going on?" Jason asked, leaning against the door-jamb, stifling a yawn.

"I'm bleeding a little and my period's not due for another ten days or so."

"Are you in any pain?" Jason asked, as if he would be able to diagnose the problem.

"No, I don't feel anything. I'll call the doctor later this morning. Go back to bed. I'll be there in a minute."

Anna sat on the toilet for a few sleepy moments. She welcomed the quiet of the house and the unusual moment of peace. Oscar and Henry didn't give her a single moment of privacy during their waking hours. They barged into the bathroom despite her entreaties for them to keep out. She could latch the door, but she couldn't bear shutting them out so definitively.

"Mama," Oscar had asked once while watching her take a tampon from the box, "are you going to put that in your bagina? You don't have a penis? You have a bagina?" She ached with love for her curious boy. Certain words she didn't have the heart to correct.

Later that morning, after talking to her doctor, Anna took a pregnancy test. The results were negative, much to her relief but also to her disappointment. When her period failed to arrive on schedule two weeks later, she locked herself in the bathroom and stayed seated on the toilet as she watched the test strip turn pink. Tears of both joy and sorrow streamed down Anna's face as she decided she would keep the news to herself until she was certain she could hold on to this pregnancy.

When she'd become pregnant with Oscar and Henry, she'd told her family right away. But now, all reason aside, Anna feared that the schism she felt in her life would manifest physically somehow. Her hold over this conception felt tenuous. She decided she wouldn't even tell Jason, as though by remaining silent she might prevent the worst from happening.

"ANNA, ARE YOU sure you're not pregnant?" Jason asked her a week later. "Your breasts look like your pregnant breasts." He gently held both in his hands as she straddled him with her long, thin legs and let her hair drape across her face. "Move your hair and let me see those gorgeous eyes."

"Shh," Anna quieted him as she flipped her hair to the side and put a finger to her husband's lips.

They didn't get much alone time, and Anna didn't want to lose the opportunity. The boys had been put to sleep in their own beds for a change, so Anna and Jason had theirs all to themselves. Still, their bedroom was nearby and they woke easily. Oscar especially possessed uncanny extra-human radar. Whenever his parents so much as began kissing, he would awake from his sleep and yell, "Mama, I want you!"

Anna moved slowly up and down above Jason. She braced her weight with her arms, keeping him inside her just to the very tip and then pushing down fully against him, so he filled her completely. She rose above him again, again, again, her eyes closed in sensual meditation.

Jason persisted. "Anna, seriously, you've been in a peculiar mood lately. What's up?"

She stopped moving and opened her eyes, looking down at him. "Yes, I am pregnant," she said without joy. "I'm pregnant and I feel like shit and I feel like I'm going to lose the baby because my life is so screwed up right now!"

Anna rolled off her husband and curled up on the bed next to him. She began sobbing silently. The words "my life" echoed in Anna's ears, leaving her painfully aware that she didn't include her husband or children in her current predicament.

"Hey, hey, this is good news. Why didn't you tell me? Didn't you think I'd be happy about it?" Jason was smiling broadly, and Anna could see how happy he was about it. This made her only more upset.

"Jason, what are we going to do with three? I can barely handle the job with two kids. Three is going to put me under. And now more than ever I have to keep my job, or how else can we afford it?" Tears ran down Anna's face.

Jason took Anna's shoulders and tried to get Anna to look at him, but she turned her head away. "Baby, one more kid isn't going to put us under. We'll be fine."

"*You'll* be fine, Jason." Anna turned back to look directly into Jason's eyes as anger overtook her tears. "*You* don't have to leave the house every day to go to a job. *You're* not the one who worries about whether the nanny, and the mortgage, and the 529 plans are paid in full each month. *You* won't have to work through nine months of pregnancy. *You* will be fine. *I*, however, will not be fine. And I don't even know what I'm saying, because more than anything else, I want another child. I just don't know if I can handle it all." She broke down again into sobs.

Jason pulled her toward him and wrapped his arms around her body and buried his face in her neck. "Anna, listen, if you don't want to work anymore, let's talk about what we can do. I'm sure we can find a solution." Jason's tone was calm.

"Jason, you don't make any money. What do we do for money if I don't work? What do we do for health insurance? Seriously, what could we possibly do?" She didn't mean to say it with contempt, but she heard the words come out thick with it. "Do you even know how much money we spend every month? You don't. You're so preoccupied with your drawings that you don't take a minute to think about the household income, much less how you could contribute to it."

"That's not true, Anna. I do think about it. I've got a lot of different projects going right now; one of them is sure to pay off." His voice had a hard edge to it now.

"What payoff? Have you ever done the math? It'll take three of your projects seen to completion just to get you out of debt. And that's only if they all go through. By the time they're finished, you'll have so much more debt that you won't be any further along. If I don't work, we lose everything. Money isn't magic, Jason, it doesn't come because you need it. Why do I even have to say these things to you?"

"I'm not a fool, Anna. Of course I understand the situation. I don't plan on being broke forever. I really believe that the work I do will give us a payday." Jason's voice had suddenly grown tired. Anna knew this conversation cost him, but she did nothing to make it otherwise. He continued: "But if you're going to make me say it, yes, until then, we depend on you to make the living for the family."

"So how do we pay the rent then, Jason, if I don't work? Admit it, I have no choice."

"But you can't say that you work only to make money for the family, because that is only part of it. You love it, Anna. You work for you, and you know that. I'm not saying that it isn't difficult; I'm saying that it isn't as simple as you make it sound."

Anna knew there was truth to what Jason was saying, but that didn't mitigate the resentment she was feeling toward her husband. Her mother had made the same point to her months earlier. Anna and Isabel had been clearing the table after a Ducci family dinner when Marie, Mama Ducci, suggested, "Anna, you look tired. Go take a break. Isabel and I can take care of the dishes. Jason can watch the boys for a few minutes."

"Don't be ridiculous, Ma, I'm fine. Certainly fine enough to clean up after dinner," Anna argued.

"You do too much. Go rest," Marie insisted.

"Not doing the dishes is not the rest I need," Anna said, taking the bait and regretting it immediately.

"Boy, oh boy, men have it made these days . . . you do it all, don't you? No, Anna, what you need is more help at home." Marie landed the point in a self-satisfied tone.

"Don't tell me what I need!" Anna hated being so predictably defensive.

Her mother's expression grew serious as she stood in front of Anna and grabbed her hands. "Sometimes you have to admit that you need some help. Don't wait until it's too late."

Anna shook her mother's hands away. "Too late for what? What the fuck is that supposed to mean?"

Isabel stepped in before it got too ugly. "Enough bickering from you two. I need help with these pots and pans."

Anna had a hard time making her mother understand that Jason was not the problem. One of the many things Anna loved about her husband from the very beginning was his willingness to shoulder his share of the domestic duties. Jason didn't have macho issues and was not averse to the work historically allotted to the mislabeled "gentler" sex. He'd just as soon wear an apron as a tool belt, or take the boys to the park as chair a board meeting. Anna had never met anyone like him before. She knew all this in her heart, knew that one of the reasons she could stand to be with Jason was that he gave her the room to fully develop outside of their life together. Every other man Anna had ever known couldn't bear, in the end, that Anna had a life apart from the one they shared. Jason was different.

"Jason, I feel crazy right now, and I don't think it's because of the raging hormones of early pregnancy." Anna was speaking calmly again. "I feel like I have to—that we have to—make a change, and I can't imagine what that would be. I'm scared that I'm just going to stop—stop being able to pick up my children when they cry, stop being able to smile at them, stop being able to appreciate what you and I have together."

CHAPTER THREE

Beth

BETH PEERED DOWN from her office window at the protestors crowding the length of the block. Momentarily doubtful that they could exist this late in human development, she
checked her desk calendar as if it might provide a clue. Having
confirmed that the twenty-first century had indeed arrived—
but had not improved her understanding of why people still
behaved with such vehement ignorance this far along in so
called civilization—Beth registered the date, June 21. It was
eight years ago to the day that she had found out that her husband was HIV positive. She had witnessed his slow decline
ever since. While advances in education and medicine had finally made inroads to controlling the virus, all this had done
for Beth's now ex-husband, Paul, was to give him a false sense
of safety he worked hard to maintain.

Beth's phone lit up with calls. She ignored them, letting her
assistant intercept the barrage, and picked up the open line to
call Maggie, her head of PR. "Maggie, remind me not to get
out of bed on this date in the future." She was referring to
the situation with Paul and the one at hand, but then thought

better about opening up that subject. It would waste precious time neither of them had at the moment.

"Sure thing. Hang on a sec, Beth. Lily just emptied an entire box of Rice Krispies into the toilet, including the box, and I'm trying to fish it out of the bowl . . . Okay, tell me, what's up?"

Beth switched her attention to the more immediate crisis and gave Maggie a quick breakdown of the situation developing outside the office. "Can all these people really have such a problem with underwear? They're worse than animal rights activists. Anyway, I'm sure this is all good for us, so no reason to complain about it, right?" Beth was more amused than annoyed.

The new line of lingerie for pregnant and lactating women was selling 50 percent faster than they had forecasted. In the past month, overall sales had shot through the roof with the launch of RHM's first two print ads, reproduced and displayed in larger-than-life-sized backlit boxes in the storefront windows and strategically placed around the city and on billboards along local highways. The madness of the day proved the ads had touched a nerve—activists from both sides of the aisle were going nuts. The public display of sheer nursing bras and oversized lacy thongs for women in their third trimester had apparently sent people reeling. Beth wondered if it was the products themselves that were considered offensive or that RHM had enlisted America's sweetheart, tennis pro Agnes Seymour, to model the pieces while nursing her newborn.

Beth railed against the mob below for a few minutes as Maggie listened patiently on the other end of the line.

"Are you ready to get all of this down?" Beth had finished with her tirade and had moved on to discuss the specifics.

A masterful multitasker, Maggie was ready.

"Okay, so we've got Page Six and the *Times* trying to interview me and Seymour," Beth said, her voice a staccato of excitement. "*New York* magazine wants to do a story on RHM. Can you handle them, or do you want me to?"

Sacha popped into Beth's office to give her an update, which made Beth hoot with delight.

"Apparently CNN is already on the street interviewing the protestors, and the fire department is on the way. They're burning our nursing bras out there—how is that even possible?!"

Maggie jumped in. "I'll take the print, since I can do that by phone. You hang on for the cameras and the fire department. Try to be neutral—don't fan those flames if you can help it," she warned Beth. "Let's allow the story to play out a bit. I'll be there in an hour."

Beth knew that Maggie's plans to make it over to RHM were less than realistic. She always had the best intentions, but her life at home was all chaos all the time.

Sacha buzzed in. "Jessie is on line three."

The one person to get through at any time and under any circumstances was Beth's daughter, Jessie.

"Maggie, hold on for a minute, I've got Jessie on the other line . . ." Beth switched lines. "Hi, sweetheart. What's up?"

"I'm here with Hanna doing my homework," Jessie said in a quiet voice that gave away her concern for what followed. "Paul just called and he sounded funny. It was weird. It was like he couldn't breathe. He was looking for you. Do you think he's okay?"

"I don't know, honey, but I'll call him from here," Beth

tried to reassure her. "Don't worry . . . Listen, things are a little hectic today at the office, so I might be home a little later than usual. It won't be too late, around seven thirty or eight. If you get hungry, have something with Hanna. You don't have to wait for me. Okay? I love you."

Beth made it a habit to be home no later than 6:30 P.M. so she and Jessie could have dinner and still have time together before Jessie's bedtime. Most nights, once Jessie was tucked in, Beth worked in her home office between 9:00 and 11:00 P.M. The days were long but doable. Provided that she had time with her daughter, everything felt manageable.

"But, Mom, Paul's voice scared me," Jessie said, near tears.

"Oh, honey, I'm sorry you're scared. I promise I will call him right away and that everything will be fine," Beth lied, even though she was certain Jessie knew it was a lie.

Beth hung up with Jessie and picked up the line where Maggie was on hold, but she was no longer there. They didn't have to properly finish the conversation for Beth to know Maggie would already be on the case.

Beth went back to the window. She heard the sirens heading her way when Sacha buzzed in again: "Isabel is on line one."

If anyone else besides Jessie got through to Beth, it was Isabel. They'd met in college after a year of circling each other suspiciously and bonded, finally, over the contempt they shared for their sorority sisters. Beth and Isabel had been inseparable ever since. Their lives often veered dangerously close to each other's.

One night in particular had solidified their friendship, occurring during graduation week at their midwestern college, on a particularly drunken evening when families of both graduates were visiting the campus to celebrate. Beth's father was in between wives two and three (there would be five in total), and Isabel's brother was just finishing medical school. Beth and Isabel were manic with end-of-college festivities. They'd been living on fumes for the past few weeks and their respective families seemed to catch a contact high.

Isabel's parents peeled off after dinner to go back to their hotel. Anna was away at a conference and unable to make it. So Beth and Isabel's brother, Bobby, and Isabel and Beth's father, Albert, made two odd couples as they headed downtown to a dance club. The night was a blur, though Beth did remember her father telling her at one point in the drunken evening that he wanted to take Isabel back to St. Louis, buy her a cello, and give her cello lessons.

"But, Dad," Beth told him, "Isabel wants to live in New York City and she has no interest in playing the cello."

Beth also overheard her father, the head of the university's obstetrics and gynecology department, tell Isabel that he knew every nerve ending in her pelvis. He was a bit eccentric, old Al.

Bobby fell hard and fast for Beth, a petite but strong-limbed and equally strong-willed redhead with a spray of freckles across her nose and the body of a young boy—narrow hips and waist—but with perfectly formed small breasts that needed no bra to stand firm. She managed to be cute and dangerous at the same time. Bobby wouldn't be the first or last to fall at the small, elegant feet of Beth Mack.

The morning after the debauched evening, Isabel crawled into bed with Beth. Bobby had left just an hour before to slink back to his hotel room.

"So, who cuffed who?" Isabel lifted the handcuffs off the bed frame and let them clang against it.

Beth, barely awake, muttered, "Does it matter? The real question is whether I should call you Mom or Auntie Isabel. You first. What happened with Big Ole Albert? I stopped paying attention when I saw his tongue in your mouth . . ."

Isabel considered the implication for a foggy, hungover moment before catching on.

"Oh, ugh, Beth . . . *Gross!* That must have been too weird for you to see me kissing your dad. Jesus, Beth. I made out with your dad—what the fuck . . . ?"

They both fell out of bed laughing. Beth was relieved when Isabel, struggling to shine some light on the recesses of her intoxicated mind, realized that Big Al's seduction stopped at the kissing stage.

"How did you stop him?" Beth had to ask.

"I told him I didn't want to cheat on my girlfriend. It puzzled him enough to make him stop cold. I think I successfully scared him away."

"You clearly don't know my father."

"Yeah, well, I intended him to think it was you I was talking about. That was my stroke of brilliant inebriated logic in the heat of the moment . . . He can't be that fucked-up, can he?"

"I don't even want to think about it!"

The two friends, still on the floor, lay silently for a few minutes, partly reeling from the moment and partly because they were both still a little drunk. It was going to be a wretched day.

"So, what about you?" Isabel asked. "Don't tell me you might be carrying my brother's child."

"I get pregnant if someone smiles at me when I am ovulating. I'm afraid we didn't use any protection and my ovaries feel like monkeys are hanging off them." Beth wrinkled her nose and scrunched her eyes shut to push away the thoughts of an unwelcome pregnancy. "How stupid am I? Let's hope your brother and I are not a fertile pair."

Exhausted from the festivities of the night before, they climbed back into the bed and snuggled under Beth's comforter. They slept through most of the morning in each other's arms until Isabel snuck out and returned with supersized hot coffees and McMuffins—hangover food of the gods.

Five weeks later, Beth and Isabel traveled back to downtown Columbus, this time to the Planned Parenthood clinic where Isabel held her hand the whole way through the termination. Beth never told Bobby about it.

Beth and Isabel continued to help each other out of jams in the years that followed college. They covered for each other when necessary, and for a few years when they first arrived in New York postcollege, it was necessary on many occasions.

THE SOUND OF the protestors was muted but audible from Beth's third-floor office. Beth picked up the line where Isabel was on hold, "Hey, Is, how're you feeling?"

"I think I have gestational schizophrenia," Isabel said without saying hello.

"Get used to it. This is just the beginning." Beth was only half paying attention, since her phone continued to ring and Sacha continued to barge into her office, giving her updates about what was happening on the street. She told Isabel that this wasn't a good time to talk. They stayed on the phone for only a minute or two, as opposed to their usual twenty-minute riffs.

Part of Beth wanted to get in the mix with the protestors, to meet them face-to-face, talk to them, ask them *what the fuck* they could be thinking. Would that be dangerous? Would it just make for an ugly media story? Her mind flip-flopped about what to do. Too agitated to sit in her office or answer any of her calls, Beth got up and headed for Anna's office.

Anna was standing at the window and seemed to be talking to herself.

"The fire department should be here any moment. Lucky us . . ." Beth was making some calculated decision based on what she'd just observed.

"Don't these people have anything better to do with their day?" Anna whined.

"Thank them, Anna. They will make our year, I promise!"

"Aren't you scared that some nutjob is going to go postal?"

"No, Anna, I really am not worried about it. And all the press about this is more than we can afford to buy. I love these freaks out there doing our jobs for us." Beth could turn almost anything to her advantage, and she knew Anna admired her for it, even as she was appalled by it. Beth was okay with that.

"Listen, Maggie is on her way here for a meeting in a bit. Stick around if you can so we can strategize. I'm going to watch the firemen do their thing . . ." Beth left the offices and headed downstairs to watch the drama unfold.

As she walked through the store she heard a loud thud and glanced up to see something bouncing off the storefront window. The plate glass cracked down the middle.

"They hate our underwear and wear wooden shoes . . ."

Beth said aloud as if it were the beginning of a common nursery rhyme. It was a game she sometimes played with Jessie. After what she'd been through with Paul, all of this was child's play.

Beth surveyed the store, which looked a little worse for wear. She'd sent the saleswomen home in case things got ugly, so the store was empty and quiet compared with the ruckus outside. Beth had considered the possibility of violence, but she didn't want to admit so much to Anna. Since they had to close the shop, they had lost an entire day's business. Still, Beth was certain they'd more than make up for it online. With all the attention the controversy was causing, sales would skyrocket. This was all working out fine as far as Beth was concerned.

She took a long, slow breath, resolved that all was for the good. With one last scan of the store, her eyes rested on a tear sheet of one of the Agnes Seymour magazine print ads lying on the counter by the register. It was wrinkled and torn at the edges, and at first Beth figured the ad had gotten caught in the melee of the day. She picked up the page to discard it in the trash bin but froze when she saw that someone had torn holes in the paper where Agnes's eyes and breasts had been and there was a target drawn with heavy black marker across her belly. An arrow pierced her infant's heart and horns had been drawn atop his head.

"What the fuck?" Beth said aloud. She crumbled up the page and threw it in the trash can with a frisson of understanding that it was an angry world out there. Beth tried to shake off the incident. *What a fucking day . . .* she thought, and then, *Oh, damn, I forgot to call Paul.*

She picked up the store phone and dialed Paul's number.

"Paul, hi, it's me, Beth. Jessie said you'd called at home . . ." She was speaking into his machine when she heard someone fumble with the phone in an attempt to answer it.

"Hey . . . hi," an unrecognizable voice, labored and raspy, said on the other line.

"Who is this?" Beth asked.

"Beth, it's me." Paul could barely get out a few words without stopping to take a long, slow breath. He sounded like he was drowning in air. "How are you?"

"How am I? Paul, what is going on?" Beth had talked to him a week earlier and he'd sounded fine. His health wasn't great, but he didn't sound like an iron lung.

"I think I have pneumonia again . . ." A weak inhalation followed before he managed to squeeze out, "I'll probably be headed back to the hospital soon."

Beth breathed heavily into the receiver as if to lend her breath to him. That he wasn't in the hospital already made Beth truly angry for the first time today.

"I spoke with my mom earlier," Paul continued. "She told me that I was supposed to"—he took another long intake of breath—"take care of her in her old age." His voice broke. "She also said that she knows she will go to heaven and she doubts she will ever see me there." Paul was barely able to finish the sentence for the lack of oxygen he was unable to pull into his lungs.

"Paul, just stay away from her. The last thing you need her to do right now is make you feel guilty for dying, for Christ's sake! Can't you ask Helen to keep her away?"

Helen was Paul's sister and the only one in his immediate family with the slightest clue about the real cause of Paul's failing health. His mother tried to convince herself that her son had some unidentified chronic illness because he worked so hard and because Beth had left him with a broken heart. Her mean-spirited response to his decline told Beth that his mom knew better, but keeping the lie alive that her son wasn't gay made her self-righteous. So much for the strength of the Christian spirit. Paul could rest assured that his mother prayed for his soul every day, but she would do nothing to soothe his flesh and blood suffering on earth.

Paul was silent for too long, and Beth thought maybe he had fallen asleep. Then she heard him pull a slow, painful breath. "Beth, why did you leave me?"

Conversations with Paul over the years inevitably veered toward this question, more so lately than ever before. She had never really understood the power of denial—the word was tossed around so cavalierly—until she realized that Paul truly didn't understand why she'd left him. He had never even admitted his homosexuality to her. In many ways this broke her heart more than anything else.

"Oh, Paul, please don't ask me to go there. I loved you. I still love you. What can I do to help you now?"

Paul wasn't responding. Beth could tell he was still on the phone only because of the heavy rasping noise his breathing made.

"Paul, Paul, are you there? Please answer me." Beth heard the phone crash to the floor. She hung up and called 911. Then she dialed Helen's cell phone. When Helen answered, Beth realized that she was there with Paul. She could hear sirens in the background.

"Helen, what is going on?"

"We're on our way to the hospital. I'll call you later," Helen said. She was crying.

"I'll meet you there."

"No, Beth, please don't. Mom will be there, and she doesn't want to see you. I'm sorry. Please, just wait for me to call you," and she hung up the phone.

Beth stood for a moment considering her options. Should she bully her way into the hospital or respect Paul's mother's wishes?

"When will this day end?" she asked herself out loud. Beth sat down on one of the store's armchairs and slipped into a thoughtful, dreamlike state, not quite asleep, closer to meditation. It felt like she was there for only a few minutes, but by the time she regained awareness, the crowd had cleared, the window had been taped, and the firemen were gone—she'd missed them, dammit—and someone was knocking on the front door. She saw Isabel's beautiful face peering through the storefront window. She smiled at the sight of her friend.

Isabel was almost three months pregnant and had the unmistakable satisfied glow of a woman who wants to be pregnant and is. Beth was happy and relieved for her best friend, who'd been trying to conceive for the past two years. For many of their friends, it had become all too common to miscarry or to be unable to conceive at all. "It's what we get for waiting so long," Beth had once told Isabel, and regretted it immediately.

Beth filled Isabel in on the telephone conversation with Paul. Isabel listened attentively as she always did, but Beth knew her friend was at a loss as to how to help her.

"His mom still doesn't get it?" Isabel asked.

"No, she still blames me for his illness, which makes no sense whatsoever. You'd think she would have a clue between the pneumonia and KS." As frustrated as Beth was, she stuck by her word not to out Paul while he was alive. It was his dying wish.

They talked for a bit more and Beth left Isabel with a quick hug and returned to her office. She made another phone call to tell her office manager to have the window replaced tomorrow. As she jotted down notes of things to discuss with Maggie and Anna, Sacha poked her head in the office.

"Maggie called and said she can't make it into the city to meet with you and Anna. Something about her stepson having sprained his ankle playing basketball—she had to go pick him up . . . I told Anna, so she's already left for the day," Sacha said. "If there's nothing else to hang around for, I think I'll head out as well . . ."

"Thanks for keeping your cool today, Sacha . . ." Beth thought to tell Sacha about the vandalized ad, but then thought better of it. Sharing it with someone would help exorcise the image, but she didn't want to scare her assistant. *Best it stay in my head for now*, Beth thought. *Maybe I can talk with Maggie about it later.*

Instead, she bid Sacha good night. "See you tomorrow . . . Thanks again!"

Beth was suddenly weary and happy that the meeting had been canceled. Now she could surprise Jessie by getting home earlier than expected and take them to Jessie's favorite burger joint for dinner.

Maggie's cancellation wasn't a surprise, whatever the particulars this time. Maggie had enough to do, raising her own daughter at home in addition to the pressure of running her own consulting business. The extra work of taking care of her two stepchildren for a year while their mother was in France seemed to have put her responsibility quotient over the top. Maggie's husband, John, wasn't a bad guy, but as far as Beth could tell he didn't make Maggie's life any easier, that was for sure.

Beth grabbed her purse and ran out the door. When she got to the street, she was surprised to see Isabel still hanging around in front of the store. She lifted her eyebrows to ask her friend why just as a taxi pulled up and Christopher Bello emerged to beckon Isabel inside. Beth just rolled her eyes and raised a hand for her own taxi. She didn't bother asking where they were going. The day had held enough surprises; she could wait to get to the bottom of this one.

NO MATTER WHAT kind of day she was having, the moment Beth started for home, she began to feel an anticipatory joy. Jessie was like a present waiting for her every night when she got home. That Jessie had arisen from the tragedy of Paul's life deepened her gratitude for her daughter even as it tinged her immense joy with sadness.

As Beth put the key in the door she heard Hanna say, "Jess, I think your mom is home already . . ."

Before she could push the door open she heard Jessie running toward it, shouting, "Mom! Is that you?"

"It's me!" Beth called, pocketing her key and waiting for Jessie to open the door. Ever since Jessie was old enough to reach the handle, she loved to push up on her tippy-toes to open the door when her mother came home from work and jump into her arms. It was a point of pride when she was three, and now that she was seven, the homecoming every evening was ritual. Like her mother, Jessie was strong and lean, but compact, so Beth was still able to pick her up easily.

Hanna had already prepared dinner, so Beth canned the idea of going out for burgers. The three sat down together, as they had for many evenings before, and shared a meal of chicken and dumplings.

After dinner, Hanna kissed Jessie and Beth good-bye. Once they were alone, it was clear to Beth that Jessie was in a talkative mood.

"Why did Paul call you here today? He didn't sound like himself on the phone. Didn't he know you were at work?"

"I think he just forgot. He wasn't feeling too well." Beth was hoping Jessie wasn't going to be too inquisitive.

"Is Paul going to die?" Jessie always referred to her father as Paul, though she addressed him as Pop in person.

Beth knew this was an unavoidable conversation. "We all die, Jess, but Paul will probably die sooner than he ought to since he is very sick. I'm sorry that's true, but it is."

"Why is he so sick?"

Jessie seemed to be trying to pry something out of her mother. Beth understood Jessie's natural curiosity, but she had a hard time navigating it. It had taken years for Beth to come to terms with Paul's HIV.

"He has something called an autoimmune deficiency. That means his body is no longer able to fight off illnesses. When you or I get a cold and we get better all by ourselves, it's because our body fights the cold and wins. Well, Paul's body doesn't know how to fight anymore, so he can't get better. Does that make sense?"

Explaining it now to Jessie made it new for Beth all over again. She shivered for a moment and hoped Jessie didn't pick up on it.

"Why won't his body fight?"

"It lost its ability to do that."

"Why?"

"Because he has the AIDS virus."

"How did he get the virus?"

Beth felt that old surge of anger over Paul's illness and worked to push it aside. She wanted to assure Jessie that she couldn't get the virus from her father but wasn't quite ready to explain the details. Beth understood that Jessie would be worried, and she wanted to respect that. Still, she was stymied.

"We don't know how he got it, but you don't have to worry about getting it. You are healthy. Okay?" Beth thought she sounded unconvincing; Jessie had touched a button.

"Will you get the virus and die too?"

Beth knew that she and Jessie were HIV negative, but macabre fantasies haunted Beth where her status as a healthy person would be revoked by some previously unknown trait of the virus. It had taken three years after Paul's diagnosis for her to stop periodic testing, and then only because her doctor had told her to stop punishing herself for testing negative in the first place.

Beth finally believed it. "No, sweetheart, I won't get it either."

Beth's silent but constant angst was that somehow either she would be taken away from Jessie or Jessie would be taken from her.

. . .

THE NEXT DAY at the office, things were a little quieter, if only for the fact that there weren't hundreds of screaming protestors outside the building. The press continued to call, and Beth turned down one request after another to make TV appearances. She had been tempted by a last-minute invite by David Letterman the previous day, having been a fan since her college years, but knew he would have gotten the better of her. Instead, she and Maggie got RHM model Agnes Seymour on the show, which worked out perfectly. They showed the ad on the screen several times and Agnes talked about what fun she had modeling for the shot. She talked openly about nursing and expressed confusion about those who would find it anything short of natural and beautiful. Letterman had a ball with that one but stopped short of being disrespectful. The audience cheered Agnes.

Beth was so pleased with the way the backlash was playing out, she began strategizing for the next series of ads. She ran into the marketing director's office. "Sally, can you get me twins? I want to do before and after shots for a series of ads."

"You want me to find twins who are pregnant?" Sally asked.

"No, not pregnant twins, someone pregnant *with* twins. I would love to be able to shoot the mother during her pregnancy, while she is giving birth, and afterward with the babies. We'll even design hospital gowns for the delivery. They had a problem with one infant? Let's give them two."

Sally frowned at the last thought. Beth saw her disapproval and checked herself. She knew she had a tendency to cross the limits from provocation to bad taste.

"Okay, maybe not the delivery gowns, but twins, I definitely want twins. Get your assistant on it now." When Beth got fired up about something, she tended to bully her way through it and wanted results immediately. It was a problem before she owned and ran a company. Now it was her privilege to be aggressive.

Beth went to find Anna to see what she would think of the twins idea. Anna, more conservative than Beth, often was not ready to back Beth in taking risks, especially if it would help the bottom line. Anna had a clear way of thinking through to the economic effect of any decision. With Anna's recent fragile mood, however, Beth couldn't be sure what to expect.

Anna's door was closed. Beth knocked and opened it slightly. "Anna, can I come in?"

"Of course." Anna sounded tired.

"Hey, you okay?"

"Yeah, I'm fine. Just tired. The baby was up all night teething. I got three hours of sleep. Yesterday morning, when I was spending a few minutes with Jason and the boys in the backyard before I left for work, Oscar turned to me and said, 'Mama, leave now. We're blowing bubbles with Papa. Go, now!' He didn't want me around."

Anna struggled like no one else Beth knew with being away from her children every day. She and her three-year-old, Oscar, had an intense bond that had begun in utero. Anna had cried for a month after coming back to work after maternity leave.

"Jessie used to do that too, except she would kick me out of the house when Hanna came. I used to think, *Great, my kid prefers her nanny to me, what am I doing wrong?* Then I realized that kids try to establish routine to make order out of their world. 'In the morning Mom goes to work. I accept that. Morning comes, time for Mom to go.' They sense your ambivalence and it makes them uncomfortable, so they impose order by saying, 'Leave now.' You know Oscar has no idea he's hurting your feelings, right?"

"I know, I know. I overreact because I don't want to leave him. It's not that I don't want to come to work, but I also don't want to leave. It all makes me feel crazy." Anna's eyes filled with tears and streamed down her face. "I never got used to it. I don't know why. I thought it would be easier once Henry was born, but it isn't."

Anna hadn't taken a real maternity leave when she'd had her second son. Things were so busy at RHM that she worked every day from home and went into the office for meetings. Six weeks after Henry was born, she was back in the office full-time. Beth understood that Anna never felt that she had spent proper time with her boys during that early stage. Maybe that was why she never quite adjusted, although Anna had never once complained about it.

"Listen, Anna, you've been struggling with this for a while now and I've been thinking about it. Would it help if you took a sabbatical? Maybe you could stay at home for a month or two and see if it works for you. When I need you for strategic decisions, I'll call. In the meantime, Eric can handle the day-to-day financials. Consider it makeup time from when you had Henry." Eric was Anna's incredibly competent associate, and Beth knew he could handle things just fine for a few months.

It was a calculated risk: Beth was counting on a change of heart from Anna and a renewed commitment to her professional life after some extended time at home. Anna was a whiz at what she did, and Beth would do whatever she had to do to keep her—even if it meant giving her up for the short term.

Beth added, "If after a break you want to come back, then you can come back fresh. If you decide 'profession be damned, I'm staying home with my kids,' then just help me make the transition of finding someone to fill your position. Think about it." Beth didn't believe for a second that Anna would opt for a stay-at-home motherhood, so this last statement stung in her mind like the lie that it was. Still, she hoped it sounded convincing in the delivery.

Anna perked up noticeably. "I will. Thank you, Beth."

Beth thought better than to bring up the twins idea just then. Instead, they covered some important catalog questions and she headed back to her office.

She called Helen. "How's Paul doing?"

Helen was speaking in a whisper all the time now, in an attempt not to burst into tears. "He's in and out of consciousness. The doctors don't know yet if he'll recover from this bout. They can't seem to pinpoint any one problem. I'm afraid he's just going to let go . . ."

Beth could barely hear her. "He won't let go so easily. Your brother's will is stronger than that. Let me know if anything changes, for better or worse."

Beth was long past crying for her ex, yet there were times when the knowledge that he would die before Jessie was a teenager felt impossible to grasp. Jessie would lose her father, and as complex as their history was, a love bond persisted that had sustained them as family.

CHAPTER FOUR

Isabel

"SO WHERE ARE we going?" Isabel asked Christopher as he ferried her to his apartment on the Upper West Side. She was excited to be out of the dreary workday and into the realm of evening.

"I have tickets to see *Othello* at the Delacorte," Christopher coolly announced, as if tickets to Shakespeare in the Park at the Delacorte Theater could be had by anyone at any time. Located in the heart of Central Park's west side and nestled on the flank of a rocky rise, the Delacorte provided an intimate theater venue against a spectacularly dramatic backdrop. Most people waited in line all afternoon for free tickets to the evening's show. But Christopher had bypassed this inconvenience, either paying a steep price for the privilege or cashing in on a serious favor.

"Your favorite, Christopher Walken, is playing Iago. It should be hilarious. I thought a picnic in the park before the play would get you home and to bed earlier than if we waited until afterward to eat."

Isabel happily let Christopher take charge of the evening;

watching Walken channel malevolent Iago would be the perfect way to turn a crummy day into a glorious one.

Christopher lived across from the park in a classic six. He'd had the apartment since he first came to New York seventeen years ago and paid one-quarter of the market price on his lease due to the rent control laws not meant to protect the likes of Christopher Bello. He lavished the money saved by the criminally low lease on the apartment's luxurious interior. The inconspicuous lighting offered a rosy glow that simmered on and off silently upon entering and exiting each room. Guests always looked their best in Christopher's apartment. The modern furnishings, custom built to fit the space perfectly, were hewn from walnut, outfitted with thick, tufted cushions and cost a small fortune. In spite of the clean lines of the apartment interior, there was a lushness to Christopher's home that always made Isabel think of Jeannie's prison lair in *I Dream of Jeannie*.

Back when Christopher and Isabel spent those awkward getting-to-know-you dates together, Isabel had spilled red wine on a bone-colored floor cushion. She was mortified. Christopher dismissed it and never mentioned it to her again. Like most of the people in Christopher's life, things were also expendable. Whenever she visited his home, the spot on the cushion came to feel like something she owned in his space.

Shortly after, a rare book Isabel had found in the stack of art books on Christopher's coffee table had further cemented their connection. Jean Cocteau's *Le Livre Blanc*, an explicit collection of prose and line drawings depicting sex between men, was far from a staple in the libraries of even the artiest straight men. Christopher's possession of *The White Book* intrigued

Isabel, but more, it locked into her own fascination with the artist.

"Why do you have Cocteau's *White Book*?" she'd asked him.

"It's so *louche*, I love it," Christopher told her, as if that would explain everything.

"*Louche?* Really? I always thought it quite tender and brave," Isabel retorted.

Unapologetically homosexual in a time when it was not acceptable to be so, Cocteau hadn't explicitly claimed authorship of the book when it was published in 1928. It would have been disastrous to his reputation to have so brazenly pushed the limits of polite society by admitting authorship that early in the twentieth century. Still, the inimitable drawings and prose made it clear who had created it. Isabel applauded the audacity it took to create and publish the tome, even if anonymously.

Cocteau had been a kind of hero to Isabel since she first discovered his work in Paris when she resided there in her early twenties. The artist lived without excuse, creating a body of work that defied categorization as a filmmaker, poet, novelist, painter, provocateur. Isabel lived by Cocteau's tenet: "Tact in audacity is knowing how far you can go without going too far."

As they entered Christopher's apartment now, she was delighted to see a wicker picnic basket, a white linen napkin expertly tucked around the edges, sitting atop the Carrara marble kitchen counter. Christopher had clearly called in the order and had it delivered to his apartment earlier in the day. Isabel couldn't help but wonder if he'd had a previous date who'd canceled. She figured she must be the stand-in for an otherwise carefully planned evening. How else to make sense of the tickets and elaborately prepared picnic dinner?

Christopher must have registered the moment Isabel spent taking it all in and spoke as if she'd voiced these concerns out loud: "You can get anything pretty quickly in this city if you know who to call." He grinned.

Christopher grabbed the basket with his left hand and, with a bow and sweeping motion of his right arm, ushered Isabel out the door and into the elevator. When the doors closed, he leaned over to kiss her on the chin. Isabel didn't push him away but kept her face expressionless. He was up to something, and Isabel knew better than to guess what it might be. She'd spent way too much time in the past navigating his shifty cycles of affection and distraction to know that there was no use in trying to figure out his motives now.

They crossed Central Park West through the din of traffic and entered the softness of the park, heading east toward the Delacorte. A cool and cloudless summer solstice, the park wouldn't empty out until well after nine o'clock. Cyclists rode the loop past new lovers making out on park benches. Teenagers played hacky sack in tight circles. People walked their dogs, one man carried a blind Abyssinian cat perched on his shoulder, and another sported a four-foot albino boa constrictor, beautifully marked in white and pale yellow, wrapped around his shoulders and neck. A woman played with her ferrets in the grass. A group of Latinos kicked a soccer ball around a patch of dirt just in front of the Delacorte. Under a huge willow tree, six octogenarians practiced tai chi, all wearing white linen *gi* and *hakama*. It was a time of year when all of New York City's residents and their eccentricities burst from their small spaces into this glorious extension of their homes.

Christopher and Isabel found a patch of neat grass near

a large elm, close enough to watch the soccer players but far enough to avoid getting hit with the ball. Christopher yanked a bright red sarong out of his back pocket (how had she missed the bulge there?) and spread it on the ground. He then placed the wicker basket on the corner of it and ceremoniously invited Isabel to join him: "Madam . . ."

Christopher expertly laid out their light supper of cold salmon, spears of asparagus wrapped in prosciutto, steamed edamame, sesame flatbread spread with olivata, and her favorite drink, Orangina (so the dinner *was* prepared for her!). For dessert, freshly cut pineapple and strawberries beside a tin of crème fraîche. He had managed to not include any of the things that were repulsive to her now. How he had intuited this, she couldn't fathom.

Christopher was staring at Isabel's profile as she watched the activity around her. He traced her slightly crooked nose with his finger.

"A boy who loved me broke it when he punched me in the face. I was sixteen years old," Isabel said without looking at him.

"On purpose?"

"We were stoned, dancing in the dark under a strobe light. He was this quiet, angry boy named Gordon. He missed the arm of a buddy who'd been teasing him and instead smashed my face. I remember the sound more than anything. It made a terrible *crunch*." Isabel scrunched up her nose at the thought of it. "The party stopped and the lights came on. I'd fallen to the floor and had my hands covering my nose, gushing blood. I was so high I thought the whole thing was funny. Gordon was so upset at having hit me that he got out his father's shotgun and shot up the trees in his backyard."

"What became of you and Gordon?"

"I kissed him once, but more out of pity than affection."

"Where is he now?"

"No idea."

They grew quiet for a few moments while they watched a toddler trying to blow bubbles, unsuccessfully, with her magic wand.

"Remember our boxing match?" Christopher asked.

"Yes, of course. We've had some very strange ways of expressing our love over the years." Isabel mimed an exaggerated punch at Christopher, then leaned against him affectionately.

When they were still working together, he had once given her boxing lessons as a Christmas present: ten two-hour sessions with a professional boxer. Isabel took to the sport with relish and marveled at her bleeding knuckles after the first few sessions. She hung those bloody fist wraps around her bed frame as a badge of her efforts. She loved punching the heavy bag with her training gloves. She shadowboxed for practice almost every night as part of her daily workout.

Isabel had taken eight of her lessons when she and Christopher made the mistake of sharing her favorite meal of raw oysters, french fries, and martinis (dry, up, with extra olives and dirty ice cubes on the side) late one night, heavy on the martinis. They argued over dinner, a lovers' tiff about nothing important, except they weren't lovers.

Christopher had called over the waiter. "My martini isn't cold enough. Neither is hers. Can you please take these away and bring us another round?"

"Mine is fine," Isabel told the waiter. "You can just replace my thermometer-tongued friend's drink."

The waiter imperiously picked up Christopher's drink after winking at Isabel and sashayed toward the bar.

"What's that supposed to mean?" Christopher demanded.

"Not cold enough, Chris? Seriously? Just put in one of the ice cubes we asked for. Why are you being a jerk?"

"I'm being a jerk by expecting excellent service and a cold martini? Don't set your expectations so low, Isabel," Christopher said with a smirk.

"Maybe that explains why I'm here with you," Isabel retorted.

"And what is *that* supposed to mean?"

"You're the one who sent back the drink. You're being fussy and annoying. Anyway, I'm joking, Chris, get over it."

"I'm not the one with the theory on jokes," he replied.

Christopher made believe he was pouting for a minute, then brightened. "Okay, let's settle it in the ring. Three two-minute rounds in my apartment. I'll supply the gear."

Typical, thought Isabel, *the lessons were about sparring with her all along*. "You're on," she said.

They stumbled to his apartment, where they cleared a space by pushing all the furniture against the walls of the living room. Christopher disappeared for five minutes and came back with all the gear.

"Here, put these on," Christopher demanded as he threw her a balled-up white T-shirt and a pair of gym shorts. He'd already changed into the same.

Isabel changed as Christopher watched.

"Okay, good. Now for the wraps." Christopher solemnly twisted wraps around Isabel's hands first. He helped her put on gloves, then wrapped and gloved his own hands. He set the timekeeper and pressed the button, they touched gloves, and he put up his dukes.

"Wow, you're very serious about this, Chris," Isabel said, and laughed, giddy now with anticipation.

"We said we'd fight, so let's fight," he challenged. Christopher caught her with a soft tap to the face. It didn't hurt but it shifted her good humor to bad.

Isabel lunged forward, forgetting everything her trainer taught her about footwork and balance, and barely grazed her opponent's arm. He countered the punch with another tap to the head, this one much harder than Isabel expected.

"That hurt," Isabel whined as she swung again and missed completely.

"I barely touched you. C'mon, fight back. Quit talking. It only distracts you." Christopher kept Isabel flustered with a flurry of jabs to the body. He wasn't really hitting her, but his blustery moves made her angry.

Isabel's lessons with the boxer had been only one-sided. He would hold up mitts and Isabel would punch and jab at them. Sometimes he put the mitts down and said, "Go ahead, make it count. I want you to try to hurt me." But her boxing trainer was so sweet that Isabel didn't have the heart to really have at him. She realized now that she was fighting Christopher that she probably couldn't have hurt him even if she tried.

Now she tried jabbing with all her might with her right, which threw her off balance. Christopher, quick on his feet—he'd been training for the past few years—blocked her punch and followed with an upper cut that stopped before making full contact with her ribs. The bell rang and they dropped their arms and walked around the room sweating and breathing heavily.

One minute later the bell rang to begin again, and Christopher came after Isabel with a real punch this time to the stomach, and she went down.

"What . . . the . . . fuck, Christopher! Are you out of your fucking mind?" Isabel scrambled up from her knees and took a minute to quell the nausea rising in her belly. Fury brought her to her feet and she went after him with a guttural scream that sounded like it came from outside the apartment. Isabel began punching wildly and blindly wherever she could. Off-kilter and with no strategy, she went berserk on Christopher until she finally connected with a shot to the side of his head. A feeling of satisfaction and, with it, a kind of sickness made her stop. She struggled to catch her breath. "You . . . are . . . such . . . an asshole."

"Did you think I was kidding?" He hit her again, this time in the shoulder where the pain did not deter her, and she swung wildly at his belly. At that moment, she wanted to hurt him. She wanted blood.

The bell rang to end the second round and Isabel fell into an armchair against the wall. Soaked with sweat and still feeling woozy from the shot to the stomach, she thought she would pass out. Four minutes of fighting felt like a marathon. The martinis weren't helping.

About to toss it all over Christopher's antique Persian rug, she announced, "I'm done. No more. You win."

Christopher, short of breath as well, put his arms in the air to claim victory, dancing from foot to foot. Isabel thought

about smacking him with a sucker kick to the groin—it was so
tempting—but she was too tired to lift her shaking leg. Christopher saw her eyeing his vulnerability and stepped back, placing his gloves across his crotch to protect himself. Isabel burst
out laughing at his quick reading of the situation. She pushed
off her gloves and let them fall to the floor. As usual, the absurdity of their friendship caused the irritation to abate quickly. It
reminded Isabel of something her mother would say from her
girlhood days when she and her siblings would roughhouse:
"It's a game until someone gets hurt. "

Christopher pulled Isabel up from the chair and led her out
to the terrace. She collapsed on the lounge as he picked up
the garden hose. Christopher briefly watered the plants before
turning it on Isabel, who accepted the cool water. He lay down
next to her and pointed the hose up to make a fountain of
fine spray above them. He kissed her hard and then turned his
gaze to find the few stars that shone through the light-washed
Manhattan night sky.

"Did you ever doubt your father's love?" Christopher asked
as if it were the only question in the world.

"No, never," Isabel answered without much thought.

"That's why you terrify me."

Christopher squeezed the handle of the hose harder and
showered them with a torrent. When Isabel didn't protest, he
put the hose down and took her hand. They lay silently marveling at the crescent moon punctuated at its bottom tip by a
flashy Venus. The temperature dropped suddenly—or was it
their adrenaline?—and they started shivering and went back
inside. Isabel quietly dressed and left him to push his furniture
back into place. "Nice fight," one of them had said as Isabel

closed the door behind her. She couldn't remember now why she didn't stay.

"That was one of our more interesting dates," Christopher said now as he fed Isabel a perfect wild strawberry dipped in crème. He was smiling at the memory.

Isabel finally looked at him. "Is that what it was?"

AT A QUARTER to eight, Christopher went to the call window to get the tickets. It was Isabel's favorite time in Central Park. The bats began their twilight feeding, swooping down across the field in pursuit of an evening feast of urban mosquitos. That bats found a place like Manhattan hospitable made her happy.

"Bad news," he was saying as he walked back toward Isabel. "Walken is being replaced by an understudy. Let's skip it and go back to my apartment. We can play a quick game of Scrabble and then I'll take you home."

Had Christopher known all along that there would be an understudy and just used the promise of a Walken performance as a carrot? Weren't they way past that? The thought of coercion probably hadn't occurred to him. Why would it at this point?

Isabel issued a gag order to the voice in her head and said instead, "Chris, I'm just going to go home. The picnic was lovely. Thanks for everything today, but my head is a bit muddled right now."

"Are you missing Sam?"

"Not as much as I should be, and don't ask me what that's supposed to mean because I have no idea. I'll call you tomorrow."

They walked out of the park to Central Park West, where Christopher hailed a cab for her. Isabel settled into the comfort of anonymity so particular to New York taxis. She was glad to be alone again.

Isabel stared out the taxi window as they flew down Seventh Avenue, the blur of pedestrians morphing into one sentient urban being. Contemplating the peculiar nature of her friendship with Christopher, Isabel could count on one finger the occasion of a broken heart. One time only, and it'd been by Christopher Bello. It never made sense to her, how their connection could be so lasting and yet so tenuous.

When they'd first met through a mutual friend, Isabel had found Christopher rather frail and sweet. She'd mentioned her first impressions of him to her friend, who'd laughed loud and long and assured her, "No way, he's neither of those things."

In the beginning, Christopher and Isabel shared little or no tension, and it wasn't until they worked together that she began to see Christopher as the antithesis of her first impression of him. It was this schism in her intuition that intrigued her at first. Christopher defied all of Isabel's instincts. His pull wasn't just on the surface of things; he became more of a mystery to her the better she came to know him.

The moment she'd fallen in love with him was as much a conundrum as the course of their entire relationship. After a staff meeting held in Christopher's office one afternoon at *Pink*, Isabel stayed behind after the others had left. Christopher closed the door as if he had something grave to discuss. Instead, he surprised her with an unusual suggestion.

"Let's trade pants," he announced.

"Now? Here, in the office?" Isabel asked, perplexed and

thrown off guard—something she would become accustomed to later with Christopher but hadn't yet.

"Yes, right now. The door is closed." Christopher made the idea sound perfectly plausible.

They pulled off their bottoms, giddy as children, and threw them across the desk to each other. Christopher caught Isabel's low-hipped black cotton and Lycra bell-bottoms in his left hand just as his summer-weight gray wool trousers landed on Isabel's head.

They stood for a moment facing each other, pants-less but now serious, as if the next few minutes of this escapade would infer some greater meaning.

Isabel stood in her Agent Provocateur bright green lace thong with fuchsia ties.

"I like the pink ties," Christopher told her. Isabel flashed her matching bra before Christopher encouraged her: "Go on, put on my pants."

Isabel shook out Chris's trousers and slid her strong legs into them. She pulled them up and zipped them, then tied her silk blouse in a knot above her navel, as if preparing for the rest of the day in new drag. Her butt filled the trousers nicely, but they were too long by eight inches and huge around her waist. "Hey, give me your belt," she demanded.

Christopher whipped it across the desk, and she caught the buckle before it hit her face. She threaded the belt through the loops, cinched it across her narrow waist, and then rolled up the pants legs. When she was done, she twirled around for Christopher to inspect.

"Hey, not bad, Is. You could totally pull that off. It's rather chic."

Christopher shimmied into Isabel's pants, but he couldn't close the zipper and button over his crotch, now bulging against the hip-hugging fabric. He stood before her, his smooth white abdomen peering out from her now distressed pants, crisp white cotton boxers spilling out.

"Can't say the same for you," Isabel offered. "You look ridiculous."

They were laughing uncontrollably until Christopher's assistant buzzed in with a phone call that couldn't wait. All silliness between them retreated as Christopher paced his office, barefoot. Isabel sat down in the chair opposite his desk and put her shoeless feet on the edge of it. She watched him as he spoke into the receiver, marveling at the composure of her friend and colleague despite how absurd he looked. Inexplicably, it was the sight of Christopher's flat white belly and skinny, hairless ankles peeking out from her tight pants as he paced the office, earnestly discussing how to win back an important client, that changed forever her heart. By the time Isabel pulled on her own pants again and left the office, she felt melancholy and miserable.

Everything was different after the exchange-of-pants episode. A little angry about the heart she left in the pocket of Christopher's trousers that day, she felt tricked, as if he had stolen something from her. From that afternoon on, he'd held a part of her he didn't even know he had and wouldn't want even if he did realize it. For a year she cried herself to sleep out of frustration and confusion after charged evenings with Christopher that ended with her alone in bed. Their seduction of each other held to a certain point but somehow always stopped before sex. Only after Isabel had fallen for Sam had she finally had the nerve to ask Christopher about it one night over dinner.

"Why have we never had sex?"

"It would change everything between us," Christopher said matter-of-factly as he continued to cut into the steak he was eating. He paused, then put down his fork and knife and looked at Isabel with some tenderness. "I don't want anything to change."

"That assumes it would change for the worse. Why would you think that?"

"Because sex fucks things up," he said as if it should have been obvious.

"Since when did that stop anyone? Besides, I don't buy it, Chris. You just don't want to fuck me. Which is fine, if perplexing," Isabel retorted without rancor.

This imbalance of desire worked like a charm on Isabel's heart until she had a revelation.

The ersatz couple had been inseparable over a long weekend, which started with not one, but two different stage versions of *Hamlet*. Halfway through the second one—they walked out at intermission—they raced out of the city in Christopher's new sports car to a private beachside hamlet just an hour outside Manhattan. (How he procured these spaces at no cost to himself was another bit of witchcraft on his part.) Isabel had spent two nights wrapped around Christopher in his bed. No sex: she felt as though the tensile strength of his affection was now choking her. On the second night, he spoke to her in great detail about a new girlfriend he was pursuing, a supermodel he'd recently become obsessed with. Isabel got up from the bed, pulled on a long robe, and walked to the end of the great property leading to the Long Island Sound.

She thought at first that she would have a good cry, but instead she sat on a bench facing the water. Isabel felt her heart soar away from her body, out over the Sound, black and still under the moonlight. Separating her heart from her body as a kind of surrender helped her to see clearly for the first time Christopher's pull on her. She understood his actions toward her as a declaration of a kind of love, but a kind where he had all the control. He'd created a tightrope of his affection on which she found herself willingly—if perilously—walking, with no net to catch her were she to fall. Staring into the darkness, she realized that this sort of unrequited romantic love was not love at all, but an exercise in self-annihilation. The appeal only to the suffering itself. She made a pact with herself there and then to refuse to sustain that suffering. When she stood again she had finally retrieved her heart.

After that night, Isabel maintained something else for Christopher, something she'd never felt before in her long life with men. An easy romantic affection took hold, one she could still call love, but of a different sort, and without a name.

Absent the high-wire act of seduction that Christopher relied on to hold Isabel close, the tension between them cooled. They still spent time together, but with the balance of power now neutralized, Isabel wondered how long the friendship would last.

The ride downtown was blessedly long, allowing Isabel time to daydream: the city held so many memories for her. Certain buildings, street corners, restaurants, entire blocks . . . it was impossible to watch the city fly by without visiting moments past. How would the city look to her once the baby arrived? Would its frenetic energy and controlled chaos—what made the city so seductive to Isabel—suddenly become threatening once she had an infant in her care? The thought of fleeing the city for the suburbs like so many new parents made Isabel shudder. Would having a baby end the life she had created for herself? Or would parenthood simply be a continuation of life as she now lived it, just plus one?

Isabel realized that none of these questions was answerable, but she intuited that this was the only time she would ever be alone again for a very long time. Even though she could have no idea what her life would be once the baby arrived, she was sure that her child would occupy the greater part of it—in the physical sense for certain, but also in an emotional and psychic sense. This was time for her now. And although she missed Sam like crazy when he was out of town, she was thankful for the time without him.

Sorry the taxi ride hadn't lasted longer, Isabel paid the fare and thanked the driver for the gift of solitude he'd unwittingly granted her. As she approached her apartment door, Isabel heard music coming from the other side and felt a moment of terror in her belly. She didn't remember leaving music on when she left for work in the morning. Too afraid to open the door, she pressed her ear against it and listened more closely. When she made out that the music playing was *Tabula Rasa* by Arvo Pärt, she realized with relief that Sam must have made it home.

Pärt was Sam's favorite composer, and it was his habit to play his music when he returned from work as a way to reset his focus. *Tabula Rasa* was a mesmerizingly melancholic piece, and Isabel suddenly felt sad that she hadn't been there to greet Sam. She opened the door and called her husband's name. His suitcase was lying by the door. She could see an open bottle of red wine on the kitchen counter and hear the shower running in the bathroom. Instead of interrupting him, she sat quietly on the couch, savoring the few extra moments alone, calmed by his presence.

"Hey, baby, I thought you were out for the evening."

Sam startled her. She hadn't heard the water stop—maybe she'd dozed off for a minute or two? He stood above her next to the couch with a towel wrapped around his lean waist, using a smaller one to dry off his thick dark hair.

"I wasn't feeling very well. What about your meetings in Chicago?" Isabel wanted to jump up and kiss him, but her body wouldn't comply. As Sam dropped onto the couch next to her, his towel slipped off and onto the floor. He flipped her legs over hers.

"Lead counsel had an appendicitis attack while he was on vacation with his family in Greece and couldn't make the conference call as scheduled. The meeting was postponed for two weeks. I got on the next plane home. That means I don't have to go anywhere for a while." He kissed her on the back of her neck. "I missed you."

Isabel snuggled up to Sam and held his cock in her hand. Sam was the only man Isabel had been intimate with whose penis was a source of comfort as well as pleasure.

AT FIRST GLANCE, Sam Burston was an unlikely husband for Isabel. Slick and impeccably groomed with his dark blue suits, crisp white shirts, and Hermès ties, Sam seemed to epitomize the corporate player, the kind of man who squelches individualism in service to climbing the corporate ladder, a ladder erected on the firmament of well-trained minds. Eccentrics and outthinkers need not apply. No, at first glance, Sam was decidedly not Isabel's type.

It didn't help that they met when Sam tried to pick her up in a crowded restaurant. He had spotted Isabel while she and Beth were waiting for a table. Just as they turned to leave and try their luck elsewhere, Sam touched Isabel's elbow to get her attention. "Excuse me," he said in a soft voice, "my friend and I have room at our table. Would you like to join us?"

Isabel was counting on a quiet dinner with her best friend and hoping for some sound advice about how to extract herself from Christopher's spell. Her quick assessment of Sam and his friend—suits chasing tail—caused her to dismiss them with a quick shake of the head until Beth pinched her butt in protest. Sam was handsome in that frat-boy way that appealed to her best friend. Beth had experienced a tragic few years in romance, so Isabel quickly turned her coldhearted no into a warm smile of acquiescence. Beth didn't miss a beat and sat down next to Sam. Isabel was stuck with his close-eyed, close-shaven-headed friend.

By the merciful end of what seemed like an endless dinner, Sam surprised Isabel by asking her out when Beth got up to use the ladies' room. Beth had monopolized much of the conversation over dinner with her witty repartee, by which Sam seemed enthralled, so his advance on Isabel didn't follow. She accepted the date more out of surprise than desire.

Walking through the cold, wintery night toward the subway after making their good-byes to Sam and his friend, Beth complained, "Well, that didn't go as planned . . . At least he might distract you from that elusive nutjob Christopher."

"Oh, I'm sure nothing will come of it," Isabel told her best friend. "These guys seem like throwbacks to me, playing a role that should be long gone . . . you know, the midcentury organization man. What do they do now that we no longer need them to provide for and protect us?"

"For fuck's sake, Is, the guy wants a date. That's what guys do, and unless I'm mistaken, it's what we gals do too."

"Yeah, I know . . . but don't you think that men these days are like nineteenth-century heroines? They are stuck in roles that are less and less relevant and they all seem slightly depressed to me. It didn't end well for Emma and Anna, and I don't see it ending well for them." Isabel wasn't sure if she was just trying to make her friend feel better after being slighted or if she was onto something.

"I thought Sam seemed pretty put together. If it doesn't work, toss him my way, will ya? And besides, how much of this crap has to do with Christopher?"

Isabel's philosophical reverie was broken. "Oh, Lord, I don't know. Everything doesn't always have to go back to Christopher."

It was true that during the entire dinner, she was lost in the not-so-distant memory of a naked wrestling match with Christopher in his apartment. Afterward they'd drunk warm milk with Ovaltine. Then she'd dressed and went home, as their maddening custom dictated.

"I didn't say everything goes back to Christopher. You did, Is."

Isabel and Sam's first date lasted four days and ended with them hitting the trifecta at Belmont during the Triple Crown, winning more than $2,000 on a blind bet. They forever referred to it as "the four-day date that never ended."

Sam surprised her at every turn. Nothing about him was as she expected. His bookshelves held the collected works of Nabokov, Thomas Bernhard, and Borges, as well as Carl Jung and Karen Horney. He could recite the psychiatrist's monologue from *Equus*, her favorite play. He played the saxophone, and he could dance. She'd never met a straight man who could dance with abandon but without aggression. Isabel fell in love and accepted Sam's proposal of marriage, cherishing the seashell ring they'd found at a beachside souvenir shop.

Now Isabel nodded off while gently stroking Sam. Besides vomiting and fucking, the urge to sleep often overcame her. One often preempted another. Sam carried Isabel to their bed, slipped off her shoes and dress, and tucked her under the cool white sheets.

The phone rang just as Isabel was sinking into slumber, and she heard Sam pick it up as if from far away.

"Hello? Yeah, hey, thanks, Chris. We're pretty excited . . ."

Isabel woke with a flutter at the mention of her friend's name. She raised her head from the pillow to catch the rest.

"No, she just passed out. I'll let her know you called . . . Uh-huh, yeah, man, sure . . . Okay, good-bye."

Sam quietly entered the bedroom. "Is, are you awake?"

"Hmm . . . barely . . . who was on the phone?" she mumbled.

"No one important . . . go back to sleep."

CHAPTER FIVE

Maggie

FROM THE MEDIA room across the vast loft, Maggie could hear Nino Rota's jaunty score accompanying the finale of *La Dolce Vita*. That the film wasn't clicked off immediately meant that John had likely fallen asleep in front of the TV, which also meant that he was not tending to Lily. Before Maggie had a chance to register her annoyance, she heard her two-year-old daughter's feet patter across the loft.

"Mommy? Where are you? Krispies stuck in the toilet. Come see!"

"I'm in my office, Lily," Maggie yelled. "I'm coming."

"Where? I can't see you!"

The advantages of living in a huge space were sometimes at odds with the logistics of child rearing. Maggie and John had moved from a cramped six-hundred-square-foot one-bedroom apartment in Greenwich Village to a four-thousand-square-foot loft in Jersey City when they were expecting Lily. Having to support two home offices, one toddler, and John's two grade-schoolers, space was the one thing Maggie thought might keep them all from driving one another crazy. Still,

Maggie often wondered if the move had really been all that necessary in the end.

"We occupy only two hundred square feet," she'd said to her husband one night. They were all piled on the couch eating ice cream cones and watching *Kiki's Delivery Service*. "What did we need thirty-eight hundred extra for?"

With its towering forty-five-foot ceilings, buttressed by the original exposed iron supports, and seemingly endless open space, the loft was incomparable with any Maggie had ever seen in Manhattan. Rays of light shone through the two-story-high windows, reflecting off the polished but mottled wide-planked maple floors. It would be the perfect home if it weren't in Jersey City, but that was what made it affordable. As long as they were inside, Maggie was happy. She complained bitterly, though, when she didn't feel like cooking and wanted decent take out. She would drive her minivan into Manhattan just to bring home a decent order of rice and beans, fried sweet plantains, and *ropa vieja* from her favorite Cuban-Chinese joint.

Maggie found Lily in the bathroom, peering into the toilet. Rice Krispies were, in fact, stuck against the sides of the bowl and the waterlogged box floated inside.

"Froggy hungry. Box too big," Lily explained.

Maggie then spotted the green plastic frog bobbing under the cereal box and understood everything. "Oh, I see. Honey, go wake up your father, please. I think he's on the couch in front of the TV. I'll clean this up and we'll give Froggy something else to eat."

Maggie pushed up her sleeves and pulled the rubber gloves out of the bathroom closet and the toilet brush from its holder.

Just as she began to scrub the sticky cereal from the bowl, her office cell rang from her back pocket. She'd had enough foresight to bring it with her but not enough to pull the gloves off before answering. Toilet water ran down the gloves and dripped into her ear. "Ugh!" Then, "Hello?"

"Maggie, remind me not to get out of bed on this date in the future."

"Sure thing," Maggie replied, thinking, *I'd like to have skipped it too.*

RHM was Maggie's favorite client. She'd started doing publicity and strategy for the company when it was just starting to gain momentum almost four years ago. Beth had recruited her from the New School, where Maggie worked as the director of project development and PR. Her job to connect art and commerce helped fine arts students find practical applications for their work with commercial enterprises. She'd caught the media's attention with a stunt she miraculously pulled off at the Guggenheim Museum on behalf of a skateboarding urban studies major and Sector 9 skateboards. Outfitted with four GoPros, the student rode down the spiral ramp of the iconic Frank Lloyd Wright building and out the front door. Sector 9 used photos from the stunt in its ads and the museum benefitted by attracting students and twentysomethings to the museum in unprecedented numbers. Beth had called Maggie after a profile in the *New York Times* detailed Maggie's ambitious plan for the performance piece. Beth told her that the PR event exemplified exactly the kind of audacious ambition she was looking for in a strategist.

Since then RHM had grown exponentially, due partly to generous backing from an angel investor. Beth had been able to take on huge risks in development and materials. Someone somewhere had enormous faith in Beth.

It turned out to be a good bet for the backer, because RHM, after the initial start-up costs, had done nothing but make tons of money. Much of it was reinvested into the company, which had, among other unusual aspects, the best employee package Maggie had ever seen. With the exception of two people Beth had fired, every single person who started with the company was still employed today. On the firm's fifth anniversary, Maggie placed a feature on RHM in *Fortune* magazine. The investors were more than satisfied.

Maggie worked on a freelance basis out of choice, but she was an integral part of the company. She and Beth had worked out a mutually beneficial arrangement where Maggie could budget from the reliable monthly retainer and, with a few points on the company's net profit, have a sense of ownership. Since Maggie's home life was chaotic at best, the freelance life helped her juggle it all. Over time, she and Beth had grown to be very close friends. She knew Beth well enough to let her rant for a minute or two on the phone—she would eventually get to the point.

Beth recounted the crazy day over at RHM.

"Can all these people really have such a problem with underwear? They're worse than animal rights activists. Anyway, I'm sure this is all good for us, so no reason to complain about it, right?" Beth said, signaling that she was ready for business. "Are you ready to get all of this down? Here's the deal . . ."

Maggie could hear Lily and John across the loft and knew her daughter had been successful at waking him. At least she could now turn her attention to what Beth needed her to do.

John kept the crossword puzzle and a pen handy in the bath-room for those long visits. Maggie traded her toilet brush for the pen and sat on the closed lid of the toilet to take down notes.

Beth put Maggie on hold then seemed to forget she was on the line, so Maggie hung up the phone. She absentmindedly picked up the toilet brush and, brandishing it as a weapon, went in search of her daughter and husband. They were cud-dled on the couch watching a *Dora the Explorer* video. It was midafternoon on a glorious June day and John hadn't done anything but watch *La Dolce Vita* for the 108th time. Literally. She knew because he kept a tally on the fridge and the last time she looked it was at 107.

John was an adjunct professor of film history at Rutgers University in New Brunswick, New Jersey. He was an ABD (all but dissertation), struggling to finish his doctoral thesis on Visconti and Fellini. A learning disability prevented him from mastering Italian and had slowed down progress toward his doctorate. Maggie thought the "learning disability" was more likely caused by the amount of weed he had smoked. His excuse for viewing these movies over and over again was the hope that if he watched them enough times in Italian with subtitles, his brain would eventually kick in and he would un-derstand the language. Maggie was sure his frequent viewing had more to do with an obsession with Claudia Cardinale and Sophia Loren. Not that she could blame him there.

"John, why don't you take Lily to the park? It's sunny and warm and she's been cooped up inside all day. It's crazy to stay inside. I've got to take care of the crisis over at Red Hot Mama."

"I don't really have the time. I have to get over to Rutgers by four for a student advisory meeting."

"Can you change your meeting?" Maggie asked, doubting the urgency of his schedule. "I need you here this afternoon. Rosie isn't coming today, and I have to get over to RHM this afternoon."

"Can't. No one is in the office, and I don't know how to get in touch with my student."

"Then who is supposed to pick up Jules and Justine from school this afternoon?" John's children from his previous marriage were living with them full-time this year while their mother was in France researching her book, a project inspired by the affair between Maggie and John that broke up their marriage.

"I just figured you could. Is that a problem?"

Maggie's mouth hung open, too astonished to respond with anything but "Oh, right. Sure." She often found herself acquiescing in spite of a voice in her head screaming, *Tell him to go fuck himself!*

The phone rang again, this time on the home line. It was Jules's school calling to say that he had just sprained his ankle playing basketball and needed to be picked up right away.

Maggie raised her eyebrows at John, hoping against hope that he would step up.

"I guess you should leave now, then," he said.

MAGGIE CALLED BETH and spoke with her assistant, Sacha, to postpone the meeting they'd arranged for that afternoon until the following morning. She packed up a bag for Lily and drove off in her minivan to pick up John's son, whom she resented as much as his father at the moment. The saving grace was how excited Lily would be to get her older brother from school. She took such delight in him that Maggie couldn't be angry for long. Once they were on their way, Maggie turned on the car radio. CBS News was reporting on the day's festivities at RHM:

"A crowd of more than one hundred has gathered to protest maternity lingerie at the popular Flatiron district store Red Hot Mama. Modeled by America's sweetheart Agnes Seymour and actor Milly Ling, the campaign seems to have sparked off debates about whether maternity and lingerie are proper bedfellows . . ." The newscaster seemed to be having some fun with the report.

"Wow, people really don't have enough to do with their time . . . Give me a break!" Maggie said aloud, before she turned up the volume to hear more about how the media was positioning the protests.

"What, Mommy? Why you said that?" Lily had been listening as usual and didn't miss a thing.

"Nothing important, baby, nothing at all." Maggie was aware that the vitriol she felt at that moment had little to do with the protests and was more likely the result of her frustration with John. She knew Jules would give anything to have his father or his real mother give a damn that he had hurt himself at school. Now she felt like the evil stepmother, pissed off that she was sent to take care of it all.

Maggie heaved a sigh and fought off the anger gaining momentum inside her. "What could I have been thinking?" she said too loudly.

"What, Mommy?"

"I said, what are you thinking about, Lily love?"

No matter her state of mind, there was always Lily. Whenever Maggie began to regret her affair-turned-marriage with John, she had to think only of her daughter to know that any discomfort whatsoever was worth it if it brought her the curly-headed creature now kicking her legs and humming a rambling tune in the backseat of the car.

MAGGIE HAD MET John four years earlier at the New School in Manhattan, when John was teaching an Italian film history class. One week, midsemester, Maggie received two checks and John none. The payroll system had a glitch and read Johanna Margaret Harding and John Maris Harting as the same. The two met inadvertently in the accounting office.

John, a vision of a boyish man, stopped Maggie's breath. Two-day beard, a wool beanie pulled over his head showing unruly hair, a ratty backpack slung over his shoulder, a skateboard and book under his arm. He was reading *A Cinema of Poetry: Aesthetics of the Italian Art Film* by Joseph Luzzi. That did it.

"Hey, can I help?" she offered when she overheard John explaining his situation.

"I don't see how you could, but I am so fucked without this paycheck . . ."

"I can lend you half of mine if you want," Maggie said before even realizing that she had just offered a stranger half her paycheck. *Typical!* the voice in Maggie's head screamed.

"Oh, no . . . I couldn't do that. But thanks."

Maggie was in the maelstrom of setting up the Guggenheim/skateboard stunt, which was proving nearly impossible to pull off. Beset with obstacles every step of the way, Maggie was thinking about bailing on the project.

To keep the conversation going, she asked John, "Is that a Sector 9 board?"

"What . . . ? This, oh, no, it's a Carver; the trucks are looser and it rides more like a surfboard . . . Why? Do you skate?"

"No, but I am interested for professional reasons."

"I can't imagine what those would be." His tone was incredulous, but his attention was hooked.

"I can tell you about it if you're interested . . ." Maggie said, a touch too eagerly.

"Yeah, sure, I'd love to. Do you mean now?" John seemed confused.

"Well, I have an hour before my next meeting. I mean, only if you aren't busy . . . Do you want to grab a quick coffee?"

Maggie and John headed to the corner dive diner where Maggie regaled him with stories about the stunt. Between the insurance companies, community boards, city bureaucracy, and museum donors opposing every detail, Maggie had doubts about the plausibility of seeing the project through. For the next few weeks, she and John spoke every day. His enthusiasm helped her to find the resolve to work through the obstacles threatening to derail her project.

In return he confided in her about his crumbling marriage, which had been on the rocks since the birth of their youngest, Jules, now four. Two frustrated academics who competed with each other for the attention and respect neither of them could garner for themselves, John and Georgette would tear each other's already fragmented egos to shreds. Or at least this was how Maggie pieced it all together from John's stories. Most comfortable in her self-appointed role as savior, Maggie rushed in to bolster John's spirit.

By the time he received his own check, Maggie and John had shacked up together for several sweaty afternoons in Maggie's tiny Village apartment. It was lust instigated by computer error and felt fated by the gods. They couldn't get enough of each other. Their post-class fuck and postcoital cupcake from Magnolia Bakery became ritual. By the end of the semester, they were in love and torn about what to do next. Just as they'd made the decision that John would break the news to Georgette that he was leaving, someone beat them to it.

An undergraduate auditing John's class had developed a mean crush on her instructor. John was so caught up with Maggie that he didn't notice the seductive, professor-struck student, Desi.

One afternoon, Desi followed John and Maggie back to Maggie's apartment. She waited on the front stoop of a brownstone across the street until they emerged an hour and a half later, then followed them to Magnolia Bakery. Desi hid in the playground from where she watched the lovers lick buttercream icing from each other's lips. An art major with a burgeoning talent in charcoal, Desi brought a sketch pad and pencil with her everywhere she went. She drew each scene with the voyeuristic detail and melodramatic flourish of a courtroom artist's sketch.

Her series, which she entitled *Love for Sale* (no one could figure out why), would be used effectively by Georgette later. They included sketches of John and Maggie kissing on the street, John touching Maggie intimately on the front stoop, the lovers eating cupcakes. One sketch, which must have been imagined (and with frightening accuracy), showed the two lovers in flagrante delicto. These pictures were hung in the school gallery for a week, and while they aroused some suspicions, no one could say for certain who the lovers were. Maggie and John were completely unaware. When the show was taken down, Desi had the series sent to Georgette with a cryptic note, "Because you're you."

John came home one night to the horrific surprise of an artist's rendition of his affair hung expertly on the living room walls. Georgette had left for the night, taking the children with her, to let John stew in his own humiliation. What Georgette intended as exposure became instead the curation of her marriage's demise.

When John saw the drawings hung up in his living room, he phoned Maggie immediately. "Darling, we have a problem. I know you said you'd never come here, but I think you should see something."

"What is it?"

"I'm not sure. I think it's you and me in charcoal. You have to see them." John's breath was short.

"Them? Charcoal? For God's sake, John, tell me something I can understand."

"Just get over here," John demanded. He'd never done that before.

"I'll be right over." Maggie hung up, fled down the four flights of stairs to the street, and hailed a taxi.

The intensity of the havoc wreaked by the affair bonded John and Maggie together till death. Or something. Four weeks later, John moved his clothing, books, and computer into Maggie's apartment. It all happened so fast, Maggie didn't put any sort of protest in motion, although she knew she was making a mistake. But how could she insult John just when his whole life had fallen apart because of her?

Georgette, admirably, had turned her heartache into opportunity. Months of tears ended with the publication of an article in the *New York Times Magazine*, entitled "Love for Sale." A thinly veiled account of the affair between Maggie and John, in which Georgette made an argument in favor of the nineteenth-century French courtesan.

"Mistresses today are clumsy and don't understand the implicit boundaries between sex for sex's sake and lasting marriages," she wrote. "A fling with another man or woman should not be misconstrued as a replacement relationship. Since contemporary American society doesn't provide an outlet for, or acceptance of, extramarital activity, every casual fuck has the power to dislocate a marriage." The article, accompanied by Desi's semi-erotic drawings, drew an enormous response from readers. A week later, Georgette had been offered a book deal with an obscene advance and was on her way to becoming a popular talking head on marriage and infidelity on every morning news show.

BY THE TIME Maggie arrived at Jules's school, Lily had fallen asleep in her car seat and she had the unpleasant task of waking a toddler. *It will all be fine* was Maggie's internal mantra as she wrangled her reluctant daughter out of the car. She dreaded the inevitable wounded look on Jules's face when he saw her, instead of his father, coming to his rescue.

The forlorn boy was waiting in the lobby, his ankle mis-shapen from the ACE bandage wrapped over an ice pack.

"Where's Dad?"

"Oh, he had an emergency at Rutgers and I was on my way in anyway . . ." she lied. "How're you feeling?"

"Fine."

"Does it hurt?"

"Yes." Jules was sullen. "When's Mom coming home? I thought she was supposed to be here by now."

"I don't know, Jules." Maggie tried to sound sympathetic instead of impatient. "Look, Lily, it's your brother, he has a boo-boo. Give him a kiss and help him feel better."

Maggie was trying to keep Lily from the meltdown she was about to have and quell the expression of abandonment welling in Jules's eyes at the same time.

"What do you say we go and get a banana boat at the Ice Cream Palace before we pick up Justine? We still have an hour to kill. Sound like fun?"

She took one groggy yes from Lily as a positive response and forged on.

By the time they headed to pick up Justine, the younger children were in high spirits. Justine was the more gregarious of John's two children, and Maggie felt a stronger sense of re-sponsibility toward her than she did toward Jules. She wished John would be a better role model for his son but felt that, as boy and man, they needed to work that out on their own. With Justine, Maggie thought and hoped that she could pro-vide some positive influence.

Maggie pulled up in front of Justine's school lobby with five minutes to spare. Lily and Jules were keeping each other occupied in the backseat with the pile of lift-the-flap books they kept in the car. Maggie sat back and closed her eyes, welcoming these precious few moments of not having to physically *do* anything. Her mind raced back to what was happening at RHM. It would be her job to spin the protests and controversial ads into gold ink for the company. She considered what, exactly, had so offended people.

Maggie's thoughts worked their way through the issues, as if arguing for both sides.

On the politically conservative side of the issue, she reasoned, sexualizing pregnancy and birth blasphemed conception and motherhood. The sacrosanct exploited for commercial gain.

Maggie saw RHM's approach as a celebration of women's God-given gifts. *How can I spin it so that others can see it in this positive light as well?* she wondered.

On the left-leaning side of the argument, Maggie contended, RHM's lingerie and ads were blatant objectification of women in their most exalted and revered capability. The female image turned fetish.

This, Maggie understood, could be seen as a strike against women's struggle for gender equality. *How can I help them understand that this* is *the ultimate equalizer? What can be more powerful than to own the ability to procreate, to express it sexually and celebrate it if you want?*

The two sides were really not that different. They never were. Maggie felt close to some kind of plan when Lily began to scream.

"What, Lil? Jules, what does she want?"

"I think she pooped. I can smell it."

Even as Jules said it, Maggie's olfactory senses kicked in. "Oh, yeah . . . C'mon baby girl, let's get you out of that stinky mess." As Maggie got out of the car to attend to Lily, it occurred to her that they'd been parked outside Justine's school for half an hour. "Jules, can you manage with those crutches and go check on Justine? Ask the security guard where she might be." Maggie pulled her phone out of her pocket to call John, hopeful that he might know something about Justine's schedule.

Nothing like sitting in a car seat to spread a diaper mess around. This was a five-wipe cleanup. As she wrestled her squirmy daughter in the backseat to change her diaper, Maggie tried to call John's cell and dialed the apartment instead by mistake, so she was surprised that he picked up. "John, hi! What are you doing home?"

"Hey, I'm on long distance with Georgette in Paris. Can you call me back in a few?"

"Um, yeah, sure," Maggie responded as she clicked off the phone. "'Long distance'?" she exclaimed out loud to no one. "Who says 'long distance' anymore?"

By now it was past four o'clock, the time John supposedly had to be at the university. Instead, he was gabbing away with his ex-wife in Paris while Maggie changed diapers and picked up their children from school. Something in her life had gone terribly wrong.

It took another half an hour for Justine to materialize. She'd been in the girls' locker room changing from her soccer uniform for the past hour. Maggie wanted to be angry with her for being so inconsiderate, but then thought how she'd done the same thing when she was Justine's age. Her mother called it "dillydallying."

Maggie remembered well the half-serious admonishments she'd receive when she'd left her mother waiting. Her tendency to dillydally had ended with her mother's death, when Maggie was only eleven. A lunchtime-drunk businessman plowed into her car at a red light, killing her instantly. After that, Maggie became a person of precision.

Justine, as a ten-year-old girl still safe in the realm of childhood, had every right in the world to dillydally. Maggie smiled at her as she walked through the doors.

Something else occurred to Maggie at that same moment: Jules had jumped from the car, without his crutches, and effortlessly ran into the school when Maggie asked him to check on his sister. What about that sprained ankle? Glad to see that he was physically sound, Maggie wondered about the emotional health of the boy. Instead of walking it off when he'd twisted his ankle, he'd cried for his parents, but had gotten Maggie.

The cell phone rang just as Maggie piled all the kids back into the car. It was John. "Hi, what's up?" he asked.

"What's up?" she echoed, trying to hide the contempt in her voice.

It was her fault. She always defaulted to pleasant mode even under the worst circumstances. But how could she explain to the kids that their father, while loving in ways that mattered most, was inefficient about the logistics of child rearing? It wasn't any different from her own father's neglect after the death of her mother.

Everyone does the best they can, right? A refrain that plagued her. John said it all the time. "Maggie, I'm doing the best I can!" It reminded her of her dad's advice, "Just do the best you can." *But what if the best you can do sucks?* Maggie wondered. *Where does that leave you?*

"What's up? Oh, not much, we're on our way back now. Hey, do you have any ideas for dinner? The kids are starved." She wasn't even going to begin to question him about the student he stood up.

"Why don't you pick something up on the way home?"

"Righto." Maggie clicked the phone off. She was getting close, very close, to action that didn't bode well for her future as a married woman.

When she got home, John was at his computer, working away on his thesis. She understood that he had the best of intentions but wondered when he would admit that it was futile and turn his attention to something he *could* do. Maggie heard that annoying ditty in her head again: *He's doing the best he can!*

THE NEXT MORNING, Maggie awoke to what felt like a three-martini hangover. She hadn't had one drop of alcohol the night before. She considered for a minute the likelihood that she was coming down with something. When the details of the previous day seeped into her consciousness, she realized the toxicity she felt was bred from conflict, not gin.

The lure of hot coffee was the only thing that pulled her out from under the covers. That and the 9:00 A.M. meeting over at RHM. John snored next to her, and by some miracle, Lily was still asleep in her bed. Maggie checked on her before padding across the loft to grind the coffee beans and beginning her morning ritual of brewing espresso and heating milk. Maggie looked forward to that joyous first cup of coffee in the silence of a sleeping house, before everyone else began to stir.

It would be up to her, no doubt, to wake Justine and Jules. Maggie had coordinated her meeting at RHM to allow enough time to drop them off at school beforehand. She couldn't bear to hear one more of John's excuses about why he wouldn't be able to do it himself this morning.

After two sips into her delicious coffee, she heard Lily running across the loft. She could tell from the direction of her baby steps that Lily had silently crept from her bed and into Maggie and John's room. Not seeing her mother, she began to cry out, "Mommy! Where are you?"

Maggie hopped down from her stool and ran to her daughter. She swung her up in the air and put her nose in her hair, which smelled of baby shampoo and chocolate fudge. She kissed her from head to toe. "Uh-oh, Lily my love, we've got to wash your hair this morning. Let's have some breakfast together first, then we'll fill the tub."

Maggie mixed up a big bowl of yogurt, bananas, and granola for both of them to share. Lily sat on Maggie's lap and they read *The Big Red Barn* three times while they ate. This was Maggie's favorite part of the day, just her and Lily alone at the breakfast table, no one else hovering about needing her attention. Maggie let Jules and Justine sleep past their wake-up call, not wanting to disturb this too-rare moment with her baby.

It wouldn't be so bad for them to be late, she told herself. It was the end of the school year anyway. Still, she knew her motives were completely selfish. After yesterday, she wanted a day off from John's kids.

Breakfast finished, Maggie started a bath for Lily and went to rouse Justine and Jules. Ten minutes later, all four of them were in the bathroom trying to get ready for the day. As he was reaching for a comb, Jules knocked a glass jar of cotton balls onto the floor, which shattered into a million pieces. The day had just begun and Maggie was already fed up.

"Guys, there are two other bathrooms in the house. Why don't you each use one of them so we're not tripping over one another? Get out of here now, please!"

No doubt triggered by her stern voice, Jules began to wail that he'd been cut by a piece of glass. After thoroughly searching his hands, Maggie could see no wounds. He'd told her two different fingers hurt, on separate hands, so she figured he was just in a state of panic.

"Jules, honey, you're fine. You didn't get cut. Now go and let me clean this up," she demanded, and pointed out the door. Maggie didn't care if she sounded harsh at that moment—there was that evil stepmother rearing her ugly head again—all she wanted was a few more moments of peace with her daughter. Blinking away tears of frustration, she began to clean up the broken glass.

Lily, enthralled by the bath, didn't notice the commotion. By the time Maggie had cleared away the mess, she was ready for her after-bath snuggle. Wrapped in a towel, Maggie held Lily close. Maggie loved to track Lily's growth by how she fit along her own body. When she was an infant, Lily's whole body had flopped easily over Maggie's shoulder and Maggie could hold her with one arm. Now Lily's head fit where her whole body used to and her legs stretched down to Maggie's hips. It was a measure of time passing more quickly than she could register it in the day to day.

Even after her bath, Lily had a strong scent that Maggie

found intoxicating. Maggie understood how animals could identify their young through smell alone. She felt close to her own animal instincts when it came to Lily. This greatest gift stripped away what civilized life brought, leaving something atavistic in its place, often and miraculously felt as love.

The trials of the morning behind her, Maggie dropped Lily off at Rosie's for the day and loaded the big kids up in the car to head into the city. If the rest of the morning went smoothly, she would be only fifteen or twenty minutes late for her meeting with Beth, who would understand the delay without need for explanation. Still, her heart was racing from the way the morning had unfolded.

Maggie was too late to drive around looking for a legal spot on the street near the office, so she decided to pay the exorbitant parking fees—*Dammit!*—and put the car in a lot instead. She grabbed her bag and hoofed it the few blocks to RHM, pulling out her phone to call John as she walked. Before she could dial his number, she was stopped dead in her tracks in front of a bus stop shelter. Her jaw dropped—along with her phone (screen side down, *dammit again!*)—at the sight of the image affronting her. The side panel held one of the RHM ads featuring a stunning Milly Ling, now defaced with big, angry black Xs covering her eyes and breasts. A crudely drawn target with an arrow in the bull's-eye covered the actress's abdomen. Maggie shuddered at the violated picture. Feeling shaken, she picked up her phone, now with a cracked screen, and pressed John's number.

"John, hi, it's me." She didn't even wait for John to respond. "Listen, I can't do this anymore. You slept through the entire nightmare this morning. From now on, you have to help. You don't help, your children don't get to school." It was a gutless threat—the kids had only five more days left until summer break—and Maggie felt churlish making it.

"Sure, Maggie. If you'd said something, you know I would have helped." John's voice was steady and earnest, which drove Maggie crazy.

"That's the problem, don't you get it? Why do I have to ask you to help me with your children?"

"I was sleeping, Maggie. I didn't know."

"John, just don't talk. It makes me angrier . . . I'm about to get to work and I'm already late. I gotta go." Maggie clicked off the phone.

As soon as she hung up, she regretted making the call at all. She knew John wasn't so much negligent as he was distracted. Lost in her silent debate, Maggie walked right into the police barricades still strewn about the sidewalk in front of RHM, bruising her left thigh. As she rubbed the pain out, she looked up. There was a violent gash in the green-tinted translucent storefront window that caused Maggie to shudder and reminded her of the job she had to do.

Just as Maggie turned to open the doors leading to the office, she was startled by a man standing next to the doorway. He had blue eyes, neat close-cropped hair, full lips, and a gloriously strong nose. One glance and he was a striking fright, another and he was strikingly beautiful. Maggie stopped cold in her tracks and her belly caught an unexpected butterfly before she regained her senses. She shook him off and brushed just past him to enter the building. When the door closed behind her she exclaimed to no one, "What the hell was that?"

Up on the third floor, Maggie greeted the staff at RHM,

emboldened to see them full steam ahead after the drama of the previous day. She headed straight for Beth's office.

"I just got hit by the thunderbolt. Either that or I just looked into the eyes of a serial killer," Maggie said breathlessly.

"Ha! Very good—*G-1*, Michael in Sicily when he first sees Apollonia." Beth and Maggie shared an obsession with *The Godfather* movies. Maggie especially appreciated the films since John didn't get them, stuck as he was in the rigid curriculum of what he considered "real" Italian films.

"But what's this about a serial killer?" Beth asked as an afterthought.

"Oh, nothing really. There was this guy standing outside the door downstairs who caught my eye. It was the strangest thing . . ."

Sacha poked her head into Beth's office, announcing that everyone was waiting for them in the conference room.

"Things with John not so great?" Beth asked affectionately as they headed to their meeting.

"Fuggedaboutit," Maggie said, and laughed.

THE STAFF OF RHM was assembled and ready for business. Seated around the large bamboo conference table, the principle executives of RHM gave brief updates of the fallout from yesterday's protest. It had been covered in all the local newspapers except the *Wall Street Journal*, though a journalist from the paper had called, interested in doing a story on Beth and the company.

"Looks like we have our work cut out, but this is a good thing for us." Beth exuded confidence, which trickled down to every employee of RHM. "Anna, can you give us an update on sales?"

"Well, the overall sales were up for the month, and even though we had to close the store early yesterday, we've already beat last June's numbers by fifty percent and we still have eight days to go. Catalog call-in and online sales made a noticeable jump in activity last night and this morning, no doubt from the news coverage. The store is jammed already, though it's too early to tell if customers are buying or just curious window-shoppers. All in all, things look more than promising." Anna's voice was strong and authoritative, but Maggie thought she looked wiped out.

"Just as Beth suspected," Anna summarized, "the protests haven't seemed to hurt us at all, at least from a sales point of view."

Maggie spoke up out of turn with a burst of inspiration. "Why don't we organize a roundtable discussion on mother-hood to be televised on one of the news programs? If people are yelling about what pregnant women should and shouldn't be wearing, and what we should and shouldn't be selling them, maybe we should start a dialogue around the issues. We can have call-ins and really make things lively. If we can't do it for television, I can always try to place the story in a women's magazine." Maggie was so accustomed to jumping from one thing to another that ideas often got blurted out the moment they materialized. Suddenly self-conscious at the outburst, she began to apologize. "Sorry to interrupt, Anna . . ."

"I love the idea," Beth decided, already thinking ahead, "but who would put it on the air?"

"I'll find someone."

Maggie spent the day at RHM, where she began making a round of phone calls to take the temperature on her roundtable idea. By the time she was wrapping things up, she looked at her watch to see that she was running late. The day had slipped by so quickly and Maggie had to leave right away to be on time to pick up Lily. Usually Rosie either came to spend the day at Maggie's apartment or she picked up and dropped off Lily herself, but her car was in the shop all week. John's Harley—even with the sidecar—didn't accommodate a toddler.

Maggie said a quick good-bye to Beth and Anna and left the offices. As she walked toward the parking garage, she realized she had gotten so carried away with pitching the roundtable that she'd forgotten to tell Beth about the defaced ad while she was at the office. She picked up the phone to call her but then thought better of it. The past few days had given them all enough to process. Another angry critic wasn't going to change anything. Maggie pocketed her phone.

As she neared the end of the street, she got a prickly feeling. When she turned to investigate, she was astonished to see the blue-eyed man from the morning. *What are the odds?* she thought.

Blue Eyes unnerved her, though she couldn't immediately pinpoint whether it was in an attracted sort of way or in a threatening one. She dismissed the coincidence of seeing him twice in one day as an it's-a-small-world moment. Over the years, the false intimacy of coincidences with strangers on the streets of New York gave Maggie a sense of security. She had always felt that the city was her first and most constant lover—and a generous one, presenting plenty of opportunity for philandering of one kind or another.

PART TWO

LATE SUMMER

CHAPTER SIX

Anna

ANNA LAY IN bed, exhausted by the day's activities. The family had decided to spend the last two weeks of summer in Montauk at Anna's parents' bungalow, an optimistic attempt to have some quiet family time, as if there were such a thing with two toddlers. The boys were, at least for the moment, asleep after an active day at the beach. She could hear the hum from the television turned low in the living room, where Jason watched the History Channel.

Anna welcomed the time alone and tried to expel the caustic thoughts fogging her mind. She couldn't shake the fear that she wouldn't be able to hold on to the fragile life forming in her womb. She wanted only to rest, but instead she was spending her vacation running around the South Fork of Long Island, shepherding Oscar and Henry to the beach and back. Anna feared that her favorite place on earth with her favorite people on earth was turning into more burden than joy.

That Jason had the time and energy to watch TV enraged her. No matter how much he shared with Anna the daily demands of parenting young children, now that she was pregnant again, she needed Jason to do more now so she could give this new baby the sustaining body it needed to thrive. Her frustration was taking its toll.

Earlier in the day while they were all at the beach, she had lost it with him for a misperceived infraction. Jason had returned to the car for the toy trucks they forgot to pack in the wagon. Henry and Oscar wanted to splash in the shore break, but Anna feared that the undertow current might pull them away from her. She grew impatient waiting for Jason, who seemed to be taking his sweet time returning to the beach. *I bet he bumped into a friend and is yakking away while I'm left to mind the boys*, she thought bitterly while she tried to distract the kids. By the time Jason finally appeared, she had worked herself into a state of fury.

Anna attacked Jason as he walked toward them on the sand, triumphantly holding his sons' favorite trucks. "What took you so long?"

"The shovel on the backhoe fell off of Oscar's truck. But I found a way to fix it!"

"Really, Jason? You *had* to fix it *now*?" she huffed. "You couldn't have waited until we got home? The boys wanted to swim and I can't take them both into the water alone. You were gone for over half an hour!"

Jason didn't take the bait. Instead, he dropped the trucks in the sand and swept both boys up in his arms as he ran with them to the water's edge while they shrieked with delight.

The fact of her anger made her feel even more miserable. *What if all this negativity jeopardizes my baby?* She wrestled her mind to focus on all the good things about their lives together.

. . .

BEFORE ANNA MET Jason, she had given up trying to work out a conventional arrangement with a man. She no longer had faith that any man could give her the freedom she needed while supporting her in helpful ways. Anna had grown to accept that what she needed was too much to ask of the other sex. She wanted freedom from caretaking fragile egos. She wanted a partner who would encourage, not hinder, her dreams; a good father to their children, a lover, a best friend. It didn't seem like too much to ask, yet the right man eluded her.

When she was in her early twenties, Anna had been in love with an eccentric Australian playwright, Mick Wilkinson. The couple spoke of marriage, but Anna was only a few years out of college and wasn't ready to settle down.

Mick, on the other hand, was ten years older and ready to put down roots. He had traveled during his twenties, satisfying a surf obsession by seeking waves in far-flung locales. He'd surfed Indo and Japan, the Gaza Strip, and the frigid waters off Scotland. He rode tidal river bores and ship wakes in the Great Lakes and epic swells at Mavericks. Mick's experiences offered a window into a life played out in stark contrast to Anna's sheltered suburban upbringing. He could navigate any situation with humor and ease, and Anna couldn't resist his laid-back approach to whatever came his way. For two years, Anna was enthralled by Mick's free-spirited soul and ability to take whatever he wanted for himself in life. These very qualities led him to make a fatal relationship blunder.

During a New Year's Eve party they'd held in their Hell's Kitchen apartment, Mick decided to surprise announce their engagement. The problem was he had yet to propose. He'd thought the surprise would flatter her. He was very wrong.

Two weeks later, Anna broke off the engagement she'd never accepted in the first place and broke Mick's heart by moving out soon thereafter. Anna, convinced that between lust and everlasting love, an imbalanced power dynamic threatened even the most devoted couples. She was not hopeful for a satisfying partnership.

After, Anna entered a decade of dating and long-term affairs that ended with her unwillingness to make peace with the stubborn gender divide she encountered in each of these relationships. Determined to have a child, Anna planned to conceive with her friend Joe Ballard. Joe had never quite recovered enough to settle down with someone after the devastating loss of so many friends during the AIDS epidemic of the '80s and '90s. Anna and Joe had been partners in their otherwise partnerless lives. They traveled together, knew each other's families and were family to each other for years. Through Joe's breakups and Anna's, they were always there for each other. After a year of talking about having a child together, they consulted with an attorney to draw up the necessary paperwork for custody and childcare arrangements. Anna's desire for children far outweighed her need for a husband. A friend for life seemed as good a partnership as any, and traveling down the path of the unconventional underpinned her protest against relationships past. This was the way to go. Anna had been sure of it.

ANNA HAD JOINED RHM at its inception. She and Beth had camped out in Beth's living room until they found the right space for the fledgling company. They were on a tight budget, liquidating their 401(k) funds and mining their limited cash reserves to launch the company. Just after they announced the start-up, additional working capital came from an angel investor, though the details were vague. A lawyer contacted them to let them know that an anonymous partner was giving them $5 million. In exchange, the investor expected only repayment of the capital over ten years at little interest and a minor share. When Beth investigated, she and Anna were assured that the source and the offer were legit. Anonymity was the only other imperative. Beth was close to saying no until Anna convinced her otherwise in an unusual reversal of their standard risk-averse versus risk-tolerant roles.

"We're protected, so why not go with it?" Anna encouraged.

"Because what if the investor turns out to be some kind of screwball who steps in and tries to take over?" Beth insisted. "I can't believe someone would make such a generous gesture without a catch."

"But the lawyers already gave the offer a thorough vetting and there's a safety valve if they try to step in," Anna pushed. "I say we go for it. It will give us an edge in the marketplace. Do you know how quickly we'll be able to respond to demand with that sort of cash padding? This could make us!"

"Okay, fine. But, Anna, you better be right . . ."

The company green-lighted the deal with a signature and a prayer.

It was Anna'a favorite time, professionally speaking. Working around the clock and sharing an assistant, she and Beth created the culture that would become the enormously popular—if incendiary—RHM. With some of their investor money,

Beth found an expansive raw space in the Flatiron district and hired Jason Schwartz, a talented and affordably uncelebrated architect, to design RHM's offices and flagship store and see through their construction.

Over the course of those first months of planning the space, Jason and Beth spoke several times a day. When Beth wasn't available, Anna would pick up the line. They had not yet met in person, but Anna and Jason became flirtatious phone friends. Jason's voice was reedy and gentle, and at times, a tremulous vibrato in his speech made him sound either slightly nervous or as though he was quelling excitement. Anna couldn't tell which. Her mental image of him was of a slight, nerdy man with a small chin. She felt soothed whenever they spoke and she came to think of him as a friend.

On the flip side, an outrageous acquaintance had once told Anna that she sounded like a "big, fat dyke" on the phone, which she took as a compliment. Her tenor voice held traces of bass tones, and when she laughed it came as a hearty bellow. Anna assumed that Jason had formed a similar picture of her in his mind.

When the future site of RHM was close to being finished, Anna stopped by to take a look. She found Beth engaged in conversation with an upright, eccentric-looking man. He ran his hand sensuously over the coral stone he and Beth were considering for the floors. "I love the way stone feels alive, like skin. Synthetic materials can't replicate the sensuous—" he was saying to Beth as Anna walked in.

"Oh, excuse me," Anna said, "I didn't know you were having a meeting."

"Don't be ridiculous. Anna, you know Jason Schwartz, don't you?"

Anna inhaled sharply and blushed. Jason looked nothing like she expected him to. He was taller than she had envisioned and had a head of thick, copper-colored hair pointing in every direction. Gravity-defying hair. He was lithe and sturdy. Though not classically handsome, his appeal was in the plumb line of his posture, the sureness of his gaze, and the warmth of his smile, which made her knees buckle. The man was irresistible.

"*You're* Jason?"

He nodded slowly, eyebrow cocked, almost in apology. "*You're* Anna?" he asked, incredulous as well.

They both laughed as if they shared the same joke. Beth grimaced and asked, "Hey, what's so funny?"

"I'm not sure I even know," Anna said.

"I think if I say anything at all it will be a mistake," Jason added.

"Is there something I should know?" Beth asked. Neither was listening.

When Anna left the site, she shook off the encounter with amused indifference, knowing better than to think anything of it. She'd experienced plenty of immediate infatuations; this one would be nothing more than any other. The next day when she got to Beth's apartment-cum-office, the phone rang and Anna picked it up.

"Hello?"

"You shouldn't do that to people," Jason said without preamble.

"Do what?"

"You shouldn't be smart and funny and charming on the phone without warning people that you look the way you do." Jason's voice was shaky. Anna was enjoying this immensely.

"I'll take that as a compliment and not an insult."

"Take it how you will. Can I take you to dinner?" Jason asked.

Anna's thoughts shot like lightning from *Oh, shit, is he hitting on me?* to heart-fluttering delight at the realization that he was, in fact, hitting on her. "Um, sure."

"Tomorrow?"

"It's a date." Anna hung up the phone, flattered, skeptical, but excited. "Oh, Anna, don't even think about it," she told herself aloud.

The next morning, Anna canceled the dinner when she remembered she had a previous theater date with Isabel. She'd completely forgotten in the moment, but she wouldn't think of standing up her little sis. Part of her was a little relieved to have a legitimate out.

Jason called about a month later to try again.

"You've been laying low," Anna teased when she heard his voice.

"I didn't want to scare you off," Jason explained with complete sincerity. "Besides, I've been out on a job in Connecticut for the past few weeks. So how about we try again. Dinner this week?"

"Sure."

"Is Wednesday good for you?"

"Sounds fine," Anna said.

"Great. I'll call you that morning so we can decide where and when. Bye."

Jason and Anna met for a drink in an East Village dive bar. They never made it to dinner. They played darts, drank Guinness, and talked like old friends for four hours straight. When Anna told Jason of her plans to conceive with Joe Ballard, Jason told her, "You might want to wait on that."

"Um, well, thanks but no thanks for the unsolicited advice . . ." she answered with a vehemence she hoped would have the wanted effect of sending the message, *Back off, buddy.* They let it go at that for a while.

When Anna asked him what he was doing for the holidays (Thanksgiving was coming up), he'd answered, inexplicably, "You are my holiday."

"What's that supposed to mean?"

"I mean, I promised myself one thing for the holidays, and that was time with you," Jason told her.

"Isn't that a little presumptuous?" Anna challenged, visions of Mick Wilkinson floating through her mind. Still, she realized the flirtation in her voice distinctly overrode any objection. *What the hell was going on?*

Having forgone dinner, they picked up some fried chicken and a six-pack of beer and headed back to Jason's apartment, a compact and spare flat, perfectly arranged. He'd turned a 450-square-foot L-shaped studio into a Japanese-inspired loft, with a tatami mat bedroom above his office area. A masterful use of the limited floor plan, the space, like Jason's voice, made Anna feel calm.

The two stayed up all night talking. Anna had grown weary of those get-to-know-you questions spent on dates: Where did you grow up? How many siblings? What drugs did you take in college? The answers rarely held Anna's interest. After an hour or two of these exchanges, she could foresee the boredom that would set in as soon as a roll in the sack had played itself out.

So Anna avoided these subjects. And since she held little expectation for the outcome of this unusual date, she relaxed and let her curiosity drive the conversation. Explicit about her lack of belief in marriage, Anna made it clear that she was not looking for one. Not a typical first date topic, but Anna wanted to set the record straight. She'd long grown tired of the assumptions made by and about people of a particular age.

The conversation was by turns serious and then silly. At a certain point Anna asked Jason one of her favorite questions, one that befuddled most: "Why did the chicken cross the road?"

"Is this a test question?" Jason asked.

"Just answer it," Anna insisted.

"Okay . . . To get to the other side."

"Yes, but is the other side geographic or cosmic?"

"Cosmic. At least, that's what I always thought . . ."

"Yes! Yes! Yes!" Anna screamed with delight as she kicked her legs up and down on the couch. She and Jason laughed long and hard at this shared insight. Anna's laughter brought on a mean case of hiccups, making them laugh themselves into tears.

They sat facing each other on the couch, feet meeting in the middle, and talked until the gray dawn seeped through the long, narrow, un-curtained casement windows. At first light, Jason asked permission to kiss Anna. He rolled off the couch and onto his knees. He leaned toward her, held her face in his hands as their lips touched for a long, blessed moment before he pulled away. Jason bowed his head. He seemed lost in meditation for a moment before he raised his head and spoke.

"Remember when I told you earlier tonight that I thought you should wait on having a baby with your friend Joe?"

"Yes—I thought that was rather bold of you," Anna said, trying to hide the smile forming on her face.

"And now?" he asked.

"And now, I'm not so sure . . ." She turned her head and gazed over her shoulder before directing her attention back to him, feeling more puzzled than cautious.

Jason stared at Anna for a few seconds before taking Anna's hands in his.

"Anna, will you marry me and have our babies?"

"What?!" Anna kicked him away. "Are you out of your fucking mind?" she said, even though she knew he was serious and she didn't really think he was crazy at all. She'd felt it too.

"I knew I wanted to marry you the second I saw you," Jason confessed. "I called my best friend the afternoon I met you and told him that I'd just met the woman I was going to marry. He said I was crazy too."

"But I just told you a few hours ago that I have no interest in marriage," Anna protested.

"You mean, until you met me?" Jason said. His tone, miraculously without arrogance, held a nakedness so powerful that Anna found herself answering in a whisper.

"Yes, until you." Anna was seriously considering his proposal in spite of herself. "We haven't even slept together, how do we know whether we'll even like each other in bed?" she asked, hoping to pull them both back down to reality.

"I'm not worried about it at all. Are you?"

"No, not really," Anna capitulated. She wondered if there existed a police of reason who could step in and stop them from such impetuousness. "Can we do this?" She didn't even know whom she was asking.

Jason shrugged and raised his eyes skyward to confirm the irrefutability of what they were considering.

Anna fell back against the couch and closed her eyes. She'd been awake for twenty-four hours and the sudden adrenaline of the moment made her sleepy. Jason let her slip away and simply rested his head on her abdomen. She had no idea how long they stayed like that. Was it a minute or two, an hour? The light in the apartment had grown from a dusty gray to a more golden hue from the sunlight slicing across the studio floor. As if awaking from a dream, Anna found herself saying, "Okay, so how long do you give me to decide?"

"I'll go out and get some bagels, coffee, and orange juice. Will that give you enough time?"

"Grapefruit juice, not orange juice."

"Okay, yes, of course, grapefruit juice . . ."

"And yes, that should give me plenty of time," Anna said, not quite disbelieving the conversation they were having.

By the time Jason got back, Anna had showered and put on one of Jason's shirts. She'd even used his toothbrush, which she'd never ever done with previous paramours.

When he walked in the door, he gave her a boyish look. "So?"

Anna stood with her arms at her sides and nodded. A slightly deranged smile slowly lit up her face.

"Good" was Jason's rather perfunctory response, as if it had all been preordained and he needed only this formal acquiescence from Anna. He'd kissed her then for the second time;

this one was long and deep and delicious. He held up the bag of bagels. "So let's have some nova to celebrate."

Jason defied all of Anna's past experiences. She thought she could spend a lifetime listening to his voice. And as it was coming from the improbable physical being of Jason Schwartz, she felt humbled—humbled by the surprise that life had granted her, humbled by the challenge to her hubristic certainty that there was no man out there for her to love.

Anna felt that the decision to be with Jason had been made for her. A joyous inevitability suffused the way she felt about him. She had a harder time getting her head around how she would explain to her family—who had finally adjusted to the fact that she was about to have a child with Joe—that she was now on the road to the one thing she'd been certain she didn't want.

When she called her parents the next day to tell them she was getting married the following week, they surprised her in that they were not surprised at all. Anna thought for a crazed moment that somehow they'd conspired to make this happen, even though she knew this was the first they'd ever heard of Jason Schwartz. Her mother was so calm it was unnerving.

Anna took the case against herself since her mother wouldn't. "But I barely know him. Don't you think this is crazy?"

"Honey, it's the way I felt about your father when I first met him. I knew instantly that he was the man I would marry."

Anna wanted to tell her mother that she was nothing like her and Jason was nothing like her father. Her situation resembled nothing of her parents' life. Anyway, things like this weren't supposed to happen, not to her, not now. But Anna couldn't figure out who or what she was protesting. Was it the chance for happiness with a loving husband and family? The fact of the matter was she wanted it very much; she just didn't believe it was possible before she met Jason.

ANNA HELD GREAT affection for her father, Nick Ducci, and their relationship had always been strong, both in spite of—and possibly in part because of—his Old World Italian patriarchal attitudes. He was strong and affectionate and believed in always doing the right thing. On the surface of things, he ruled the house. Protective of his family, they always came first, second, and third. Nick could be loud and intimidating; he didn't hide his emotions. When angry, he shouted; when happy, he'd laugh long and loud. He cried when something made him sad or unbearably happy. Nick Ducci filled the house with his big heart and even bigger opinions.

Anna's young boyfriends had always been terrified of her father. Anna silently loved him for it even as she outwardly chided him for being so intimidating. In her heart she knew she could never love a man who was afraid of her father. She wanted someone to stand up to him the way she always had. She'd admired his fierceness most and tried to imitate it even as a young girl.

Still, growing up in a predominantly Italian enclave of family and friends, Anna was most affected by the ways in which women were subordinated to men. As an adult she could never get the picture out of her head of large family dinners where this was played out. At the table, the women's chairs were often pushed slightly farther back, so that they were seated behind their husbands who dominated the food and conversation.

While the men leaned forward, elbows on the table, presiding over the scene, the women kept their hands on their laps or by their sides. The positions spoke of generations of dominance.

She had first become aware of it during a Christmas Eve dinner, when she was just a girl of eleven or twelve. The traditional multicourse Christmas Eve Feast of the Seven Fishes took days of preparation and lasted hours. It began with an antipasto of marinated baby artichokes, olives, roasted peppers, sliced raw fennel, and provolone. Then came the pasta course, always served three ways: linguini with lobster tails, linguini with crab claws, and *aglio e olio* with anchovies. Next came the main course: fried smelt, flounder, scallops, and *baccalà* salad.

After dinner, the men would sit over espresso and wine, cracking walnuts and smoking cigars, as the women cleared the table and spent those same hours hand-washing all the dishes, scrubbing the kitchen, and preparing dessert. The men never lifted a finger during those dinners.

But that Christmas Eve, when her mother had called her into the kitchen to help with the dishes, Anna had put up a fight. Her brother and male cousins were not asked to help and she was damned if she was going to.

"But, Mama," she had objected, "I want to stay at the dinner table and eat walnuts with Papa and Grandpa."

"You belong in here with the women, not with those noisy, stinky men!" Anna's mother disapproved of the cigars the men lit after dinner. "Come here!" she insisted.

"No, I'm staying here with Papa!"

Anna sidled up to her father in the chair next to him and reached for the walnut cracker and the basket of nuts.

"Anna, do you want a little wine? You can have a bit with

some seltzer," he offered as he poured her some red wine into a juice glass and topped it off with some seltzer.

"Thank you, Papa." Anna nodded, making sure that she didn't seem too eager.

"Drink it in sips. Don't gulp it down."

Anna took a sip of the diluted wine. She liked its grapelike bitterness and the bubbles that tingled her tongue. She picked a walnut from the basket and worked to place the round walnut shell between the two arms of the nutcracker, but it kept slipping out. The walnut shot across the table and hit her grandfather's belly. The men chuckled, and her father said, "Anna, give it to me, let me help you."

"No, I can do it myself," she said with some annoyance.

She finally got the walnut properly firm in the vise and squeezed with all her might. Nothing happened. Her small hands ached but she squeezed even harder until the entire apparatus flipped out of her hands and knocked over the juice glass of wine all over her dress. The men around the table laughed at the effort—though not with menace. Anna fought back angry tears until her mother, hearing the commotion, came to the doorway of the dining room and scolded them all. Anna burst into tears and her mother grabbed Anna by the arm and dragged her into the kitchen.

"I told you to stay in here with us women," her mother admonished. Then she added more kindly, "Oh, dear, look at your dress! It's okay. We can clean it later. Here, take this"— she handed Anna a sifter filled with confectioners' sugar— "and sprinkle it on all of those cookies on the tray."

Anna refused to take hold of the sifter, but her mother pushed it into her hands and positioned them above the cookie tray.

"Just shake it back and forth like this," her mother instructed. Anna stood motionless for a moment, and as soon as her mother let go of her hands, she turned the sifter over, dumping all the sugar on top of the cookie tray, and threw it on the floor. She ran out of the house ignoring her mother's shouts.

"Anna, you get back here this instant. Isabel, go get your sister!"

Anna ran down the street, past the neighbors' houses lit up in blinking multicolored Christmas lights. She ran in the cold late-night air until her lungs hurt and snot ran from her nose. She heard Isabel's calls from down the street, which somehow penetrated her mortification. Anna turned around and slowly walked home, choking back sobs and shivering from the cold.

She thought her mother would punish her when she reentered the house, but instead she put a blanket around her daughter and asked, "What, Anna? Why are you so upset?"

"I wanted to sit with Papa" was all she managed, her body stiff with refusal to submit to her mother's affection. Her mother was weak, she thought, enslaved by her husband like most women. One thing she was sure of, she would never be like them.

TWO AND A half decades and two children later, Anna and Jason had created a loving bond in the life they had built together and nurtured over the past five years. On some level she had been relieved when Jason intuited the fact of her pregnancy on his own. It was less of a burden now that she didn't have to carry it alone.

Jason tried to distract her and cheer her up by planning family day trips on the weekends. They drove to Coney Island and had dinner in Sheepshead Bay. They took the subway to the Bronx Zoo, where Henry laughed at the wallabies and a blind llama spit on Oscar much to his disgusted delight. When she grew tired, Jason took the boys on the giant slide and climbed with them up the jungle gym. Anna watched them, all the while praying for the health of the new baby.

Now they were all together for an end-of-summer bit of family time before the demands of the fall season began. At the nanny's request, Anna gave her a well-deserved two-week vacation, though Anna regretted it immediately.

It rained the first two days they were in Montauk, which would have been a welcome relief from having to do anything at all but for the pent-up energy of the boys. They had their mama all to themselves now and they weren't going to miss one moment.

In between downpours, Anna suggested Jason take them out of the house. "Henry, Oscar, Papa is going to take you to the farmers' market and you can climb on the hay bales! Mama is going to stay home to rest a little. Then we can play when you get back, okay?" Anna did her best to sell them on an outing without her.

"I want you to come too, Mama!" Oscar asked.

"No, baby, I am going to stay home and take a nap."

"Okay, I will stay home and take a nap with you," Oscar suggested, clearly believing he would do that, nap with her, which of course he wouldn't.

"You have to help Papa with Henry, okay?"

"I don't want to go with Papa and Henry! I want to be with you!" Oscar was now close to wailing, which got Henry riled up as well.

"I stay too," he managed, but it sounded like "Ay-yay do," which made Oscar laugh through his tears.

Anna looked to Jason for help, but he just shrugged. "Come on, boys, let's leave Mama alone for a few minutes at least. I need your help in the backyard." Oscar and Henry dutifully followed their father to the yard, but only five minutes later Anna could hear Oscar's footsteps running through the house looking for her.

"Mama, where are you?!" He sounded close to panic.

"I'm in my room, Oscar . . . What's the matter?"

He said nothing, but found her in bed and crawled in with her. There was nothing she would rather do than curl up around her little boy and sleep. But just a moment later, Henry waddled in, face and hair covered in dirt, which he planted all over the duvet.

"Where's Papa?" Anna asked them, trying not to show her annoyance.

"Papa?" Henry asked.

She crawled out from the covers, picked up Henry, and went in search of her husband, who was picking tomatoes.

"Jason! I thought you were going to take them."

"They wanted their beautiful mother. I can't say I blame them." He smiled and kissed her. "Here . . . let me take Henry. Go back to bed—take Oscar and maybe you can get him to nap with you."

THIS DANCE WENT on for days. While Anna craved the love and attention of the boys, she desperately needed time to herself that she wasn't getting. She made it to the fourth day before breaking down.

Jason found Anna silently sobbing in front of the television. She had an arm wrapped around each son while they watched a *Bob the Builder* video. Tears streamed down her face, her eyes swollen into slits. She made no sound and the boys were so rapt that they hadn't noticed. They'd spent hours on the beach earlier, had had their baths, and were blissed out watching their favorite show.

"Anna, what's wrong?" Jason had been fixing the grill all afternoon and was covered in grease. He was wearing a tool belt and work clothes. Henry looked away from the screen and pointed to his father and said, "Bob!" clapping with pride at having made the joke. Oscar fell off the couch laughing, which made Anna laugh through her misery.

She squeezed her boys tight to her and kissed them on the backs of their necks—Anna loved the soft hollows just below their hairlines, loved to bury her face there. It tickled Henry and made him squeal with delight.

"Anna, what's the matter?" Jason sat down on the couch with them.

Anna couldn't bear to try to explain to Jason how she was feeling since she didn't understand it herself. Exhaustion didn't quite cover it, because what she felt was more terrifying. It was the same feeling she'd felt before, the feeling that she would just stop. *Stop.* She was the Energizer Bunny and her batteries had finally died. Now what?

Anna wiped away the tears and straightened up. "Can you

watch the boys while I go take a bath? They've already had theirs and they've had their snack. I haven't planned anything for dinner—maybe we can just go to the Lobster Roll."

The Lobster Roll was a favorite seafood shack just a few miles west on Montauk Highway. It was one of the first places Anna took Jason when they'd gotten together. Since they didn't know each other when they married, they'd dated post-nuptially. Each place they'd visited in those early days held a special discovery for them.

"Of course, take your time," Jason said as he picked up Henry and leaned in to kiss Anna.

"Don't let them fall asleep. If we can get them to dinner and back here before they pass out, maybe we can get them to bed early."

Anna retreated to the bathroom, where she closed and locked the door behind her. She wished she could use the aromatic bath salts she kept for those rare moments she had alone in the bath but wouldn't dare take the risk. She let the room fill with steam, then cooled the temperature of the water using the cold tap, making the water tepid, not hot.

Anna slipped into the bath and closed her eyes. She took a long, slow breath in through her nose, and on the exhale through her mouth she was distracted by Oscar's wails downstairs. "I want to see Mama! I want to watch her take a bath . . ."

Jason tried to console him. It didn't work. Next, she heard her three-year-old's footsteps on the stairs.

"Mama," Oscar called, "I want to stay in the bathroom with you."

"Oscar, honey, please go help Papa take care of Henry. I'll be down in a few minutes."

"But, Mama, I want to be with you!"

"Oscar, please," Anna begged. There was silence on the other side of the bathroom door and Anna thought for a moment that Oscar had gone back downstairs.

"I'm not Oscar," he said quietly, but loud enough for Anna to hear him through the door.

Oscar loved to pretend he was one of the many characters he encountered over the course of the day. Whenever he did this, it changed his mood immediately.

"Who are you?"

"I'm Bob."

"Oh, okay, Bob. Can you help out with Henry?"

"He's Pilchard," he said, referring to Bob the Builder's cat.

"Right, Bob. Papa needs help taking care of Pilchard. Mama will be finished with her bath soon."

"Mama?" Oscar's voice was tiny now, barely audible from behind the door. He often made his voice smaller when he was pretending, as if assertion would make it less real. "Are you Wendy?"

Wendy was Bob's helper . . . or something.

"Yes, baby, I'm Wendy. Pilchard needs you downstairs. Wendy will be down soon."

"Okay, Wendy. I'm Bob."

"I know, Bob. See you soon, Bob."

It worked. Anna could hear Oscar run down the stairs, bursting with newly found resolve, his voice now big with excitement. "Papa! Where's Pilchard?"

Anna smiled. Oscar's demands came from some sweet place that dissolved her frustration. The very fact of his existence made her heart break every day. She worried about him—he somehow felt too fragile for this world. Henry, on the other hand, possessed an innate fierceness, attributable, perhaps, to his status as second son. Still, Anna thought the genesis of their differences occurred at a genetic level. Henry was a Ducci; Oscar was a Schwartz.

Anna thought about the new baby. She fantasized about a third son, a houseful of boys. She closed her eyes in silent reflection.

The bath had already gone from warm to almost cool when Anna opened her eyes to search for the submerged washcloth. The water was cloudy and she had to feel around for it. It took a few minutes for her to realize that the bath was tinted pink. In the center of the tub a cloudy suspension of crimson held her attention for a moment. Another second brought the realization that she was bleeding. She stood up quickly, losing her balance. She slipped back down, falling hard on her backside. Anna screamed, then heard Jason running up the stairs a moment later.

"Anna! Anna, are you all right?" Jason yelled as he flung open the door, breaking the meager lock.

Anna, too stunned to answer right away, doubled over from cramping as the water grew to a brighter red. She looked up at Jason, eyes wide and mouth clenched tight. She felt a regret she'd never known before this moment.

"Take the boys downstairs," Anna managed between sobs. "And call the doctor. Ask him what I should do. I started hemorrhaging before I slipped, but the fall made it worse."

Anna pulled herself from the tub and started trembling

uncontrollably. She managed to pull a big bath towel around her shaking body and sat down on the toilet, where she watched as the life literally drained out of her.

Jason came back to tell her he'd left a message with her doctor's answering service, who said they would find the doctor right away. "Let me help you get to bed," he offered.

"No, Jason. Just leave me alone. Please. Get out."

Lying in the darkening bedroom an hour later, Anna was filled with anger. She played over in her mind the demands of her daily life, this vacation that wasn't a vacation, and her frustrations solidified around Jason for not picking up the slack. Just as she feared, her body had been pressed to the limit and her premonitions of losing the baby had come true. Her mind raced with the quotidian scenarios of her daily life: pushing her way through the crowded subway; jumping into taxis uptown, downtown, and back again; meetings and lunches; racing home from work. Every evening she inhaled her dinner as the boys climbed all over her, followed by the ritual of bathing them and getting them into bed. This rigorous routine began at five thirty every morning and ended after nonstop activity at 10:00 P.M. if she was lucky. Awakened three or four times during the night to minister to the needs of her boys, she didn't rest even in sleep.

How had this happened?

ANNA COULDN'T LOOK at Jason for an entire week following the miscarriage.

"Anna, please talk to me," Jason pleaded. "Don't shut me out. I'm sad too."

"You're sad? I'm sorry you're sad. I'm sad too, and also furious and in pain and hormonal and everything else I don't have a name for . . . I'm sorry you're sad, but you can't possibly know what this feels like."

"Help me understand," he said.

"You can't."

CHAPTER SEVEN

Isabel

SAM WAS HOME more than usual for the six weeks following Isabel's outing with Christopher. With her husband around, Christopher's pull lost much of its strength, until Isabel wasn't sure if she had dreamed that Christopher had called and spoken with Sam that night or if it had really happened.

Life fell into their couple-rhythm of work, dinner, movies, and baseball games, sometimes even venturing to Yankee Stadium. They had the occasional evening out with friends. Isabel was feeling better; the nausea had mostly abated except for when brushing her teeth, which had turned into a race to finish before she threw up. Once she was done, she didn't feel sick for the rest of the day.

During her seventeenth week, Isabel and Sam saw the baby for the first time via ultrasound. Isabel fell in love instantly. Until then, her pregnancy had felt too abstract to attach any substantial feelings to the life she was carrying. But seeing the slow-motion movement of her baby boy's hands made him real, transforming her fetus into a child. Her child, her little boy. Isabel knew from that moment on that her heart would belong to her son, and even if she had no idea how that would manifest, she surrendered to this force of nature not her own.

NEARLY TWO MONTHS went by after their picnic in the park before Isabel saw Christopher again. He showed up at Isabel's office, unannounced, one afternoon in mid-August. It was testimony to Christopher's brashness that he would come to the offices of *Pink* even though there was a good chance he would bump into the Turtle.

"What are you doing here?" Isabel asked as he barged into her office.

He held an envelope in his hand. "I have a present for you and I wanted to deliver it in person."

He made no outward acknowledgment of Isabel's belly, which had popped, a softly rounded bump through the colorful and clingy Missoni dress she wore. He seemed to accept her pregnancy with a calculated nonchalance. There was no way he wasn't affected by it, but Isabel also couldn't guess how. She wanted to explain to him how she felt completely transformed, not so much physically, despite the obvious ways her body had changed with the demands of pregnancy. Rather, her entire being seemed to have shifted with the understanding that she was going to be a mother. What that meant was still a mystery to Isabel, but she felt Christopher looking at her differently, as if wanting to know what Isabel was feeling inside when, of course, he couldn't. She didn't know herself.

Christopher handed her the envelope. Inside was a handwritten letter sealed in a glassine bag. She turned it over and immediately recognized Cocteau's unmistakable signature and star. Her heart leaped. She pulled the letter from its protective sleeve and slowly deciphered the scratchy script. The letter was from Cocteau to his friend Coco Chanel and alluded to the child he would never have. The little-known story was that he had, in a moment of rare heterosexual activity, impregnated a girlfriend. The baby was lost—the story didn't follow whether from termination or miscarriage, and this letter did nothing to resolve that question. He did admit that it was one of his only regrets in life.

Isabel had mentioned to Christopher years ago the fantasy she entertained that she'd discovered Cocteau's daughter residing on the Upper East Side of Manhattan, now an old woman. She couldn't believe that Christopher had remembered her outlandish fantasy. Giving her this gift at this particular moment in their friendship signified something she couldn't quite fathom.

Isabel placed the letter back into the bag and slid it inside her desk drawer, which she locked. Without a word, she took Christopher's hand and led him out of her office, out of the building, and to his apartment.

They exchanged no words. Ten years of foreplay ended in silence as Isabel unbuttoned Christopher's shirt and slipped it off his slight, pale torso. She unbuckled his belt and stood back to watch as he stepped out of his trousers. She thought for a moment of the pants exchange in Christopher's office so many years ago. How silly they had been then; they were not now. Isabel lifted off her dress and stood squarely in front of Christopher as he gazed on the fullness of her naked body. Keeping her eyes on his, she pushed Christopher down on the daybed and mounted him, her belly and breasts engorged and dense. She felt stronger than him, heavier, and she liked it.

Isabel was touched by how tentative Christopher's movements were, how unsure he seemed about where to place his hands and mouth. How unlike the man she'd always known. She whispered: "I'm not that fragile, Chris. Just fuck me the way you've imagined for the last ten years."

Christopher's face grew stern for a moment before he flipped Isabel onto her back with one arm, pushed her legs up in the air, and penetrated her with more aggression than she expected. She liked that too.

They lay in each other's arms afterward. Tentative again, Christopher gently placed his hand on her belly. "Will I feel the baby move?"

"You won't be able to feel him yet. I do, just slightly. It feels like bubbles." Isabel covered Christopher's hand with her own hand. "You can call him 'him.' We know now that's it's a boy."

"Another man around to adore you. How do you feel about that?"

"How can I complain?"

Isabel's thoughts bypassed Sam and returned to the Cocteau letter. She'd been searching for years for a firsthand reference to the incident of his fatherhood. It had haunted her. Baffled by how Christopher could have found it, she began to ask him. "Christopher, that letter, how did you—"

He put his finger to her lips. "Don't ask me anything about it. Just accept it as a gift from one friend to another."

"Okay. Fair. New question—got anything to eat? I'm starving."

"No, but they make a wonderful turkey Reuben at the shop downstairs. I'll order one up."

"No, don't. I'll pick one up on the way back to the office." Isabel dressed and was headed out the door in minutes. She returned to give Christopher a lingering kiss and then left him lying naked in his bed, feeling like it was every pregnant woman's right to have a lover.

Isabel returned to the office disheveled and flushed from sex. The Turtle stood outside her door. "Was that Christopher Bello in your office earlier?"

"Yes, it was," Isabel answered, meeting his eyes in a challenge.

"Are you two friends?" the Turtle asked, knowing full well that she and Christopher had shared a bond for years. He was digging for information and she wasn't about to give it to him. The Turtle's face colored as she stared him down.

"Very good friends, yes."

"He's an . . . interesting fellow."

"Oh, you have no idea . . ." Isabel baited him.

"Uh-huh." He stared at Isabel with bulging cyes. The Turtle's unnerving habit to stay focused on someone's face even when it was clear the conversation wasn't going anywhere had further served to cement his place as a dickhead early on at the office.

Isabel picked up her messages from Tina. Once she'd returned all the phone calls and answered the more urgent e-mails, she automatically called Beth. Relieved that Beth was in a meeting, Isabel thought twice about whether she wanted to share her afternoon tryst with anyone, even her best friend. Maybe this was something she wanted to own for a while.

Later that night when she got home, Isabel curled up with a copy of Rebecca Solnit's *Wanderlust*. Sam was back in Chicago. A photograph from their wedding day stood in a frame next to where she laid her head. She stared at it and smiled a bit sadly. If Sam had been home, she wouldn't have gone to Christopher's apartment. That was certain. She wondered, in the spirit of Cocteau, if she had pushed past the limits of audacity. But her ambivalence about what she'd done was mitigated by the gratitude she felt. In the silence of the apartment she shared with her husband, Isabel solemnly acknowledged thanks to him for being away, grateful for the time with Christopher and for the time, now, alone. Like the letter Christopher had given her, her tryst with him felt like a secret gift, one she would cherish in sacrosanct privacy. She stopped herself from answering the obvious question: What if she had gone too far?

Isabel's mind wandered to when she and Anna were young girls, those years between her first Holy Communion, when Isabel turned seven, and then later when she was confirmed, at eleven. The sisters often played a game on a fallen tree that crossed a small stream in the wooded land just behind their suburban home. They would walk along the narrow branch, trying to balance without falling off. To one side was the rushing shallow stream; to the other, the safety of the bank. They would start out crossing it slowly. With each trip across the log, they pushed each other to go faster and faster. The game would end, inevitably, when one of them fell into the water.

For Isabel the game held its own secret power. She imagined that falling into the stream was a kind of forced baptism: you fell because you needed to purify your sins. If you landed on the bank, dry and secure, it was because you had earned the

solidity and sanctity of the earth. Isabel's efforts to avoid falling into the stream were not always rigorous. Didn't she need
a baptism to cleanse her? That's what catechism had taught
her. Once fallen, she would try to imagine what had prompted
her need for absolution. She was too young to make any intel-
lectual sense of her internal game, but the images accompanying it had stayed with her as a kind of silent visual rumination
throughout her adolescence.

When her cell phone rang later that night, she let her voice
mail pick it up, suspecting correctly that it was Christopher
calling. She didn't want to spoil the sense of solitude she had,
just her and her baby. Isabel undressed and crawled into bed.
Lying naked in the dark with her hand on her belly, she waited
for signs of life from her womb. As if to answer his mother's
wish, the baby moved a limb across her uterus, drawing a line
from the inside. It was the first time she had distinctly felt his
presence. She whispered into the darkness, "Good night, my
angel, good night," and fell fast asleep dreaming of the growing boy inside her.

When she awoke the next morning, Isabel listened to the
message on her cell.

"Hi, darling. It's your lover here. When will I see you again?
Say it will be soon."

As long as she had known him, she had never heard Christopher smitten in this way, not with anyone and certainly not
with her. He seemed to have released all his strategies, ex-
posing a neediness Isabel couldn't believe existed in him. At
another time, she wouldn't have trusted it (though she would
have been enthralled by it all the same), but she didn't need to
trust Christopher now. What happened yesterday was about

her, not about her and Christopher. After their communion, what Christopher didn't and couldn't possibly know was how unreachable she was to him.

BETH CALLED ISABEL at the office that day to invite her to lunch. Isabel's meeting had been canceled earlier that morning so she was free.

"Meet me at Tommaso at one." Da Tommaso was always good for a table, and the food, service, and people watching were top-notch.

"Either pregnancy has become fun or you've been up to something," Beth observed the moment she sat down.

Isabel avoided her friend's inquisitive stare. "It must be the clothes," Isabel remarked, and smiled coyly. She was wearing one of Beth's creations: a nearly sheer eggshell linen-and-cotton sleeveless dress that hugged her full body. A plunging neckline boasted of her pregnancy breasts. Diverting the conversation from Beth's comment, Isabel asked, "So, what news is there of the backlash after the protests? I see all kinds of editorials on it. It's incredible that they haven't grown tired of bashing a lingerie line!"

"Maggie's been brilliant. She's making sure that there are pieces about the structure of the company and how we're one of the most progressive in terms of accommodating working mothers. It sends the message we're supportive. The whole thing is ridiculous. I mean, how do these people think we become mothers anyway? What kills me is the actual mothers who hate what we are doing. They must have missed a big part of the fun of conception or they wouldn't be complaining so loudly." Beth suddenly seemed distracted by something and changed tracks. "Have you talked to Anna?"

"Yes. She seems tired. Why? Do you think it's something more?" Isabel felt a twinge of regret that she'd been neglecting her sister lately. It was hard for her to see Anna struggle. As the younger of the two, Isabel wanted Anna to have figured out all the tough stuff already. It was an unfair expectation, and she knew it.

"Nothing is particularly wrong, but she seems depressed to me. I think she might be angry with Jason because he gets to spend more time with the kids. She seems to blame herself for not being able to balance it all neatly. She doesn't understand that it doesn't get balanced neatly—it just rocks back and forth every day and the job is to try not to get too seasick. Anyway, I think she could use an ear," Beth said.

"I'll call her after lunch. Maybe I'll go home with her tonight after work. Sam won't be back until tomorrow." Isabel felt an unexpected loneliness at the thought of her sister's frenetically full household contrasted with her empty one. She put her hand on her belly and the feeling disappeared. Even with Sam gone as much as he was, she rarely felt lonely. Before she was pregnant, Isabel always had friends around. After she conceived, she reveled in the companionship she felt with the baby inside her. She was never alone now. With Christopher, her life almost felt crowded.

"How is Jessie dealing with Paul?" she asked.

"I'm never sure from day to day what I should tell her and what I should keep from her." Beth's bottom lip quivered for a quick moment and then stopped.

"Do you think she wouldn't understand?" Isabel asked.

"I think she understands that he's very sick. And it feels wrong to not answer her questions honestly. But what do I tell her? 'Jessie, your father is gay, but he can't really accept it, and no one else knows, but he's dying of AIDS, even though there are drugs he could take to help himself, but instead he's committing suicide by self-loathing . . .'"

Beth hung her head, and Isabel grabbed her hand from across the table.

"I'm sorry, Beth. It just sucks in every way."

"And Paul's mother is still in so much denial that she blames me for making Paul sick. She doesn't think twice that Jessie and I are healthy—how would that be possible?!" Beth's voice had gotten louder as she went on, but then she paused and it simmered to a whisper. "I couldn't visit him when he was in the hospital because his mother would have freaked if she saw me there. And even if I barged my way in, I couldn't have dragged Jessie into that drama. But she kept asking to visit. The whole thing is a fucking mess." Beth looked drawn and tired in a way that Isabel had never seen before.

Isabel shook her head. "I don't know . . . maybe we underestimate what children can handle. Jessie's a smart kid. Keeping people in the dark has never helped anyone, young or old. But then, I don't know yet what it's like to have a kid on the other side. Ask me once this little guy is born and I might change my mind."

Isabel became quiet again. Beth eyed her as though she sensed there was something her friend wasn't saying.

"What, Is?"

Isabel looked at Beth and opened her mouth to tell her friend about her time with Christopher, but no words came.

She realized she was nervous about Beth's response. For all of her bravado and brashness, Beth was solidly conventional when it came to her love life. It was what had attracted her to Paul, who on the surface seemed a very straight, corporate, chivalric guy. Of course, surface impressions clearly hadn't been worth a damn. Still, Isabel knew Beth wouldn't approve of her transgression, especially given the fact that the very good man she married deserved better.

"Is there really something in this world you couldn't tell me?" Beth asked, sounding offended.

"I saw Christopher yesterday," Isabel blurted out.

"Is that unusual?" Beth didn't catch on as quickly as she normally did. This wasn't good.

"This time it was."

"'Saw' as in 'fucked-saw?'" Beth narrowed her eyes when she said this.

"Maybe . . . yes."

"Christ, Isabel."

"Can we not talk about it? I'm still taking this in myself. Saying it out loud just made it real."

"What about Sam?"

"This isn't about Sam, Beth. It isn't even about Christopher. It's about me."

"Uh-huh."

Isabel felt herself growing annoyed by her friend's implicit judgment. "Forget it, Beth. Let's talk about something else."

"Sorry, Isabel, but it isn't *nothing*, you know . . . Maybe I was right when I called you the Black Widow . . ."

Isabel winced at the reference to their one falling-out, years ago when they were in their late twenties. They'd been out at a jazz club with a guy Isabel had just started dating. A few hours and several drinks into the evening, Beth had pulled the guy aside and told him, "Beware the Black Widow . . . She weaves her web and she's been known to eat her lovers when she's done with them." The comment did nothing to deter her date, but Isabel saw Beth's not-so-playful warning as a breach of their friendship and wouldn't speak to her for weeks. Beth later claimed she was trying to be funny. They'd finally kissed and made up, but Isabel had felt stung by the comment for years, knowing there was some truth in it. Still, Beth had never again mentioned the Black Widow reference. Isabel had long ago pushed the comment and their tiff about it into the memory junk heap of low moments. That her friend was referring to it now hurt her more than she cared to admit.

"Seriously, Beth? Can we not go back there?" Isabel asked in a sharp tone.

"I don't know, Is. You have a wonderful husband—there aren't a lot of them out there, you know—and a lover. All I've got is a closeted, dying ex-husband." Beth squeezed her eyes shut even before the words were completely out. "Well. That sounded as horrible as it is."

"Maybe you're right. I am being selfish." Isabel paused to consider it for a moment. "But I can live with that." She didn't offer any more, letting Beth choose the conversation's direction from there.

"Let's skip it for now."

The two friends sat in silence, not uncomfortably, for a few minutes until Beth turned their attention elsewhere: "Listen, Maggie is trying to put together a panel discussion on motherhood. She is in touch with KinderCo about sponsoring it and trying to place it as part of a series of roundtable discussions on family issues. Would you be interested in doing it? All of the participants will be mothers, and she wants one to be an expecting mother. You certainly would have a lot to bring to the table." She said this as both an offer of reconciliation and a provocation, but smiled to let Isabel know nothing had changed between them. "What do you think?"

"Will you be involved?" Isabel asked.

"Yes. Probably Anna as well. Maggie might even do it. We're still looking for one or two others. Maggie is going to see if there is a problem with three of us being connected to RHM, but part of this is to try to set the record straight—whatever that is—and it might be better if we know who's involved so there are no scary surprises. I'll keep you posted."

Beth and Isabel spent the next hour over chamomile tea and biscotti, catching up on each other's family and laughing about past debacles. Christopher wasn't mentioned again.

Isabel loved hearing stories about Beth's crazy father, who was now on his fifth marriage (fourth wife). Beth asked about Isabel's brother, Bobby, who'd married a gold digger who swigged white wine during the afternoons while he saw patients as an endocrinologist at Cedars-Sinai in Los Angeles. During Beth's brief affair with Bobby, Isabel and Beth had fantasized about being sisters-in-law, but thankfully, it hadn't turned out that way. Bobby, a loving and supportive brother, was not the best husband. He was generous to a fault—and unfortunately that generosity didn't stop when it came to his dick. He'd had affairs with his yoga instructor, the dog sitter, and an ER nurse—so predictable it was cliché. Each time he was caught with his pants down, he repented and promised to stay fully committed to his wife. Isabel couldn't fathom why they stayed together. And, as much as she missed her brother, she was happy they were a safe distance across the country.

She considered briefly their parallels in infidelity, but then dismissed any similarities between herself and Bobby. Isabel had never cheated before and didn't find the prospect of it titillating in any way. Her intimacy with Christopher felt like an entitlement, not to betray her husband, but to act with complete and utter self-concern. Aware that her argument wouldn't hold with anyone—not even with Sam, who accepted her fully—Isabel hoped it wouldn't come to a point when she would be forced to explain herself.

WHEN ISABEL GOT back to the office she called Anna and arranged to spend the night with her sister's family in Brooklyn. She was not entirely truthful when she told Anna that she needed some family time.

Christopher had left a message on her voice mail. He was "desperate" to see her—his word—but Isabel stuck with her plans to go to Anna's. It was the first time she had ever had even a hint of control in their friendship. Thinking back on her conversation with Beth over lunch, she smiled at how right Beth was: Isabel felt sublimely selfish. And it felt okay. Her heart now belonged to another boy—one with different kinds of demands, demands she couldn't begin to comprehend. Until he entered the world, she was going to enjoy every moment of living only according to her own wishes. Christopher could wait.

Anna and Isabel met at the subway station to ride to Brooklyn together. They couldn't get seats, so the women stood with the crowd.

"You'd think someone would offer you a seat. Do you want me to ask someone to get up for you?" Anna said quietly to Isabel.

As soon as Anna said it, there was a tap on Isabel's elbow from a sturdy, elderly woman who'd stood up and pointed to her seat.

"No, thank you," Isabel told the woman. "I'd rather stand." She turned back to her sister and said, "Balancing takes my mind off the pressure on my bladder. Sitting just makes it worse." Isabel leaned against the pole to steady herself as the train lurched forward. "How are you doing, Anna? You seem tired." Isabel knew how much Anna hated to be perceived as anything short of Superwoman. She trod lightly.

"I just miss the boys when I'm at work. I feel like they'll be teenagers in no time and I'll have missed some vital part of their development because of my job. I'm scared and sad and exhausted."

"Sweetheart, you're tired because you have a demanding job and two small boys who get your undivided attention when you're home. That doesn't leave much time for yourself," Isabel said, hoping she sounded supportive, not critical.

"I don't need time to myself right now. I had plenty of that before the boys. I need more time with them."

Isabel wasn't about to argue, so she let it go. The train pulled into the station, and they were pushed out of the subway car by the mass of commuters also exiting the subway car. Anna provided a human shield for Isabel amid the commotion.

The sisters arrived at the Ducci-Schwartz home at seven

o'clock. While most families around America would be gearing up for the children's bedtime, Anna's sons hadn't had dinner yet, let alone a bath and quiet time. Jason had dinner simmering on the stove, three-year-old Oscar was playing *Big Action Construction* on the laptop in the living room, and Jason and the baby played catch with a sparkly red bouncy ball.

Anna kissed each of her men hello. Isabel noticed how her sister's mood changed considerably just walking in the door. While she looked dull and lethargic at the end of the workday, it was clear that Anna's family gave back to her, many times over, the energy they no doubt consumed. Still, the wear and tear of being the breadwinner and mother of two was evident. She and Jason had a respectful, loving, sexy thing going between them, but Isabel wondered how long Anna would be able to keep it up. Anna's patience seemed endless . . . until it wasn't anymore. This was, until now, her unbroken pattern in past relationships. She'd always walked out when she'd had enough, leaving plenty of baffled and broken hearts in her wake.

Isabel had admired her sister's decision to forgo traditional parenthood when she had planned to conceive with her friend instead. But meeting Jason changed all that. With him and the boys filling her life, she now finally had something worth the effort it took to sustain. Beth's concern about Anna was founded, though. Isabel suspected that it would be her career Anna would walk out on this time, not her man.

By the time they all sat down to dinner it was close to eight o'clock. Once they'd finished, the boys were wound up into their before-bedtime frenzy. Oscar ran across the living room to the couch, where he jumped up and flipped his feet over his head against the back cushion. Then he fell over, jumped off, and ran back to the other side of the room to do it all again. This happened at least eight times in a row. Meanwhile, Henry ran up and down the hallway throwing and kicking his red ball, squealing with delight each time his foot connected to make the ball fly. Isabel was always astonished at how two small humans could make the same amount of noise as an unruly crowd. Jason apologized: "They're laughing now and in about five minutes they'll be in tears. Just wait . . ."

Jason's patience impressed Isabel. She wondered how she would fare under similar circumstances. Sure enough, five minutes later, Oscar had a tumble off the couch and bumped his forehead on the coffee table. He began to laugh and cry hysterically at the same time, as was his habit, while Henry, following his brother's lead, started bawling for no apparent reason. Isabel watched with wonder as Anna calmly whisked Henry up and to bed with a promise to read him his favorite book, *Tuesday*. Jason grabbed Oscar and brought him in for his bath. As quickly as the chaos had ramped up, the household became hushed.

Isabel followed Jason into the bathroom. "You can finish what you were doing; I can give Oscar his bath."

Once Oscar was dressed in his stripy pajamas and ready for bed, she handed him over to Jason, who had just finished cleaning up the kitchen. Isabel kissed them all good night before heading up to the guest room on the top floor of the brownstone, where she pulled out her phone to call Sam from the coziness of the blankets.

Beth's reaction to Isabel's tryst with Christopher earlier in the day played over in Isabel's mind. She wasn't feeling guilty, but rather something more like bewilderment. Isabel didn't buy into guilt. As far as she was concerned, guilt was just another lie people told themselves: a culturally acceptable way of wanting things both ways—questionable behavior and absolution all in one!

Still, the riddle as to why she enjoyed intimacy with Christopher, when she knew it would hurt Sam if he were to find out, puzzled her. She was certain only that her need to compartmentalize and act selfishly was stronger than her sense of preserving the "sanctity of marriage." Isabel had made a vow of commitment in her marriage to Sam, but not one of exclusivity. It was a bit late to raise the matter with him now. *What if Sam is doing the same with an old fling in Chicago?* she asked herself. The thought didn't raise any bile. *He might be* was the answer that made her smile with the understanding of how foolish it is to believe that anyone ever owns another person. She realized it was likely that Sam might not feel the same; she would keep it to herself to protect him and what they had.

She dialed his number. "Hi, it's me," she whispered as if sneaking a call to her own husband.

"Are you home?" Sam asked.

"No, I'm spending the night at Anna's. It's crazy-town here with the boys!" They laughed as Isabel described her nephews' pre-bedtime meltdown antics. But then she grew serious. "Watching Jason and Anna tonight, I wonder how we're going to do it with you gone all the time."

"Is, I'm not going to travel like this forever, I promise. I just want to close this case and use it to gain leverage for more control over how I spend my time going forward," Sam told her confidently. He always had a plan—it was one of the things she loved about him.

"Will that be possible? Won't there just be another case behind it? And then another?" Isabel didn't usually press Sam on his work, but the realities of family life had struck her hard tonight.

"Baby, we'll figure it out and make those decisions. Don't worry," Sam assured her. "I wouldn't abandon you to raise our kids alone."

"No, of course you wouldn't. I know that," Isabel said, believing every word of it. "I miss you." Isabel did. She missed him terribly.

"Same here. I'm so sick of these people and sick of this job, especially because it takes me away from you. I swear I'll find a way to spend less time away once the baby arrives."

"I'd like that. Junior will like it too." Isabel was so wiped out she nearly fell asleep holding the phone for the few seconds Sam was disrupted on the other end.

"Issy, are you still there? Is?" Sam said loudly.

"Yes, I'm still here. I'm just zonked. When are you coming home?"

"I'm trying for tomorrow night, but I'm not sure yet. I promise I'll make it home for the weekend."

"I hope you do. Good night, Sam."

"Good night, my love."

JASON WAS ALREADY up and making coffee when Isabel came downstairs the next morning. She had awakened unusually early and thought to get a head start by arriving at the office before the day cranked up. By ten o'clock, her schedule would fill quickly with phone calls and meetings and client crises.

The sound of the television so early in the morning captured Isabel's attention. There was something disturbing to her about the unmistakable upbeat background music of most shows on television. Even wars had catchy musical themes. If perversity were to take a form for Isabel, that would be it. This morning the box was tuned to a show featuring a lithe, angular brunette with her hair pulled back in a tight chignon and dressed in black leather leggings under a sleeveless amber silk blouse. The tag under the speaker's name read, GEORGETTE FONTAINE, INFIDELITY EXPERT.

How could someone be an expert on infidelity? Was she a professional cuckold or repeat offender? The whole thing seemed more absurd than real, so it took Isabel a moment to realize that this Georgette Fontaine was not only someone she sort of knew but also that she was talking about something Isabel herself had just committed.

"The thing about adultery today," Georgette was saying, "is that none of the boundaries apply. Sex for sex's sake never hurts anyone, but stealing another's spouse after an infidelity makes it injurious and unnecessary. One could say that the courtesan was a sanctioned whore, yes, but there was a place for her in society, and an accepted place at that—not so different from the Japanese geisha. I say the geisha or courtesan has a rightful place in our culture and we should not be so quick to hasten the disappearance of these very commonsensical practices."

Jason walked into the living room as Georgette was pontificating on the tube and handed Isabel a cup of coffee. "You indulging?" he asked.

For a moment Isabel thought he was referring to the subject on the screen and hesitated before realizing he was talking about caffeine, not extramarital sex. "Um, yes, one cup in the morning. Thanks, Jason."

"Do you know that's Maggie's husband's ex? Maggie from Red Hot Mama?" Jason asked, referring to the woman speaking on the screen.

"Yeah, I was just putting that all together. Why would anyone let herself be labeled an 'infidelity expert'? I guess she has every reason to be pissed, but why humiliate yourself in front of a national audience?"

"I know some friends of hers and supposedly she claims that she's famous now that she's been on *Oprah* and the *Today* show," Jason said as he stared at the screen. "I feel sorry for her. Couldn't have been an easy thing to go through."

"I guess. Still, some people will trade their dignity for a little attention in a heartbeat." Isabel caught the contempt in her voice and thought better than to further engage in the topic. Who was she to judge? Georgette somehow exuded both haughtiness and warmth; Isabel found herself held rapt.

"The other problem, as I see it," Georgette continued, "is that women are able to keep affairs private, while men seek either forgiveness or justification. This male need for acknowledgment brings an affair that is best played out privately into the open where damage is done. Women have the sense to engage without a third witness. Why do we think only men have affairs? In the heteronormative realm, women are the other part of that equation. Women just don't need to talk about it."

The conversation continued in silence in her own head. What would Georgette think of Isabel's entanglement with Christopher? Would she consider it "sex for sex's sake" or injurious adultery? Who in the world could be the arbiter of such judgements?

For a moment, Isabel thought she'd exclaimed the last bit out loud and turned to Jason to see if he acknowledged it. He didn't seem to have heard—or maybe she didn't actually give voice to her thoughts. They both stood silently in front of the blue light of the television for a minute more. Then Jason pecked Isabel on the cheek before turning to leave. "I'm going to get some work done before Anna and the boys wake up. Good to see you, Issy." He headed down to his office on the ground floor.

Isabel was tempted to ask Jason how he thought Anna was doing, but then thought it better to mind her own business. She was concerned for her sister, but Anna would resent the concern if Jason were to tell her she'd been asking after her. While fond of Jason, Isabel wished for her sister's sake that he could better provide for his family. Or maybe Isabel was just projecting her own discomfort with the arrangement onto Anna. She wondered if it was sexist to feel that way.

Without belaboring the thought, Isabel headed for the subway and a quiet early morning in the office.

TO HER DISAPPOINTMENT, the Turtle was already there when Isabel arrived. She tried to sneak by without him seeing her.

The Turtle called, "Hey, Isabel, come on in and let's chat."

"Fuck, fuck, fuck," Isabel lamented under her breath, then louder, "You're in early, Larry. Something happening here?"

"I have to fly up to Boston to make nice to an account who was offended by a story in the magazine. Thought I'd get some stuff cleared off my desk before heading to LaGuardia. I did want to speak with you about maternity leave, though, so it's good you're here. How long do you think you'll be out?" That the Turtle was wondering at all betrayed an ulterior motive.

"We get six weeks, and I'll attach three weeks' vacation to it, if that's okay with you. So I'll be out for about nine weeks." Isabel felt defensive and willed herself to sound casual. She hated herself for asking permission from this putz and a half for the time that was rightfully hers to take.

"That's fine. When do you plan on leaving?" The Turtle seemed anxious to have her gone.

"When I go into labor and head for the hospital. Hard to say, Larry, when exactly that will be." Isabel wanted to tear his head off.

Larry smiled a constipated smile. "What I meant to ask is when are you due?"

"January third." Isabel unconsciously put her hands over her belly as if to protect her child from the passive aggression emanating from the man in front of her.

"Ah, a New Year's baby. Well, great! That's just great! Thanks, Isabel." The Turtle's voice, unnaturally high during the exchange, made him impossible to read, although she knew that whatever he was thinking, it was not in her best interest. Isabel got out of there fast, resentful that he had spoiled her morning.

AFTER HER CONVERSATION with Sam the night before, Isabel had counted on his return that night, only to be disappointed to learn that he was going to be stuck in Chicago for the entire weekend. His team was coming close to having to testify in the landmark case they were working on, and they still had some loose ends. Isabel understood. There were plenty of weekends she had to spend at the office herself, leaving Sam to fend for himself. For better or worse, there'd be plenty to keep Isabel occupied.

As if to answer a call for distraction, Beth phoned to ask Isabel if she could hang out with Jessie for part of the day on Saturday. She had to take care of some legal matters concerning Paul and needed to meet with him at the lawyer's office. Isabel was glad to help. Jessie was a self-possessed kid, funny, intelligent, and a delight to be around. Isabel felt honored that Jessie not only agreed to spend the day with her mother's best friend but also that she specifically requested it.

ISABEL OFFERED JESSIE a fantasy day. She told her young friend that they would do whatever it was she wanted to do as long as it was in Manhattan. She gave her $100 to spend as she wished. The first stop was the Central Park Zoo to visit Gus the Polar Bear. Isabel thought Gus's pacing from glass wall to the rocks and back again, a routine he'd had for as long as Isabel could remember, was a clear sign of his depression. It seemed a cruel fate for the bear to be stuck inside the same structure day after day, year after year, repeating the same exact motions for hours on end. To Jessie, however, the fact of a polar bear living in Central Park was enough to delight her. After Gus, they visited the silly penguins—ditto on depression and delight.

Isabel felt a sense of wonder at Jessie, who, while still very much a little girl, had a definite sense of herself. At such a young age, she already possessed a personal style and all the makings of the remarkable woman she would surely become. Isabel was drawn to Jessie in both a maternal and sisterly way. She could remember that age as if it were not that long ago. Isabel often thought about how today she was more as she was at six or seven years old than she was as a young woman. Those wobbly pubescent years and the ones following into the late teens and early twenties, filled with self-doubt: those were years when being female felt most precarious.

The attention commanded by someone still in the act of becoming who she would be felt essential to Isabel and brought home the enormous responsibility she carried in her womb. She placed her hands on her stomach instinctively. *How different will it be to raise a son?* Isabel pondered. *Will I be able to know what's in his heart the same way I would a little girl?* She felt ready to give herself over to her son, but she struggled with the not knowing what her life would be like once he was born. *Will my priorities rearrange once my boy arrives? What if they don't? What kind of mother would I be then?*

Famished by late afternoon, Isabel and Jessie decided to indulge in a snack of sweet crepes at a SoHo café.

Isabel ordered a decaf café au lait. "Jessie, do you want a hot chocolate or something?"

"I want a coffee too. Can I?"

"Does your mother let you have coffee?"

"Sometimes she lets me, on weekends."

"Okay—it's a weekend and it's a special day. *Café au lait pour deux, s'il vous plaît!*" Isabel told the waitress.

Isabel wanted to ask Jessie about her dad and struggled to find a way to broach the subject with her, but in the end, she let the subject go. They shared a butter and lemon crepe and a chocolate one with fresh strawberries.

"What was your favorite part of today, Jessie?" Isabel asked.

"Every part!"

"I liked the penguins in the Central Park Zoo," Isabel said. "They're so funny—part bird, part sea animal—so strange!"

"I like zoos," Jessie offered, and then hesitated before continuing. "But then I think how trapped all the animals are and it makes me feel sad inside. Will they all die there?"

"Yes, I know what you mean . . . and I imagine they will die there. I'd never thought of that before." Isabel paused, lips pursed. "But some animals are born there too, and I like to think they are well taken care of in their zoo home."

"I hope so," Jessie said quietly.

Halfway through their snack, the waitress brought over a handwritten note and told them the gentleman who had been sitting just two tables away sent it. The note read: "The crepes are on me. What a beautiful mother and daughter you are!" When Isabel looked over to thank him, the table was empty and he was nowhere in sight. Isabel inquired about the man to the waitress. "Oh, that was Robert, the owner of the café. He said to come back any time."

Isabel had promised Beth to have Jessie home by five o'clock. They'd made plans for dinner out and a movie, but by the time they made it back to Eighteenth Street, Isabel was so spent from trekking around New York all day that they decided to order in Chinese and watch Netflix instead.

ON SUNDAY MORNING (the old Catholic in her screamed: *A day of reflection, not indulgence!*) she met Christopher at the Loeb Boathouse café before walking through the lush summer green of Central Park to his apartment, where they spent the afternoon in bed. In the moments with her lover—borrowed, transitory— their passion came tenderly, rather than with urgency.

Sipping tea while they lounged side by side on a double-wide chair on Christopher's terrace, Isabel demanded, "Tell me a story about when you were seven." Inspired by her time with Jessie the day before, Isabel had a sudden curiosity about Christopher as a boy.

"I don't remember much before I hit puberty . . . I know I was lonely at seven . . . and at eight and nine . . ."

"What about your sister? Didn't you spend time with her?"

"No, we existed in our own spheres. I don't know why, but we never connected. Maybe that contributed to my loneliness. She was only a year older, but she seemed worlds away from me. My parents worked all the time, so I never saw them, or at least we never spent any meaningful time together."

"That does sound lonely," Isabel said as she entwined her foot with Christopher's. "Do you have a favorite moment from your childhood?"

"I can't think of any. Though I do recall very clearly, when I was about eight or nine, I poured extremely hot hot sauce into a soup spoon and covered it with grape juice and offered it to my sister to drink." Christopher's smile widened devilishly at the memory.

"Did she take the bait?" Isabel was certain she had or he wouldn't be telling her the story.

"Yep, and then she immediately spewed hot sauce and grape juice all over the dinner table. We both got into trouble, though I don't know why. It was entirely my fault."

Christopher and Isabel cooked dinner together that evening, a light meal of tabbouleh and grilled chicken breasts. In their domesticity, Isabel found herself missing Sam more than ever.

THE FOLLOWING WEEKEND, Sam was stuck in Chicago again. Christopher seemed to have radar for Sam's coming and going. On Thursday, less than an hour after Isabel spoke with Sam, Christopher called. After several entreaties, she gave in and met up with him for dinner. Dinner turned into breakfast and into dinner again, until she realized that they hadn't left each other's side for two and a half days.

Sam's schedule barely allowed him to be home one day a week. Isabel didn't feel abandoned as much as sad for Sam, because she knew it meant a lot to him to be with her throughout the pregnancy. She'd never seen him so happy as the first time they saw the baby on the ultrasound during the amnio test. Sam shook with pride and excitement as he held Isabel's hand throughout the process. He wasn't squeamish or frightened, the way she'd heard so many husbands were. One friend had her husband out cold on a hospital gurney next to her, having fainted at the sight of the eight-inch needle going into his wife's uterus. He'd hit his head on a hospital cabinet and had to get six stitches.

Sam, so secure in who he was, never pulled any stunts to draw attention to himself. He didn't even bother correcting the nurse when she called him Mr. Ducci. Even so, Isabel couldn't explain how it did nothing to mitigate the sense that she was on her own. Sam's sense of autonomy had always been okay with her, but now that she was going to be a mother, she couldn't know what she might need and from whom.

ISABEL DECIDED TO participate in the panel discussion as a favor to Beth and Maggie. On the crisp October day of the taping, she traveled uptown to Bloomberg studios on Park Avenue at 8:00 A.M. When she arrived, Maggie was pacing outside the building while Beth sucked hard on a cigarette. Anna hadn't arrived yet.

"I can't fucking believe it. How could they do this?" Maggie was yelling at no one in particular, but Isabel guessed the comments were directed at Beth.

"Let's look at the bright side . . ." Beth's tone was less than convincing, and she didn't even bother to suggest what the bright side might be. She was clearly enjoying herself.

"Hey, Maggie. Hey, Beth. What's happened?"

"The show was one person short so the producers said they would provide a mother for the roundtable," Beth explained. "Well, they provided a doozy . . . We just walked into the green room and there she was. I have to say she was incredibly cool, considering. Maggie almost plotzed on the spot."

"Who are you talking about?" Isabel asked Beth before their attention was diverted by the producer coming out the front door just as Anna emerged from a taxi. Taking in the scene, Anna flashed a look around that clearly said, *What the fuck?*

The producer pulled Maggie to the side, and whatever magic she spoke appeared to calm Maggie down. Maggie turned to everyone and said with characteristic enthusiasm she always managed to muster, even in the toughest of times, "Okay, let's go, ladies!" Beth squashed out her cigarette and held the door open as the women filed in and up to the green room where the fifth participant awaited them.

CHAPTER EIGHT

Beth

ONCE PAUL HAD recovered from respiratory failure—miraculously, the doctors said—he was back to work two weeks later. Just before Labor Day, he called Beth as though nothing had happened.

"Do you and Jessie want to come with me to the South of France? I have a few meetings in Monte Carlo. You guys can hang out while I work for a few days, then we can drive down to Portofino and Santa Margherita and fly out of Florence. What do you think?"

It seemed crazy to Beth to take Paul up on it, considering the potential downsides—he could get sick while they were away, they could be at each other's throats the entire trip, Jessie would miss school. But they'd be gone only a week, she slowed down and rationalized, so anything that came up could be dealt with by simply flying home early if necessary. And if it all went smoothly, Jessie would get to spend time with her father, time she would not have in the future.

"Okay," she told him. "Jessie would enjoy it."

. . .

APART FROM BEING the inspiration for the roundtable on motherhood, Beth hadn't thought much about the protests earlier that summer. The fallout had simmered to an occasional outburst from individuals online, easy enough to ignore. Beth had relegated the events to a kind of ad hoc marketing effort with the net effect of an increase in awareness about what RHM had to offer.

RHM planned to launch its next series of ads now that marketing had found twins in a stunning tenured professor of mathematics at Harvard. Forty years old and having suffered three miscarriages, Dr. Rebecca Crane was fortunate enough to have naturally conceived twins, a boy and a girl. She was distinguished in her career, and she was game. They had a photo shoot with the professor at eighteen weeks, when she was just starting to show with a slight, sexy swell, and would have another at thirty-two weeks when she was nearly to term, then wait for the call to let them know when Dr. Crane went into labor. Photographers were at the ready, hoping to shoot Dr. Crane just before and right after she gave birth. Beth couldn't wait to see what this new campaign would bring to RHM.

The Tuesday after Labor Day, Sacha walked into Beth's office holding an envelope and piece of paper. All the color had drained from Sacha's face. She handed the items over to Beth and stepped back as if from an explosive.

A manila envelope, addressed to "The Head of RHM, Beth Mack" (odd enough), contained a photocopy of Agnes Seymour from the previous ad campaign. Her breasts and belly and baby had been scribbled over violently with bright orange pen ink as if to erase them. On the reverse side, the sender had copied a centuries-old illustrated poem entitled "Ode to the Death of a Young Maiden." The image lay askew on the page and the entire thing looked to have been created in haste. Beth thought back to that defaced print ad from the day of the protests and felt a jolt of recognition. Could this be from the same sick fuck?

"God, the world is populated by lunatics." Beth ran her hands through her hair and held them there. "Let's hope this is someone's bad idea of a prank," Beth said in an unsuccessful attempt to make them both feel better.

"Where did you find this?" Beth asked Sacha.

"It was sitting in my in-box. It looks like someone hand delivered it. There's no postmark or address."

"Did you show this to anyone else?" Beth held the paper gingerly.

"No, I brought it right to you," Sacha told her. "What should we do with it?"

"Let's take it down to security."

Beth explained to the building guard about the magazine tear sheet from the day of the protests and handed over the new missive. She wished now she hadn't been so dismissive about it. The guard looked at the note and nodded, telling Beth he would share it with his security company. The fact was there was really nothing to be done since the threat was not deemed overt or needing immediate action. Beth chose to consider it idle until, well, until proven otherwise.

Beth thought about canceling the trip to France and Italy, but she couldn't bear to disappoint Jessie, who was looking forward to time with Paul.

One week later Beth, Jessie, and Paul flew Alitalia to Nice, where they rented a Mercedes station wagon, then drove to the small town of Menton on the French-Italian border.

While Paul entertained business partners, Beth and Jessie worked their way along the coast from Menton to Beaulieu-sur-Mer to Cap Ferrat. In the small beachside village of Villefranche-sur-Mer, Beth bought a small drawing at the Chapelle Saint-Pierre, a church used for many years as a storeroom for fishing equipment, by an artist in homage to the sailors he'd met there. Isabel's birthday was around the time the baby was due, and Beth picked up a sweet *Madonna and Child* watercolor she'd found in the chapel shop as well.

Jessie loved swimming in the Mediterranean and delighted in the lack of swimsuits.

"Why don't we swim naked at home?" she asked.

"Americans are pretty uptight about nudity. It goes back to the Puritans." Beth paused and turned her full attention to her daughter. "Does that mean anything to you?"

"No," Jessie answered, distracted. "Mom, is Paul going to die soon?"

Instead of answering immediately, Beth offered to buy Jessie an ice cream as a distraction. Mother and daughter sat quietly on a stone wall, staring out at the water and licking their Miko ice cream bars. Beth leaned over and kissed Jessie's lavender-scented hair from the local shampoo they used the night before.

"Is he, Mom?"

"Oh, honey, we don't know. Your father is not well and he will die from his illness, but we can't say when. We can hope that he gets better, but the truth is it's not likely."

Beth saw tears well up in Jessie's eyes as she stared out over the water, and Beth pulled her close.

"I'm glad we all came on this trip together," Jessie now said, resolute.

"Me too, Jessie . . . me too."

ON A DAY when Paul didn't have to work, the three of them climbed the narrow hilltop streets of Èze and had dinner at La Chèvre d'Or. They watched a group of old men play *boules* on a small patch of dirt and sipped chilled white burgundy on a trellised patio overlooking the *petit moyen* and the sea. There was an unexpected ease in the way they related to one another that added a fresh layer to Beth's sadness over the inevitability of Paul's failing health.

In spite of his weakness, Paul made great effort to play with Jessie. One afternoon, as they were walking through town to the beach, he ran ahead up an alley and disappeared. When Jessie followed him but then couldn't find him, she called out to him, "Pop, where are you?"

Paul had found a way through one of the small shops to come up behind her, shouting in terribly accented French, "*Je suis ici!*" which made her jump with surprised delight.

Jessie followed suit, announcing, "Now I'm going to hide!" A frenzied game of hide-and-seek ensued between father and daughter along the steep cobblestone streets.

Watching them play reminded Beth of why she fell in love

with Paul in the first place. He could make any place home. She'd never seen him uncomfortable, not in any social setting, nor in solitary repose. What was so perplexing about Paul was the comfort he seemed to have in his own skin even as he couldn't admit to his most basic physical need. How did men and women less self-possessed than Paul fare so much better with accepting their desires?

Relieved from his professional commitments, Paul was now free to enjoy their little vacation without interruption. The day after their escapades in Èze, in the soft light of early morning, the three headed into Italy and drove down the winding roads of the Italian coast toward Portofino. They parked their car so they could walk by the water. Just as they reached the marina, the sky grew greenish and dark, and gusts of wind blew over the Lavazza umbrellas meant to shelter the tables at a small café. The locals ran to batten down their small boats, and three large black-and-white short-haired mutts barked and ran wildly in warning.

Beth, Jessie, and Paul made it under an awning of a small trattoria facing the inlet just as fat drops of rain began to fall. The storm cleared the streets quickly by forcing people to seek shelter indoors, and the town became eerily abandoned. The rainwater on the cobblestones intensified the salty, musty smell of the old Italian port, and for one quick moment Beth experienced a feeling of timelessness as if they had all died together and existed now in some otherworldly limbo. Beth, both discomfited and calmed by the moment, held fast to Jessie as they watched Paul staring past the churning water of the marina toward the horizon. The momentary fracture in time was repaired when the maître d' appeared with a grandiose *"Buongiorno, signore, signora, e signorina!"* and served up a plate of olives, salty pecorino and great big chunks of thick-crusted bread.

They spent the afternoon enjoying a multicourse lunch of quick-fried and salted bait fish, *prosciutto di Parma*, focaccia, and *cacciucco*. Jessie, having befriended the owner's seven-year-old daughter, played happily for hours, the language barrier no impediment. Paul and Beth shared a bottle of Lambrusco and were feeling the soporific effects of the alcohol.

"She's remarkable, our Jessie," Paul said wistfully, more to himself than to Beth. "The thing that makes all this so hard"—Paul swept his hand across his body—"is knowing I won't be around to watch her grow up. It's where I lose my faith in God." Paul pressed his lips together in an unsuccessful effort to stem his tears.

PAUL HAD ALWAYS been devoutly Catholic. When he and Beth were first dating, it was important to him that Beth attend Sunday morning Mass with him every week. Beth had no truck with religion, having grown up in an atheist household, but she made the effort to accompany Paul to church as a way to get to know him better. She admired his devotion and found beauty in the liturgical ritual. Paul's submission to the tenets of Catholicism seemed to contradict his fierce intellect, and yet it was this very conundrum that made her feel that she could trust him. He seemed at home in mind and spirit.

But the sermons and prayers of Sunday Mass left her cold. Worse, the politics of the Church seemed supremely misogynist to her. She couldn't imagine how any woman could wrap her head around such blatant patriarchal bullshit.

"Would you ever convert to Catholicism?" Paul asked her over brunch one Sunday after church.

"No, Paul, I couldn't. It would be hypocritical. In fact, I'm not even sure that I'm comfortable attending Mass with you anymore. It feels like a lie," Beth told him.

"I respect that. But I don't know how we can be together if God isn't central to your life."

"Well, that's something you need to think hard about because I don't see it changing," Beth replied. "I don't see why love between two people on earth needs something more to connect them. Love is mystery enough for me." Paul grabbed her hand in solidarity and the subject never came up again between them.

Paul had planned on becoming a Jesuit priest until, at the age of twenty-two, he had changed his mind and gotten his MBA instead. By the time he was twenty-eight, he had made a killing as an investment banker. However, he'd always struggled to understand his conflicting desires and never quite made peace with any of his choices. When he met Beth, he'd believed that she was his salvation. His struggle with her lack of faith ultimately dissolved in the bond they'd created together. What Beth couldn't know at the beginning was how she was the first and only woman Paul had ever fallen for. Paul's love for Beth transcended the limitations that entrapped him in life and faith.

From the start, Beth was drawn to Paul's easy sense of humor, which lacked any meanness whatsoever. She'd never met a man who laughed so easily, who didn't sulk and wasn't jealous. This scored high points for Beth. In May of that year, on Beth's twenty-eighth birthday, Paul threw her a once-in-a-lifetime party. Since they'd known each other for only a few months, Paul had Isabel help plan the party and invite guests. He'd rented a hundred-foot schooner to sail around Manhattan. A three-star chef prepared dinner, served by a waitstaff. The unseasonably warm night, illuminated by a full moon and cloudless sky, seemed ordained to capture Beth's heart, as if Paul had made a pact with Mother Nature herself to bestow magic on the evening. By coincidence, Tony Bennett was giving a performance on one of the Hudson River piers. The boat set anchor for an hour to listen from the water. At the end of the evening, as they left the marina and walked along the river, Paul gave Beth a strand of black Mikimoto pearls. When he proposed a month later, Beth didn't hesitate for a moment.

People often mistook the couple for brother and sister. More fraternal than romantic, the strangers' assumptions weren't entirely off the mark. They never could get the sex right. While Beth tried to address what the problems might be, Paul insisted that his strict Catholic upbringing had created inhibitions. Once they were married, he'd promised, his resistance would lift.

For all of Beth's worldliness, she chose to believe Paul. When someone asked her if she could name the most important reason why she married her husband, Beth replied quick and sure: "Trust. I trust him."

Less than a year later, Beth's concept of trust had been thrashed to bits when she found out that Paul had contracted HIV by having unprotected sex with countless men before and during their marriage. Beth felt betrayed by Paul's infidelity, but she was furious at the risk Paul had taken with her life and their unborn daughter's. Worse, the way Beth learned the truth further crushed her belief that Paul's concerns ever extended beyond reinforcing the lie he lived.

Paul had donated blood for his father, who was about to undergo surgery due to cancer. In spite of Paul's O positive blood type, which meant he was a universal donor, he was reluctant to donate the blood. When Beth questioned him about it, he replied, "I can't stand the sight of blood."

"Really? Your father has cancer, Paul, get over it and give up the blood," she commanded.

Three weeks later, Beth received a phone call from the hospital saying they urgently needed to speak with Mr. Marchand.

Beth picked up on the tension in the caller's voice. "Can you please tell me if there is a problem? This is his wife."

"I'm sorry, ma'am, we can't do that. It's a private matter. Please have him call the hospital as soon as possible. It's urgent." The doctor's voice held tight. Clearly something was very wrong.

Beth first thought, *My God, Paul has leukemia.* Further complicating her chain of morose projections, her period was two weeks late and she suspected that she might be pregnant, the result of an unusually successful evening of sex with Paul a month earlier. They'd met for drinks after work and then polished off a bottle of Cristal with dinner. Later that night in bed, Beth successfully coaxed Paul into hours of lovemaking.

Beth called Paul out of a meeting to tell him about the phone call from the doctor. Terse and distracted, he told her, "I'm very busy today, Beth. Please don't interrupt any more meetings with this nonsense."

"Paul, the doctor said it was urgent," she said. "How can you say it's nonsense?" Beth's voice turned shrill in concern and confusion.

"I'll call him tomorrow."

When Paul got home that night, she screamed at him. "For Christ's sake, how can you not want to know why the doctor is calling you with urgent news? News he can't even tell your wife! What is wrong with you?" She hated herself for flipping out, but she sensed that something terrible was happening to them.

Paul stood squarely in front of her as if to physically block her. The veins across his forehead pumped to the surface, looking like they could burst from the strain. "I couldn't get the doctor on the phone, but I left him a message. Don't worry. Everything will be fine."

Paul seemed far from fine, and Beth couldn't understand why he was acting so strangely.

He softened then and pulled her toward him. "Listen, sweetheart, let's just crawl into bed and make love."

Furious about his refusal to take the phone call seriously, the last thing Beth wanted to do was have sex with him. "Paul, not now. I'm really not up for it."

"How can you turn your husband down? I'm trying to make this work." Paul held her hands in his and pulled her, slowly, into the bedroom.

From some archaic sense of marital duty she didn't even know she had, Beth climbed into bed with Paul that evening and reluctantly allowed him to have sex with her. She lay there, motionless, biting into the flesh of her palm, as he mindlessly thrust away. When she broke through the skin of her hand with her teeth she didn't feel a thing. Paul didn't notice the blood.

The next morning, Paul awoke as if he hadn't a care in the world. Beth questioned the urgency she'd felt and wondered if she had exaggerated what had transpired the day before. They had a quick breakfast together before Paul left for the office. As he closed the door behind him, Beth called out, "Paul, please speak with the doctor today. Put my mind at ease."

That evening, Beth came home from work to find Paul sitting on the couch listening to Wagner full blast on the stereo. Paul had never arrived home from work before Beth.

"Wow—what're you doing home?" she asked, genuinely surprised and momentarily delighted. Paul's vacant stare shifted her delight to darkness. Something was very, very wrong. Her pulse spiked.

Paul turned his head to follow her as she walked over to the stereo and turned the volume down. He stood up from the couch looking like a stranger to her, as if another being had inhabited her husband's body.

"Paul?"

"I spoke to the doctor." He paused.

"And . . . ?" Beth couldn't stand it any longer.

"I have it."

Beth looked at him with impatience. "You have what?"

"I'm HIV positive."

Beth's nonsensical response was to laugh as if it were a sick joke, although she knew with dead certainty that it was not. Her knees gave out and she fell onto the rug, which somehow lacked substantiality—*was it floating?* she wondered—beneath her feet. Breathing heavily, Beth felt as if she would faint. It took a few minutes for her to feel gravity again.

"No, Paul. How can that be possible?"

"I don't know," he told her as he stood eerily still, not offering any insight as to how his life had just been cut short.

"What do you mean you don't know?" Beth said, her voice tremulous with shock. "You must know something."

But Paul stood his ground, recalcitrant, unapologetic. Beth crawled to the couch, and climbed onto it like a two-year-old would, uncertain again if gravity would keep her grounded. She vibrated with adrenaline.

"Now what, Paul? What do we do now?"

Beth's comprehension of the world shifted violently that evening. Nothing would ever look the way it had before the moment Paul uttered the fatal words, "HIV positive." She heard them over and over and over again in her mind, trying to trace her way back to the moment when she should have known that her husband was a ticking time bomb.

The week that followed felt like a dream as Beth tried to understand how he might have contracted the virus. He lied at first when she asked if he was gay, saying, "Beth, come on. I have a hard enough time having sex with women. Do you think I'd be able to perform with men?" He sounded convincing, so Beth believed him. She still trusted him.

Paul speculated that Beth's boyfriend before Paul, who had a sexually promiscuous and multi-gendered past, was responsible for the virus in their midst. Of course, this theory assumed that Beth was positive as well.

ONE TORTURED WEEK later, Beth's results came back. She had tested negative for HIV and positive for pregnancy. It was early morning when they got the call.

"Paul, *please*. Just tell me the truth," Beth said, trying to breathe steadily.

"I don't know the truth," Paul said.

"You know some things. Like: How many men? Is there a man you love?" She needed some facts. Truth, what was that?

"No! I love only you, Beth."

Paul sounded resolute, which made Beth angrier. He moved away from the confrontation, ducking into the kitchen under the pretense of pouring another cup of coffee. She followed him.

"That's fucking bullshit! You used me to cover your shame. Just fucking tell me what's going on, Paul—at least grant me that respect!"

Finally he turned to face her. "Men, Beth?" he said through clenched teeth, hands working into fists. "There have always been men. In high school, in college, at work, when I travel."

"And you didn't—don't—practice safe sex? How could you be so stupid?"

"I hated myself. Hate . . ." Paul's voice tempered to a defeated whisper. "Maybe I should just kill myself now and get it over with."

Beth glanced at the knives in the wooden block on the counter as a plausible threat and moved to place herself between them and Paul. He turned away from her but stood, unmoving, for a few uncomfortable minutes. She was afraid of Paul at this moment. If he was capable of such a dangerous lie, what else could he do? When a life comes miserably tumbling down, what morphs a thought of action into a fatal reaction?

When Paul walked away and out the front door, Beth tried to muster the strength to go after him but could only stand in dazed relief.

FOR WEEKS BETH wandered around in a haze and didn't tell anyone the news of Paul's health status. If she just kept it to herself, she unreasonably reasoned, it couldn't be real, it wouldn't be true. And indeed, it wasn't until she told the story to Isabel, a few weeks later, that it all came rushing at her as her new reality.

Beth and Paul continued to live together for a few months after the two phone calls that had altered their lives irrevocably, during which time Paul seemed to have found an insatiable sex drive. Before the news of his HIV status, he had to be seduced into sex. Not so now. He became desperate to sleep with his wife though she adamantly refused him.

Beth lived in mortal fear for her health and the health of the baby she was carrying. Paul's desire for sex disgusted her and filled her with contempt. She could barely look at him anymore and cringed whenever he tried to touch her. She wanted to kick him out of their apartment, but for the first time in her life, she found herself crippled by terror. He continued to threaten suicide, and Beth found herself caught between being fearful that he would act on his threat or, worse, that they all—Beth, Paul, and their unborn child—would become a New York horror story.

Paul moved out in August after several entreaties from Beth. She'd been spending nights at Isabel's to give Paul space, or at least that's what she told him. Only once he was out of her daily life could Beth express the rage she felt toward him. In the months that followed, Beth refused to speak with him except to remind him that she thought him a coward. Pregnant with Jessie, Beth felt murderously protective. Paul never let up on his entreaties to try to make Beth understand. He swore that he hadn't tried to infect her during that last night they'd made love. He didn't even know of his status yet, he argued. He claimed he was trying to convince himself that all was fine. But in Beth's mind it didn't matter. His denial overwrote his instinct to protect her and that freaked her out more than anything. Why else would he have postponed talking with the doctor if he hadn't known at least on some level?

There was no way to know what was in Paul's heart and mind; surely he believed the story he told himself, and Beth found a small part of her wanting to believe him as well. Maybe she had to. What would it mean to admit to herself the possibility of Paul's coldhearted ability to blatantly disregard the welfare of his wife and baby to the extent of infecting them with a deadly virus? What kind of love allowed for that? None that Beth had ever wanted to know.

Over the course of years, Beth had slowly allowed Paul back into her life with the realization that love can confound with messiness and even cruelty. Once she accepted Paul's dread about who he was, she began to sow the seeds of forgiveness. In that way, they became a kind of family.

PAUL, BETH, AND Jessie spent two nights in Portofino before flying back to New York. On the final evening, Beth made an excuse for staying back at the hotel so that Paul and Jessie could have a date for dinner at the waterfront restaurant where Jessie had met her new friend.

They returned hours later, still laughing about how Paul had mangled the little Italian that he knew while insisting on speaking to the waiters in their language. Beth's heart ached watching Paul and Jessie together. Their daily lives had little to do with each other. Still, when they did see each other, Jessie brought out a childlike sense of play in him, a quality often displayed in his life before his HIV status, but now only revealed when he spent time with his daughter. They loved each other, that was certain.

Time stood still for the three of them in that ancient Italian town, and Beth was caught in an emotional whorl that her sensible self bucked with every last ounce of energy. She couldn't wait to get back home, to get back to work and to the routine home life with Jessie that anchored her.

CHAPTER NINE

Maggie

MAGGIE COULDN'T GET Blue Eyes out of her head.

She had seen him only one day over the summer: sitting alone on a park bench across from RHM, scooping up the remains of a Wendy's Frosty from the yellow-and-red cup. He wore khaki shorts, a white oxford button-down, and lime-green converse high-tops. She thought she detected a whiff of amber as she walked past him. Maggie caught his cool blues for a moment and smiled flirtatiously. Nervous that he would think she was coming on to him—okay, she really did find him inexplicably attractive—she quickly crossed to the other side of the park with unnecessary determination considering her destination of the local bodega for a coffee. Maggie opted instead for a Häagen-Dazs ice cream bar. Seeing Blue Eyes made her suddenly feel famished.

Talk to the man for goodness' sake, Maggie encouraged herself. *What do you have to lose?*

Frozen treat in hand, Maggie walked back across the park toward Blue Eyes, resolved to say hello and at least open up the opportunity for conversation. Distracted, she had torn open the wrapper of her dark-chocolate-covered ice cream on a stick, but had forgotten to take a lick. The temperature had been hovering around 90 degrees all week and the ice cream bar couldn't hack it. Before she reached the park bench, the entire bar slid off the stick and onto her sleeveless white silk chemise. Maggie stood in disbelief for a few seconds, looking down at the blob of ice cream and chocolate on the ground in front of her. When she looked up, Blue Eyes was walking toward her. "Oh, nuts" was all she could say, a phrase that always made Lily laugh when Maggie said it.

"Tough break," Blue Eyes said as he sauntered past her. His voice, octaves higher than she expected, caused Maggie to jump at the sound of it. Maggie avoided his eyes, focusing instead on the orange-capped pen clipped inside his shirt pocket.

Mortified, Maggie headed straight back to the office, hoping she wouldn't bump into anyone she knew along the way. No luck she would go unnoticed—Beth and Isabel happened to be walking back from lunch at the same moment.

"Yikes, does it hurt?" was all Beth could muster before she broke down into hysterical laughter.

"Just tell me it isn't your favorite shirt," Isabel pleaded.

Maggie laughed loud and hard so she wouldn't cry. The shirt was new and from her favorite designer. She'd spent a small fortune on it as a reward to herself for simply getting through her days. "Easy come, easy go," she said lightheartedly, as if by saying so she could make it true.

"Don't worry, I'll find you something in the store for you to wear home. You'll get a nice breeze on your breasts since there's no belly to support the generous cut of our tops. Want another white one?" Beth ran into the store before Maggie could answer.

Isabel and Maggie made their way upstairs. Maggie hadn't seen Isabel since she'd popped. "You look, as they say, radiant. How're you feeling?"

"Exhausted and slutty," Isabel responded without further elaboration.

"Yes, I remember it well," Maggie said wistfully. "When are you due?"

"Right after the New Year. But I can't imagine waiting that long." Isabel patted her neatly protruding belly.

"Have a lot of sex and you won't have to. You know, semen softens the cervix—a too-little-known tip for the ladies."

"I'll keep that in mind . . . How's darling Lily?" Isabel asked. "Has she hit her terrible twos yet?"

"No sign yet. I'm keeping my fingers crossed that having two stepchildren and a useless husband with a self-righteous ex-wife makes me exempt."

Isabel giggled at the epic diss. Maggie gasped and covered her mouth with false modesty as if to say, *Did that come from me?*

"I'm not sure I want to know more right now . . . I'm going to stop in and say hi to Anna. See you in October, if not sooner." Isabel gave Maggie a quick hug and left.

Beth came back and handed a shirt to Maggie. "Do you want to tell me what happened, or is it better left to my imagination?" Beth was clearly having too much fun seeing the normally impeccably neat Maggie in such a state of mess.

"Remember that guy I saw a few months ago in front of the store—it was the day after the protests—I said I got hit by the thunderbolt . . ."

"I remember, but I don't think you told me much about him."

"I don't know anything about him to tell. I mean, he's actually a little creepy, but in a sexy way." Beth raised an eyebrow, which Maggie ignored. "He must work around here or something . . . Anyway, I saw him in the park and I was about to say hello and *bam*! I got hit with a thunderbolt of chocolate ice cream. Needless to say, Blue Eyes and I didn't speak."

"Blue Eyes?"

"He has inhumanly blue eyes. It makes him a bit scary."

"I'd be careful if I were you," Beth said. "There are a lot of crazies around . . . I gotta get back to work." She pecked Maggie on the cheek and ran off to her office.

Maggie ducked into the bathroom to change. In keeping with Beth's vision for RHM, the office bathrooms were thoughtfully designed to accommodate the women who used them—with dressing room, shower, towels, and products to cure every beauty and hygiene need. It looked like a bathroom in a suite at the Four Seasons Hotel.

Wearing the shirt Beth gave her from the store, a cap-sleeved cotton jersey tee with a satin-trimmed, plunging neckline—designed to show off those wonderfully engorged prenatal breasts—Maggie had the very definite desire to be pregnant again. Considering the state of affairs at home, she also knew that considering another child was insane. It would add stress to their marriage, not fix it. But Maggie wanted another in spite of John, which made the need even stronger.

As an only child, Maggie wanted to give her daughter what she herself missed out on growing up. Now that Lily was over two years old, she and a sibling would be three years apart even if Maggie got pregnant soon. If she waited to see how things went with John, the gulf between them would be even bigger. *And face it*, Maggie thought, *it isn't going to be getting any easier to conceive after forty and that's coming up fast.*

Maggie had loved being pregnant. She never experienced morning sickness, and while she was slightly tired during the first trimester, during the second and third she possessed inhuman energy. When she wasn't working, she spent gloriously romantic days and nights with John. They ate home-cooked meals by candlelight and cuddled naked on the couch watching Italian films. They spent many weekends tucked away in a bed-and-breakfast at the beach, in the Berkshires, on the North Fork. They took road trips with no particular destination, just to be cocooned together in the car for hours on end. Once, after a picnic in a state park in Pennsylvania, they made love on a picnic table under cover of blue spruce rising above them. John doted on her every moment. She felt full and fortunate and happy.

The sense of endless romance ended with Lily's birth. As smooth as the pregnancy was, giving birth was equally as difficult. Maggie had heard the old wives' tales predicting the course of events: If you have a bad pregnancy, delivery will go well. If your pregnancy goes without a glitch, count on something going wrong when you are giving birth. After five hours of pushing, Maggie still had the wherewithal to be curious. "Doc, can you tell me why I'm having so much trouble?"

"It's hard to tell exactly what's happening." The doctor's matter-of-fact tone only served to further infuriate Maggie.

"It doesn't help that the vagina curves up. The baby has to go against gravity to come out of the birth canal, making it more difficult to push. I'm sorry to report that, but it's true."

Maggie blew out a torrent of air. "God really fucked women, didn't he? Couldn't he have made it a little easier for us? What was he thinking?" she exclaimed in complete frustration. She also meant it to be funny, but she sounded more angry than comic. Truth was she did have a bone to pick.

As soon as she said it, she regretted it. The delivery nurse who had coached her through much of the labor wore a small gold crucifix around her neck.

"I'm sorry if I offended you . . ." Maggie managed through labored breathing.

"Honey, I've been through it three times myself. You do have a point!" She let out a hearty belly laugh, making Maggie relax for the first time in hours.

After twelve hours of labor, a reluctant Lily was coerced from her haven and into the world. She opened her eyes plainly and gave the doctor a scornful look. The truly scary part came afterward when Maggie, already exhausted from hours of laboring and pushing, continued to bleed. Her placenta would not disengage from her uterus and her blood pressure dropped precipitously to dangerous levels. Just as she was about to slip from consciousness, a doctor gave her a dose of something that pulled her back.

As the pain threatened to absorb her, she felt the lifeblood slipping from her. Her only thought was to hang on so she could at least see her baby. After several unsuccessful tries, her doctor called on a woman intern who was walking past the delivery room. She was petite and her hands were small and nimble enough to reach into Maggie's uterus to pull out the placenta, allowing the clotting that saved Maggie's life.

Maggie held Lily in her arms and cried from relief when she awoke the first time after delivery. She called Beth. "I'm holding her now. She's asleep against my breast. She looks like John already, is that possible?" John, exhausted from the stress of watching what Maggie endured, slept in the reclining chair next to her bed.

"Not only possible, but necessary," Beth was quick to respond. "All first children look like their fathers when they're born. That's nature's way of making sure they don't eat them. How're you feeling?"

"Battered. Happy. I'm going back to sleep now. Talk later."

When she awoke, there was a beautifully wrapped package embossed with the Red Hot Mama logo beside her bed. Inside, a delicately designed nursing robe in jade linen with magenta silk piping. Beth had a prototype handmade just for Maggie.

The year following the birth of Lily was unexpectedly sweet and mellow after the torrent of sexual activity that had marked the beginning of John and Maggie's relationship and the violence with which their daughter entered the world. While difficult for them to get much time alone, they basked in the wonder of their baby girl. By the time Lily was six months old, her face seemed to magically transform into a mini Maggie. Assured of safety from suspicious paternity—at least according to Beth—Lily grew wide-eyed and developed dark curls of impossibly soft baby hair. John was smitten with his beloved pair of beauties.

Maggie found comfort in John's experience from raising his first two children. He wasn't alarmed by any of the things that

Maggie found terrifying. At first, Maggie appreciated John's worry-free approach to child rearing. If Lily didn't burp properly after nursing, if she slept too long or not enough, if she pooped too much or it was a different color from one earlier in the day—John assured her there was no need for alarm.

Things had begun to change when Jules and Justine came to live with them. Georgette's sabbatical in France to finish her book coincided with the school year. Maggie doubted the necessity for Georgette to be away the entire year. What kind of mother put research convenience before her children?

With Georgette abroad, Jules and Justine needed to be ferried back and forth to school in the city every day. It fell to Maggie most days, since she was usually on the move between Jersey City and Manhattan, getting to and from RHM, taking Lily on their weekly outings. The more she did, the more she gave up trying to get John to pitch in. This gave her less time with Lily and absolutely not a single minute to herself. By the end of the school year, Maggie was ready to do anything to have Georgette home, much as she had wished her away at the beginning.

AS MAGGIE LEFT RHM with Beth later on the day of her ice cream disaster, she spotted Blue Eyes across the street and grabbed Beth's arm in alarm. "That's him! That's the guy!" she said too loudly, as she pointed him out to Beth.

Once Beth actually spotted the guy Maggie was pointing at, she said, "He's freaky."

On the way home, Maggie thought again about Blue Eyes. She was both compelled and repulsed by the man, and her attraction to him was more curiosity than action driven. *Maybe*, she thought, *it's just me avoiding dealing with John*. Either way, he inspired her to reach for their collection of toys she kept in the drawer beside their bed. At this John took notice.

"What's this out for?" he tried to ask casually when he discovered the black vibrator left under the pillow.

"I was using it." Maggie offered nothing more.

"Alone?"

"Yes. Jealous?" Maggie teased, feeling she was onto something. If John grew paranoid about Maggie's fidelity, perhaps that would make him more engaged. Fear could be a highly motivating force.

"No . . . should I be?" He tried to keep his tone light, but Maggie could tell he was unnerved, made all the more apparent by the intense revival of his sex drive. Maggie's distraction acted like a drug on John, and she didn't harbor as much resentment for him with Blue Eyes sifting through in her fantasies.

In a moment of uncharacteristic initiative, John made plans for a weekend away at a beachside bed-and-breakfast down in Cape May, New Jersey. Rosie offered to stay with Lily in Jersey City, and while Maggie hated to leave her behind, she'd begun to harbor hopes that she and John might still be able to reboot their marriage. She realized it would be the first time they would be alone together for more than two or three consecutive hours since Lily was born.

They left early Friday afternoon, taking a leisurely drive on the Harley through the small towns that dotted the Jersey shoreline, beginning with the Asbury Park of Maggie's youth.

"John, let's drive by the Stone Pony. I think I can find it,"

Maggie said. In the mid-1970s, scruffy rocker Bruce Springsteen performed his magic with the little-known E Street Band at the Stone Pony. It took a few circles around downtown before Maggie recognized the modest concrete building. On the nearest pier sat a once-beautiful carousel house, the painted clown faces barely perceptible beneath the grime. It had been more than twenty years since she'd last visited the seaside resort.

As a teen, Maggie would flee to the Jersey Shore with her friends every chance she had, welcoming the escape from the oppressive silence of her home where she and her father co-existed as uncomfortable roommates. Maggie suspected those weekends away from the house were a relief for him as well.

Springsteen's songs of busting out and longing spoke to Maggie's inarticulate sadness. She felt that he was singing directly to her. The solace his music provided made her feel that someone somewhere knew how she felt. She rarely listened to his music anymore even though she still loved it. To this day, it made her feel melancholic. Nostalgia often instigated a sadness for Maggie that she didn't like to indulge.

Maggie jumped down from the bike and pulled off her helmet to let the salty wind blow through her hair.

"This place is strange . . . What happened?" John asked as he remained straddled across the seat of his motorcycle.

"It's had a checkered history and went bust in the late eighties. It's still trying to recover . . ."

Maggie wanted to plant herself right there and find a way to help resuscitate the decaying urban seaside town. But John seemed eager to get moving as he cranked the gears on the bike.

"Never mind all that. Let's go." She feared if she tried to make John understand, either she would begin to sound maudlin and hate herself for it or, worse, if he didn't understand, she would hate him for what he couldn't know.

From Asbury Park they rode south to the incongruously affluent Spring Lake, just a few miles down the coast. They had a lovely lunch on an oceanfront veranda amid other diners and staff throwing noticeably disapproving stares at their attire of leather pants and black helmets.

After lunch, John hopped on the Garden State Parkway toward Cape May, skipping some of the shore towns Maggie was aching to revisit. She figured they'd catch them on the way home. Instead, he followed signs to Atlantic City. It became immediately apparent to Maggie that this was where John had been heading all along. Suddenly, John seemed to know exactly where he was.

John pulled the bike into the parking lot of the casino and pulled off his helmet. "Let's just run in and play one round of blackjack. If we lose the first few hands, we leave. If we win, we stay until we lose." John's challenge was irresistible. More, the simple fact that he was taking charge already felt like a sex drug to Maggie.

"I'm all in." She caught his hand in hers.

The visit to Asbury Park had made Maggie feel old, but she felt young again by half in the company of thousands of blue-haired ladies and men with walkers. "Oh, let's spend some time here. I think I might like it." She gave a lopsided smile.

John pulled Maggie over to a twenty-five-dollar blackjack table and pushed a stool under her butt. "Luck be a lady . . ." He stacked $200 worth of chips on the table like he had it to burn, flipping one expertly between his fingers. Standing by her side, he guided Maggie through four games of blackjack, winning every hand. They were the only players at the table. The dealer, a stern, boyish Latina, showed no emotion at all as she deftly dealt cards off the deck. She placed two nines on the table.

"John, you look like you know what you're doing. Do you know what you're doing?" Maggie asked, noticing the girlish tone to her voice and not caring in the slightest.

John upped the bet. "Double down."

The dealer turned over a Jack and an ace.

John swiped two fingers above the cards to indicate that he would stick.

The dealer broke. John smiled and kissed Maggie flush on the mouth as the dealer pushed a stack of chips across the felt.

Maggie, mesmerized by the language and choreography of it all, wondered what other surprises John had in store for her.

"Look, sweetheart, we're up two hundred." John shuffled the chips in front of her. "Let's keep two hundred and continue playing with the two hundred we started with. Sound okay to you?"

"You're the boss. Anything you say." Maggie heard the words and nodded to herself to say, *Yes, that's the thing, that's it! John needs to be the boss more often.* That would change everything. The only thing Maggie felt like doing at that moment, besides continuing to win at blackjack, was to steal away for a quickie under the boardwalk.

By the time they left the table, John had won more than $500. He stepped away when he'd lost two hands in a row. His restraint gave Maggie a second wave of admiration.

They walked out of the casino giggling and flush with victory. Standing in the parking lot beside the motorcycle, Maggie kissed John as she pressed against him. "Where'd you learn to play cards, John Harting?"

"Oh, around . . ."

"So how far do we have to drive to that B and B? I'm not sure I can wait that long." Maggie pressed the palm of her hand against his cock. He was already hard.

They both laughed and flipped on their helmets. Maggie wrapped her legs around John's backside, and strapped her hands across his groin. "I'll take the fast route!" he shouted, and the rest was lost to the sound of the engine as they sprung from the casino lot and out to the highway heading south.

THEY ARRIVED IN Cape May with plenty of time to make their nine o'clock dinner reservation—John had arranged it! After a long and sexy shower together, they dressed and headed downstairs. As they waited for their table to be set up, they sat together on a swinging double chair on the wide porch of the restored Victorian Lace Inn, sipping Pernod. Just a block away from the beach, the onshore wind brought the sound of the waves as they tumbled onto the shore with soothing regularity. The briny air was tinged with a fishiness—the smell of raw oysters and clams and the long days of summer—which Maggie loved.

Spent from a day on the motorcycle, Maggie relaxed into John's arms. She'd checked on Lily when they'd arrived at the B&B and could now give herself over to the evening. With warming pastis running through her veins, Maggie dared to feel hopeful as John held her tight and rested his lips on her head.

They were slow to get up when called in to dinner, reluctant to break the magic of the moment. After a satisfying meal of sautéed softshell crabs, wild rice with cranberries, and blistered shishito peppers, Maggie and John took a long walk on the beach. The sand was cool on their feet and the ocean blacker than the night sky. It was coming on midnight and they couldn't see another soul on the beach. They walked along the jetty and found a ledge facing out to sea. The tide was out, the sea calm, and cloud cover shielded the light from the moon. They made love standing against the slippery rocks as the pulsing ocean splashed against their feet.

The next morning, Maggie and John woke up famished and ran downstairs like two teenagers for breakfast. The clouds from the previous night had blown away and the day was bright and hot. By 10:00 A.M., they had lathered up with sunblock and headed for the beach.

Holding hands, they charged the surf without toe-testing the temperature first. Maggie had loved to challenge her friends when she was a kid to do the same. The south wind from the previous day brought cold water, and, with it, a small swell had kicked up overnight making the surf rough enough to distract them from the temperature. They fought one foamy wave after another, bodysurfing for an hour before flopping down in the hot sand for a rest.

As they lay breathing hard from exertion, Maggie laughed and said, "Uh-oh, I feel old again." They relaxed there for a minute before she turned to John, suddenly serious. "John, I want to have another baby."

"What, Maggie? Are you kidding?"

"No, of course I'm not kidding." Maggie pushed herself up on her elbows and leaned over John, who remained silent. "Not only am I not kidding, I *know* that I want another child and I'd like to get pregnant as soon as I can." Maggie didn't mean to sound so demanding, but that's how it came out. "I mean, Lily is already more than two years old and I want her to have a sibling close in age, and I am not getting any younger, and my father—"

"Whoa, whoa, slow down. What are you doing?" John put his hand up to stop the tide of Maggie's argument. "Is this something you just came up with, or have you planned on dropping this one on me this whole time?"

"John, you don't just come up with the thought of another child. Of course I've wanted this all along. What are you saying? Are you asking why we haven't discussed it before? Because . . . I don't know why we haven't. But I'm telling you now that I want to have another baby. Does this really come as a surprise to you?"

"Yes, frankly, Maggie, it does." John said it like he meant it.

Maggie shifted away from John on the sand. Her mind raced to make sense of the conversation they were having even as she felt her satisfaction from the weekend slipping away. As good as the last twenty-four hours were, they weren't going to make up for what was fundamentally wrong with their marriage. John's attention deficit when it came to his wife and kids was never going to change. He didn't pay any more attention than he had to when it came to Maggie and Lily, or his two older children for that matter. *What's one more child you can neglect?* Maggie thought, but kept quiet. *It'll just fall on me any-*

way. Maggie silenced this voice for the moment, focusing instead on the way the curl of a breaking wave turned a brilliant turquoise just before it crashed in on itself.

Determined to not let this conversation ruin their weekend, Maggie tried to reframe it toward the positive in her mind. *He didn't say no; he just sounded unenthused. Maybe I ambushed him*, she reasoned, *and he was caught off guard*. Tomorrow, on one of the stops on the way home, she would bring it up again. Now she wished they'd taken the minivan, where they could talk in comfort. The motorcycle made discussion impossible.

DINNER NEXT TO the marina that evening was a sloppy affair, perfect for her mood. Determined to normalize the tension she'd created, Maggie turned the conversation instead to John's childhood. She was seduced by John's ease in the casino and encouraged him to tell stories of his father, who, she was surprised to learn only this weekend, had been a blackjack dealer in Vegas. John's upbringing had been chaotic, and he had survived it by keeping a low profile, which Maggie thought explained his own laissez-faire approach to child rearing.

They slurped raw clams squirted with fresh lemon juice and used mallets to smash Maryland crabs cooked with Old Bay. The spice stung their sunburned lips, which they cooled with long gulps from the icy Coronas they drank from the bottle. The fishing boats docked by the marina restaurant smelled strongly of fish and the sea. On the way into the dockside café, they had stopped to admire a large mako shark caught earlier in the day, now hanging by its tail from a massive hook on a piling in the parking lot. Maggie patted the shark and jumped back at the unexpected coarseness of its skin and density of its body. She laughed at how frightened she could be at something so dead.

When they awoke on Sunday morning, Maggie was missing Lily terribly. Although it promised to be another perfect beach day, she suggested that they leave after breakfast, anxious to get home and spend the day with her daughter.

Over coffee and muffins at the same table they'd had a romantic dinner Friday night, Maggie couldn't wait another minute before blurting out, "Do you want another child, John?"

"No, Maggie, not really. I have three already. That's enough for me."

"But I only have one." Maggie hated how pathetic her pleas were—she sounded like a child begging for another lollipop.

"I just don't see how we could handle it." John's use of "we" did it. Something flipped in Maggie.

"'*We*'? What '*we*,' John? You don't do a damn thing for your children—any of them. What difference could it possibly make if there was one more around for you to neglect?"

John looked away. He pushed his chair back from the table and stood up. His lips quivered with hurt and rage.

"Are you trying to ruin this weekend, Maggie? Is that what you're doing? Because you're doing a very good job. I'm going to go pack." He turned and walked away.

Maggie signed the check on the table and stood for a moment, not knowing what to do next. She'd surprised herself with the vitriol that surfaced so quickly. *Was* she trying to sabotage the weekend? The years of therapy Maggie had been through in her twenties made it hard for her to hide from herself. It wasn't so much that she didn't say and do stupid things as it was the quickness with which she realized her part in the communication breakdown with John.

The ocean had always helped her make sense of things, so she headed for the beach. Maggie sat on the wet sand, just a few feet from the rush of the surf. Chin resting on her knees, arms wrapped around her legs, she looked out over the water. She imagined what it would feel like to let a wave sweep her away in her self-contained vessel, wondered how long she would bob above the water before slipping under.

She stared unblinking at the glassy green waves. About fifty yards out, the color switched to an inky blue and, farther out still, to an even darker hue. She tried to focus on the lines where the colors changed, imagining the sea creatures that lived at the precipice of each increasing depth. As she sat, the motion of the waves lulled her into reverie. Like all those water molecules spinning in place as energy surged through them creating swell lines, the ocean seemed to move something inside her. Even as a young girl, the pull of the waves worked like a shaman on what ailed her. As she brought her attention to it, that pull now seemed to affect her lower abdomen and then deeper, in her ovaries.

"Oh, great," Maggie said into the crashing surf. "I'm ovulating." Then she grinned ear to ear at what she already knew and felt suddenly buoyant, as if she had conspired with the ocean at that very moment to create what she longed for most of all. *If the moon and the tide are linked to menstruation, why not then to conception?* thought Maggie. After twenty minutes seated in private celebration, Maggie stood and headed back to the hotel. She no longer felt any anger toward John, only thankful for the gift he had bestowed on her.

John had pulled the Harley in front of the B&B, packed up and ready to go. She kissed him like nothing had happened, and John, not one to hold a grudge—one of his more appealing characteristics—hugged her wordlessly and handed over her helmet.

When they arrived home three hours later, there was a message from Georgette on their voice mail. The original plan had her home for the new school year, which began in one week. Jules and Justine were to spend weekdays with their mother and every other weekend with Maggie and John. So Maggie was more than dismayed to learn that Georgette had lost so much time working with Jules and Justine visiting over the summer that she had extended her stay until December.

"*Tant* fucking *pis pour moi*" was all Maggie could muster in response to the news.

IT HAD TAKEN Maggie months to find the right venue for the roundtable discussion on motherhood. There was no one willing to go live with the show, but she found producers for a cable channel who were willing to tape a series of six discussions to run weekly on future airdates on topics from motherhood and marriage to divorce and family finances. Maggie would become one of the coproducers if the series was picked up by the channel.

The day before the taping, one of the participating mothers had to cancel due to a family crisis. Maggie had been unreachable all day thanks to her malfunctioning cell phone—she really needed to get the damn thing fixed—and the show's producers had taken it upon themselves to fill the slot. By the time Maggie picked up her messages later that night, she was relieved to learn that the show wouldn't have to be postponed.

Maggie had taken a pregnancy test the day before, ecstatic when the strip turned Pepto-Bismol pink. She had decided she would deal with what and how to tell John when she was a little further along. For now, she would keep it her little secret. Maggie was feeling pleasantly smug about the direction in which her life was headed until Beth opened the door to the green room.

Clothed in a long saffron duster with a bloodred silk chiffon scarf wrapped around her swanlike neck, Georgette Fontaine was huddled close to the producer, sipping a steaming beverage out of an I ♥ NY coffee mug. The two women were chatting like old friends. It occurred to Maggie at that moment that the producer had used Georgette several times as a talking head on divorce over the past few years for news programs.

Damn, damn, damn, Maggie silently cursed the two of them, until Georgette noticed her standing there and smiled. "Georgette, hi, I didn't know you were back from France . . ." Maggie managed to say, her vocal cords constricting her normal voice into something squeaky and weird.

Afterward, Maggie would have no recollection of what followed next, although she knew words had come from her mouth. The ringing in her ears had seemingly blocked all sound from reaching her brain. She turned and fled from the room, caught an elevator going downstairs, and headed out of the building. Beth followed on her heels.

Lighting a cigarette she didn't want—Beth handed it to her; had she asked for it?—Maggie paced the sidewalk. She took a few puffs before realizing it was making her sick and she threw it down on the sidewalk. She needed to clear her head before going back upstairs. Beth was saying something, but Maggie couldn't hear her.

Anna and Isabel pulled up in taxis, and moments later the producer came barreling out the door toward Maggie. Maggie threw her a furious glare.

"Are you kidding me? Georgette Fontaine?! Of all the women in the world." Maggie tried to keep calm but her voice shook with emotion. The producer put her arm around Maggie's shoulders and pulled her close.

"Listen, Maggie, I didn't mean to ambush you," the producer protested in an undertone. "The whole thing happened so fast. Georgette was in touch with me yesterday just an hour after we got the cancellation from Philadelphia. I invited her before I made the connection. My associate producer left you a message yesterday. Didn't you get it?"

"I got a message that the spot had been filled but not who was filling it." Maggie realized now that she'd meant to call the associate producer back to ask her this very question, but then Lily had snipped her finger with scissors and, with that, the day's details had completely slipped her mind.

Maggie then laughed out loud at the absurdity of the whole thing, realizing she wouldn't have felt any better knowing the night before that Georgette was on deck to join them. Until today, she and Georgette had managed to keep a civilized distance from each other. They had actually never met in person before. Instead, they maintained an abstract connection through their blended families. Things were about to change.

"Come back to the green room," the producer prodded. "Georgette is game . . . Just think of it as an adventure. The morning is bound to be nothing if not interesting. I'll even let you review the edit, don't worry . . ."

Maggie knew then that her reaction was more surprise peppered with resentment than it was mortification. What of Georgette needing time in France to finish her work? Why did John's ex have time to travel back and forth to France while Maggie took care of her kids? The avalanche of noise in Maggie's head was deafening and Maggie fought to claw her way back to a place of calm certainty, that place she had occupied only an hour earlier when thinking about being pregnant with the second child she so wanted.

She inhaled to fill her lungs—now a little stale from the goddamned cigarette—and forced herself to focus.

"Okay, let's go, ladies," Maggie announced, and corralled the group back into the building.

The women were sequestered for three hours of taping. While the first fifteen minutes were bumbling and awkward, once they each caught their stride, the discussions were heated and intelligent and often downright hilarious. By the end, Maggie was pleased as could be with the results. It looked like the series might truly work.

But the biggest surprise of all was Georgette. Maggie found her husband's ex appealing on so many levels, not the least of which was her sheer otherness. Where Maggie was accommodating and played the martyr, Georgette was rigid and demanding. Where Maggie was overly eager to please, Georgette didn't need to have everyone around her think her swell. The qualities that Maggie had vilified when seen from a distance became the very ones Maggie admired most. She smiled to herself as she thought, *I bet I could learn a thing or two from Georgette Fontaine.* One thing had become clear during the discussion: Georgette was passionate about her children, even if she didn't express it in ways that Maggie recognized. Maggie and Georgette were not in opposition; they were on the same side.

"You recovered nicely. Kudos," Beth congratulated her on the way back to the office. Anna and Isabel had gone to lunch together and Georgette had run off to a meeting with her publisher.

"Thanks." Maggie felt pretty satisfied herself.

"So now that you know her a little better, how do you feel about all that crap she spread around about you?" Beth, as ever, couldn't help herself from playing instigator.

"You know, I think I actually might like her. You can't blame her really. The guy she's married to, and whom she loves, has an affair, and when she finds out about it, he doesn't end the affair, he leaves her. It's gotta suck."

Beth raised her eyebrows, encouraging Maggie to continue.

"I can see why they were together. Maybe she's right. Maybe they should have stayed married." Maggie was thinking out loud to Beth, who listened with an amused smile playing across her lips. "I still could have had Lily . . ." Maggie gazed off before continuing. She was on a roll. "Did you see that article in the paper the other day? A scientist in Australia found a way to fertilize eggs without sperm. If they made this successful in humans, men would be irrelevant. Face it, Beth, men are over. It's the end of men," she said with a smile.

PART THREE

AUTUMN

CHAPTER TEN

Anna

BY THE TIME Jason announced his plans for a weekend away to work on his master project on the banks of the Delaware River, Anna was barely holding it together. Over the last six months, Jason had been drawing plans for a five-hundred-square-foot modernist tree house for the children of an enterprising dot-commer in the backyard of his country house. The project would make Jason little money, the price of complete freedom to design and build with no interference from the client. Jason planned to use the tree house as his calling card. Right now, the project's least redeeming quality was that it would leave Anna alone with the boys for the weekend. She still hadn't recovered from the D&C and her hormones were raging, and with them her intolerance for Jason's work for posterity.

It was a Tuesday morning and Anna should have been headed to work. Instead, she sent an e-mail telling Beth she had some urgent personal business to attend to and then she started packing a bag.

"Well, Jason, maybe you need some quiet time this week to

prepare for your fort in the woods," she told him. "I'll tell you what, you can have tons of it. We're out of here!"

"What are you talking about, Anna? What do you mean you're 'out of here'? Where are you going?" Jason asked, sounding like he didn't really believe Anna would walk out. But he started to pace and yell as he watched her pack up the diaper bag and a small suitcase. "What the fuck, Anna? If it's so important to you, I won't go. You can't just leave!"

"Sure I can, Jason. I can leave, and I can take the boys. Fucking deal with it. Go build your tree house."

"Stop it, Anna! You're freaking out. You can't leave in this state."

But Anna pushed past him, picked up Henry, draped the two bags over her shoulder, and, with her free hand, grabbed Oscar and walked toward the front door.

"Mama, where are we going?" Oscar asked her, his mouth twisting to repress the tears about to come.

"Somewhere not here, I don't know," she said to Oscar, who now began to wail.

"Mama! Why are you mad, Mama?" he managed through sobs.

Before she closed the door behind her, Anna flung her cell phone at Jason as a final *fuck you*. Jason stood helplessly in the window, and Anna found satisfaction in the tears of frustration filling his eyes. She wanted to leave him alone and scared and abandoned. It was the only way she knew to hurt him. Now he could feel what it was like to lose something sacred.

Anna had no destination at first. In the heat of her fury, she simply got in the car and started driving. As if on autopilot, she headed toward Long Island, her two little boys crying in their car seats as Anna herself sobbed in the front. She drove east and the chaotic noise was an odd comfort. *Yes, scream and cry, boys! Wail, Anna! You lost a brother or a sister and I lost a son or a daughter—there is plenty to cry about. Cry and keep crying . . .*

Eventually the boys cried themselves to sleep and Anna began to breathe evenly. She arrived at her parents' Montauk bungalow more than three hours later, spent from emotion.

With the boys parked in front of the TV, Anna lay down next to them on the couch, where she promptly fell asleep. When she awoke, the sun had nearly set and the boys were restless with hunger and boredom. Henry had crawled on top of her and was patting her head. Oscar was pressed up against her, doing his best to provide solace simply by staying close. Her three-year-old's empathic instinct got under her skin. No one sensed her moods like Oscar did. He may have been only a toddler, but he was an old soul.

As Anna awoke her first thought was that Jason would be out of his mind with worry. The couple hadn't been out of touch for this much time since they'd been together, outside of the occasional business trip. Certainly never with the boys in tow. She knew she should call him but didn't want to spoil the serenity she felt as she lay cuddling with the boys on the couch. Exorcising her anger at Jason's expense left her spent.

Evening descended and with it a resigned melancholy. Anna softened toward her abandoned husband.

She called Jason from the landline.

"Hi, it's me," she said with no affect.

"Where are you?" Jason asked. Anna could hear him struggle to regulate his tone.

"In Montauk."

"Are you and the boys okay?"

"The boys are fine. Hungry. I don't know what I am. Define 'okay.'"

"I don't know either, Anna. I don't know what I can do to help you."

"Stop, Jason. You can't help me. Or, at least, I don't know how."

Jason let out a long breath. "What if I take the train out to Montauk and then I can drive you guys back? It scares me to have you driving while you're so upset."

"Okay."

"*Okay?* Oh, good. Okay . . ." Jason paused, then continued in a more measured tone. "I'll take the next train or Jitney—whichever's fastest. We can sleep there and come back to Brooklyn in the morning. You good with that?"

"Yeah. That's fine. I'll take the boys out for something to eat and see you here later tonight." Anna's flatness was unnerving, even to herself.

Maybe this was all she needed, she now thought, to scare and inconvenience Jason since she felt this way all the time. Scared and inconvenienced. Maybe now he would understand and be able to help her figure out how to live her life without jeopardizing all she held dear.

They agreed on the drive home the next day that Jason would keep his plans in place to visit his client.

IN THE AFTERMATH Anna agreed that she needed help with the boys, so she made plans to spend the weekend at her parents' house while Jason was away working with his client. Isabel would be joining them, and Anna looked forward to time with her parents and sister. Even better, there would be plenty of hands to help with the boys. It was hard for Anna to admit she needed help, and she had to work hard not to hate herself for admitting that she couldn't handle everything on her own.

She and Jason were carefully attentive with each other in the days following her outburst. Anna made it a point to ask Jason for help when she needed it, and Jason willingly obliged. The couple worked to find a new rhythm to their household demands.

ANNA HAD BECOME much closer to her parents after becoming a mother herself. She could now appreciate the impulses behind the smothering love she'd felt from them as a child as something other than intentional smothering. She still struggled to find another word for it. She did understand that it came from a good place, if sometimes fearful. But beyond that fear resided hard-won wisdom—wisdom Anna finally let in, like light through a crack in the cellar door.

The day after Anna had lost the baby—when she was too enraged to speak with Jason and thought better than to share the news with pregnant Isabel—she'd called her mother. When Marie picked up the phone, Anna couldn't speak and instead choked out heaving sobs.

"Who is this? Anna? Isabel?" Anna could hear the worry in her mother's voice.

"It's me. Anna. Ma . . . the baby . . . is dead!"

"What baby, Anna? Who?! Please . . . tell me what happened," Marie begged. (She would admit later that her heart nearly stopped, thinking Anna was talking about Henry at first and then Isabel's baby. In true motherly fashion, she had run down the hierarchy of terrors.)

"I was pregnant but now I'm not. I miscarried last night. I lost our baby . . . I don't know what to do . . ." Anna released all of her pain to her mother, now calm on the other end of the line.

"Oh, honey, I am so sorry. I know. I know what that feels like and it's a terrible, terrible thing . . ."

"How would you know? You never . . ." Anna quickly admonished, but then asked, "Did you?"

"Yes, Anna, I did. Between you and Isabel, I lost a baby at the beginning of my second trimester. I mourned that baby until I had Isabel, and that child will always hold a place in my heart." Marie's voice grew soft and quiet for a moment before saying, "It happens, Anna. It's not something you can blame yourself for."

"Do you know what caused it?" Anna was hoping a reason might make it less painful, though she also knew that sorrow doesn't fit any equation.

"I don't know. My doctor scolded me for moving a couch while I had been vacuuming the day I miscarried. I don't buy it. Maybe it's just God's will."

"Oh, please, Ma. I can't go there."

"Okay, fine. But why it happened isn't important, Anna. What is important is that you allow yourself to heal. You and Jason can get pregnant again and you will, if that's what you want." Marie paused. "Is that what you want?"

"I don't know," Anna admitted.

"If I had that baby after you, Anna, then Isabel would not be here. The children you get to keep are blessings and how they come to you will always be a mystery. Do you understand?"

"I'll try. I'm sorry you lost a baby, but I don't know what I'd do without Is. I'll hold on to that." Anna's voice, now steady, regained its strength.

NOW AS ANNA and her mother prepared dinner on Saturday afternoon, they reminisced about those days of long preparation for Christmas dinners. In spite of the work it took, her mother remembered them fondly. "Cooking for family and friends is a great act of love," she'd told her daughter once long ago. Anna couldn't understand then how days and days of cooking a meal that would be consumed in minutes could possibly be worth it. Now, with a family of her own, she finally understood how right her mother was.

Watching the body language between her parents on this particular afternoon reminded Anna of how finely tuned Marie and Nick were to each other.

"Nick, what time do you want to eat?" Marie hollered into the family room from the kitchen, as if they didn't eat at the same time every Saturday. The habitual question was really Marie's way of saying, *Nick, you're the boss*, which, of course, he wasn't really.

"Any time you want," Nick replied, as he always did. It was Nick's way of acknowledging the respect implicit in her asking but also that he trusted her to make the decision.

Nick kissed Marie on the cheek as he passed her in the kitchen on his way to the garage to pick a bottle of wine for dinner. Marie smiled, then swatted him away, and Anna marveled at the moment of flirtation between these two people who had lived together for nearly fifty years.

Marie could anticipate Nick's every need before he even recognized them for what they were. It had more to do with empathy on her mother's part, Anna realized now, than a power struggle between them. When it came down to the major decisions, Marie usually had the final say. It wasn't about power at all, but rather a dance that had been perfected after years of living under one roof, raising a family, navigating the heartbreaks and joys in a way to keep it all going another day and then another week and then another year.

Anna thought back to her childhood interpretation of her parents' marriage and became acutely aware of how the dynamics interpreted by each family member were twisted into individual logic or, in some cases, illogic. Who's to say what is truth between two people? Today, Marie still deferred to Nick, at least in the most obvious ways, but Anna was no longer sure who was in charge. More important, she wasn't sure it mattered at all.

BY THE AUTUMN afternoon of Maggie's roundtable taping, Anna was feeling strong again. It had been almost two months since the miscarriage and she was beginning to recognize the better parts of herself again. With just two more weeks of work to go before taking time for herself, Anna was optimistic that she might be able to contribute something worthy to a discussion on motherhood.

Humbled by the previous few months, when the balance of her life had tipped into one dominated by anxiety and depression, Anna had finally forgiven Jason for what he had no control over. Her sense of vulnerability was all her own.

The couple had time to tuck away for an afternoon while the boys were at a gymnastics class with their nanny, Jenny. They luxuriated in bed for hours, making love for the first time since Anna's miscarriage.

"So you no longer hate me?" Jason asked earnestly.

"Oh, Jason, you know I never hated you." She kissed his shoulder and neck and nuzzled there.

"You were angry, though. I don't know if I've ever seen you that angry."

"I was frustrated and heartbroken and, yes, angry too. I know we can try for another baby—and we will—but before we do that, I need to understand what I really want: from work, with you, for my life. I wish it were easier, but it just isn't. I thought I knew how I wanted things to be, but I guess I don't. I think I'm angry with the not knowing . . ." She said the last part very quietly.

"How can I help?"

"Just having you and the boys in my life is all the help I need. That, and you could make more money . . ." She laughed when she said this, but she was dead serious.

"I am trying, Anna."

"Will you promise to try harder, Jason? Promise me that?"

"Yes, I will try harder. I know how hard it is for you, and I'll do everything I can to shoulder the burden with you."

"I know I was the one who said 'try,'" Anna pushed, "but can you say you 'will'? You *will* share that burden with me? Even if you don't make any money, can you at least share the responsibility?"

"I will, Anna. I will." Jason kissed her lips to seal his promise to her.

Just then they heard the front door open and the boys run into the house, Oscar yelling for their parents. "Mama, Papa, where are you? I did a big flip today!"

"Coming, my darlings!" Anna yelled back as she leaped out of bed, threw on one of Jason's large shirts, and ran to greet the other two loves of her life.

AFTER THE TAPING, Anna and Isabel went to lunch together. Anna hadn't seen much of her sister over the past summer. She'd felt remiss about not making more of her sister's pregnancy, but she also felt uncomfortable in close proximity to her sister's pregnancy in the aftermath of her failed one. Now she wondered if her protective nature for her sister had given her an outsized sense of how her experiences affected Isabel. The fact of the matter was it seemed that Isabel had barely noticed the absence of her sister over the summer, as mired as she was in the experience of being pregnant for the first time.

"So what was all that about in there?" Anna asked of her younger sister once they'd said their good-byes to the other women outside the studio.

"All that *what* in there?" Isabel asked, innocent as can be.

"All that supposedly theoretical crap about libido and pregnancy? Are you really that turned on by being pregnant?" Anna linked arms with Isabel as they walked, not really wanting an answer from her. When one wasn't offered, Anna let it go. "Italian or Japanese?" she asked instead.

"Italian. I need some bread dipped in olive oil," Isabel answered quickly, as if she'd been waiting for the question all morning.

"Is that your only craving?" Anna asked as she led her little sis into a nearby trattoria.

"That and sex."

Anna shot a sideways glance at Isabel, who was smiling wickedly. "Seriously, Is, what is up with you?"

"I've been seeing a lot of Christopher. You know how I get around him."

Anna had played witness to the past decade of flirtation and unconsummated romance between Isabel and Christopher. She knew nothing had ever happened between them, but for a moment Isabel's wistful smile gave her pause. She shook her head to clear her doubts—Isabel might go there, but Christopher, for all his mischievousness, most certainly would not. His squeamishness around life's messiness precluded it. To a certain extent, she didn't care much either way. Isabel positively glowed with health: whatever she was doing seemed to be working for her. In their younger lives together, Anna would have pressed Isabel for more information, but she had learned to back off and give Isabel space. Important things had a way of bubbling to the surface when they needed to.

The sisters sat at a table near the window. Afternoon light streamed through the plate glass, warming them. They each ordered a glass of wine and relaxed into their seats.

"So you're really serious about taking some time away from work to be with Jason and the boys?" Isabel asked.

Anna nodded. "I'm so excited. I can't imagine life without running around exhausted. Or life period, for that matter."

Anna was more optimistic than Isabel had seen her in a long time.

"Sounds great. I'm so happy for you. I bet the boys are ecstatic."

"Henry is clueless, but Oscar is on top of it. This morning he said, 'Mama, pretty soon you will not go to work so you can stay home and play with me all day?' I told him, 'Yes, I can play with you and Henry and Papa too.' I don't think he liked that very much." Anna laughed at the thought of her sweet, manipulative Oscar.

Isabel became contemplative. "I'm almost ready," Isabel said, laying her hands across her belly.

Anna thought about the past August, when she had lost the baby. She would tell Isabel about it sometime in the future when the admission that things can go terribly wrong wouldn't darken Isabel's optimism. Anna knew in her heart at that very moment how lucky she was to have two healthy little boys and for the first time didn't feel anguish over the miscarriage. She couldn't wait to share the secrets of motherhood with her little sister.

"Do what you can for yourself for the next two months, Is, because after that, what you do for yourself won't look anything like it does now," Anna cautioned.

"I know. I am," Isabel said, still lost in her own reverie before focusing again on Anna. "Do you have any trepidation at all about being at home all day?"

"No. I know it's unrealistic, but I feel like it's a vacation even though I have to use the time constructively to figure out how I want to live my life. I admit, I've never been so confused as I am now. You know, Mom was right when she said that men have it made these days. God that pissed me off, but maybe because she's right."

"She is right, but it sure got you riled . . ." Isabel teased.

"It was that obvious she hit a nerve, huh?" Anna said. She smiled, but a shadow played across her expression. "So what is it with women today? Even if we are the breadwinners, go out and work all day, there's no one at the end of the day to give us our slippers and a martini, have supper ready and put the kids to bed." As she got fired up she began to speak faster. "I mean, where is the equity? All these years fighting for the right to be given equal opportunity, and what did we get? More than our share of responsibility. I'm angry and I don't even know who the hell I'm mad at! God, it's exhausting."

"Did you ever think that maybe you like it that way? You're needed and respected at work, you're needed and loved at home. You have a happy home and workplace and a healthy income to boot. Do you think that doesn't come at some cost? I mean, face it, Anna. You aren't some passive observer. You've created the life that you wanted."

"I know. That's what is so maddening. And it isn't enough to say 'careful what you ask for,' because getting the life you want is still the prize. Sometimes I just think I can't handle what I want. How fucked-up is that?"

Isabel casually dipped piece after piece of crusty bread in the olive oil. "Maybe you're angry with yourself for being human."

"When did you become a philosopher?"

"You'll figure it out. That's what this time is for, and you know you couldn't have a more understanding person than Beth to help you come to a solution with work."

"She was the one who suggested I take the time in the first place. She's been an angel."

"'Angel' is not the word I'd use to describe Beth under any circumstances," Isabel said, and they both laughed. "But she always knows what she's doing, that's for sure."

The sisters caught up on family drama. Anna filled Isabel in on the latest from Bobby. Most recently he'd failed to make payments to dear old Uncle Sam and the IRS had garnished his income. They laughed at the absurdity of a man who makes over a million a year but doesn't pay his taxes, not because he is evading them, but because it simply doesn't occur to him to file.

"Accountant Nick got the son he deserved! All those years harping about the importance of money really influenced his son, huh?" Isabel said. She could always make Anna laugh harder than anyone. Anna thought about what her mother told her after the miscarriage and she felt a renewed appreciation for the fact that Isabel was Isabel. Anna looked forward to being able to spend time with her little sister once the baby was born. Isabel's maternity leave would overlap with Anna's sanity leave—the timing was perfect.

CHAPTER ELEVEN

Isabel

DURING THEIR LUNCH after the roundtable taping, Isabel picked up on prickly energy from Anna but couldn't place its source. She felt she'd been negligent to the concerns of her older sister over the past few months, wrapped up as she was in managing Christopher and Sam. Whatever the cause of that energy, Isabel also didn't feel the need to push. Anna would tell her if it was important enough. Besides, Isabel may well have been projecting her own prickly vibrations onto her sister. Part of her was desperate to share news of her affair with Christopher, but Beth's rancor about it silenced her on the matter. She'd tell Anna someday, but only after the affair existed in the past tense. Until then, she'd keep it to herself.

She and Anna left the restaurant warm from the wine, welcoming the bright but lowering sun and the snappish autumn air. They walked together the few blocks to the subway entrance, where they hugged good-bye. Anna was heading back to Brooklyn to spend a stolen afternoon with her boys.

Isabel decided to walk partway back to the office. Now in her last trimester, she had vigor to burn, the polar opposite of her first trimester. She handled the excess weight lightly, even reveled in the shifting cadence of her step and breathing. The only impediment was her need to stop every fifteen minutes to pee. It seemed the baby used her bladder as a head pillow.

Isabel zigzagged through the streets, walking vaguely in the direction of her office. It was coming on to three o'clock in the afternoon, and she planned on making it back to the office at least for a few hours before meeting up with Christopher in the early evening.

The bustle of Fifth Avenue pulled her into the throngs of afternoon shoppers. She considered stopping in Takashimaya, the elegant Japanese department store, to buy a tin of her favorite white tea. She would pick some up for Christopher while she was at it. As she headed down the avenue with purpose now, her eyes focused on the spires of Saint Patrick's. She missed the discreet entrance of the store and instead found herself heading almost weightlessly toward the cathedral. She hadn't been inside the church since Christmas Eve two decades earlier, when she and her family celebrated a Christmas Eve midnight Mass there. She'd been a lapsed Catholic since she stopped attending church after her confirmation. Once she was old enough to understand the exclusionary politics of the Church, she couldn't blindly go along with its tenets of ritualized patriarchy and all that went with it.

She hadn't thought much about the role of religion in her life over the past twenty-five years, but she did wonder now, with the imminent birth of her son, whether she would practice the beliefs she grew up with or turn away from religion altogether. Would it be damning not to christen her son? she asked herself as she climbed the steps to the great cathedral doors. Pascal's wager was tempting, but seemed the ultimate sin. Belief as prophylactic: only a man could construct that gamble.

Sunlight angled through the thousands of stained-glass panels, pushing rays of refracted light, cloudy with dust, onto a few chosen pews. Isabel headed for the light. She sidled into a narrow pew and sat down, heavily now, the manic energy ebbing into an echoing calm. Her heart throbbed in that sacred space and she thought she could hear it beat outside of her body.

The smell from the incense and candles brought her back to the church of her youth in New Jersey. The gold-spired Our Lady of Mount Carmel Church, where Isabel had been baptized and received her first Holy Communion, stood immodestly in the middle of the modest ethnic enclave where her parents grew up and where she was born. The family still gathered at Mount Carmel to celebrate weddings and christenings and to mourn at funerals.

When Isabel was a young girl, the church and the attending priests had intimidated her. Sunday Masses were excruciatingly endless, made more so as they were performed in unintelligible Latin. Isabel could remember the oppressive darkness inside the church no matter the brightness of the day and how her hands shook as she fumbled the donations basket. One Sunday morning just before her first Communion, instead of steadily passing the basket to the elderly woman sitting next to her, she dropped it onto the marble floor, where it rolled to the pew behind her. Her own gasp along with the clanging coins echoed through the church and she thought she would die of shame. She and Anna giggled nervously as they tried unsuccessfully to recover the basket and money now scattered beneath the knee rests and pew stands. They were shushed by a habit-wearing nun, who came to reprimand them for their disrespect in God's home.

It seemed another age ago when Isabel would, with hands pressed together and pointing toward heaven, slowly approach the altar and bend down to kiss a statue of baby Jesus. The man Jesus hung two stories above her head in ecstatic agony on a crucifix. His crown of thorns seemed most cruel to young Isabel. She knew the prick of a single thorn, and the image of a wreath of them stuck to poor Jesus's head gave her nightmares.

The images she confronted and contemplated weekly during her youth had seemingly disappeared from her consciousness. Visiting now those powerfully impressionable images made her realize that she had lived much more closely to them than she had ever known.

Isabel rose from her pew to light a candle. She said a prayer for her grandfather, whose death in her young life affected her deeply. Grandpa Ducci connected her to the Old World her parents came from and she thought of him often, especially on the rare occasions she found herself in a church. She remembered how, every time he saw her, he would sing in an operatic voice and broken English, "Here she comes, Miss Amer-eec-a!" and how her own father would laugh with delight. Her grandfather always made her feel like the most important little girl in the world.

Isabel walked to the front of the church and knelt down on the green velvet cushioned bench facing the altar. Her eyes gazed at the statue of Mother Mary, draped in a flowing blue robe, hands held in front of her, palms facing up in supplication. The mystery of Mary had always pulled at Isabel, and yet the turning point for her move away from the Church occurred when, as a teenager, she could no longer accept the concept of the virgin birth.

"Don't complicate things, Issy," her mother had told her when she'd asked how a virgin birth was possible. "It's what the Bible says. It is not our place to ask these questions."

Isabel looked at the beatific Mary before her now and saw a different truth for the very first time. Mary, far from supplicant, was all-powerful: a single mother to a man who would become one of the most influential in all of history. Why did the nuns never address that in catechism? History has focused only on the miraculous birth of Jesus, as if Mary's participation ended there. Mary was the ultimate mother not because her womb was a vessel for the Son of God, but because she needed no man to conceive him and then she raised him on her own. Isabel now understood why she was drawn to this sacrosanct place. Reciting the Hail Mary, she surprised herself by remembering every word without faltering:

> *Hail Mary, full of grace, the Lord is with thee.*
> *Blessed art thou among women, and blessed is the*
> *fruit of thy womb, Jesus.*
> *Holy Mary, Mother of God, pray for us sinners, now*
> *and at the hour of our death.*
> *Amen.*

Was Isabel a sinner? She knew that in the eyes of the Church, she more than qualified. She thought to the terrifying moments when, as a young girl, she was forced to disclose her sins to a priest behind a sliding window in the confessional box. When Isabel couldn't think of any sins she had committed— what sins does a nine- or ten-year-old commit?—she would make things up to have something to say. "I talked back to my parents . . . I was mean to my sister . . . I didn't do my homework . . ." The practice did little to convince her of her guilt then, and she was sure that a priest in a confessional box would do little to convince her otherwise now.

But Isabel did wonder, *What would Mary think?*

She closed her eyes and covered her face with her hands, as she was taught to pray as a little girl, but then shook off the shaming gesture and instead looked up, clear-eyed, at Mary on the altar. She surprised herself as she whispered in prayer, "I love Sam and I am grateful that he is my life partner and that we will have this child together."

And then Isabel asked Mary directly, "What do you make of my affair with Christopher? History claims that you were denied carnal knowledge, which seems like crap to me." Isabel actually giggled at the use of "crap" when talking to Mary. But then, she was talking woman to woman, and this frankness made Isabel feel closer to her.

"Maybe you knew a man, perhaps without your consent, though I hope without terror." Isabel bowed her head in unity at her last thought. She grew solemn. "I accept only your judgment if you see me as a sinner, and pray for your grace to absolve me."

When she returned to the office later that afternoon, she left a message for Christopher that she wasn't up to seeing him for dinner after all. Isabel went home and heated up some homemade escarole and bean *minestre*—a favorite soup from childhood that she always kept on hand.

The image of Mary stayed with her. She felt blessed.

ISABEL HAD ENTERED her thirtieth week. Her belly, now grown beyond her breasts, dwarfed them in comparison, even though her bra size had gone to a letter she didn't even think existed on the scale. *Thank God for Red Hot Mama*, Isabel thought daily as she got dressed.

Still, Isabel's energy surged, so much so that after her thirty-week checkup, she leaped off the examining table in the doctor's office much to his consternation. She felt strong and centered, seeing Christopher when it suited her, spending more time alone than she ever had before. Sam's absence was a godsend. Without him she was able to greedily cater to her indulgent need to push the limits of acceptability. She was not V Mary or Mary M—she was her own Mary, Mary, quite contrary. And it felt good.

THE HOLIDAY SEASON kicked off with Halloween. Against her better judgment, Isabel agreed to attend a flashy store opening and collection launch with Christopher. They'd often party-hopped together years earlier and had great fun ogling the fashion denizens in all their self-important glory. Isabel stopped attending these parties once she married Sam, but this was a party celebrating the collection of a mutual friend and she thought she'd accompany Christopher as a show of support for the budding designer.

Maxx Tripp's signature flourish of an imitation codpiece over the crotch of his trousers for men had become all the rage among the fashion elite. Some women had even taken to wearing the trousers in mock defiance, making them look like Annie Hall with a hard-on.

The evening had gotten off to a bad start. She'd met Christopher in front of her apartment building and his face dropped in disapproval the moment he saw her. Isabel had taken to wearing Issey Miyake's pleats once her belly had grown beyond her wardrobe. Christopher hadn't seemed to mind her fashion choice before this evening, so she couldn't figure out what the problem was now. Admittedly, her belly protruded so far beyond the frame of her body that it looked like she was wearing a Miyake tent.

He held her in a blank stare. "I'm sure Miyake didn't intend his clothing for pregnant women."

Caught off guard by the insult, Isabel looked down at her bulging silhouette as if to confirm that Christopher was addressing her. She knew the comment was meant to sting, though she was also sure that the intended barb had little to do with what she was wearing. In an effort to avoid any conversation of substance, she offered a silly retort: "I don't know . . . maybe he would be honored by it. In fact, maybe I'll suggest to Beth that she contact his company about developing a line specifically for RHM."

"Don't be ridiculous, Isabel. That would be insulting."

"Who is being ridiculous, Chris? What's gotten into you? It's okay to be sleeping with a pregnant woman as long as she isn't wearing Miyake? We're on our way to a party in celebration of codpiece trousers for God's sake. Get a grip." Isabel let herself be pulled into a nonsensical debate, a familiar pattern in their past, but one they hadn't played out over these past months.

"Why are you being condescending?" he asked as if she'd started the whole thing. "It's not the same thing. Maxx has a sense of humor built into what he's created. This," he said as he pulled rudely at the pleats of the iridescent blue dress, "this is a misappropriation of Miyake's intent."

Christopher seemed either on the verge of tears or laughter, Isabel couldn't tell which, but the incomprehensibility of his outrage made her burst out in laughter.

"I'm serious about this," he insisted. His knitted eyebrows quivered with the strain of forced bravado.

"It doesn't seem possible for anyone to be serious about this, especially you. Misappropriating the intent of a fashion designer? Really, Chris? I think you better change professions." Isabel hated herself for taking the bait. "You're losing your mind."

He walked slightly ahead of Isabel the rest of the way to Maxx's studio store. The cruel playfulness to his posture—his refusal to acknowledge that his date was just a few steps behind—left Isabel feeling foolish and uncomfortable as she tried to catch up, the additional weight of her belly slowing her down. She smiled sardonically with the realization that Christopher had brilliantly accomplished what he intended. She was, at that moment, an uncomfortable fool.

Neither spoke again until they arrived at the party. Maxx greeted them with raised eyebrows. He'd witnessed Isabel and Christopher in action when they'd worked together.

"What a surprise to see you two together," he trilled.

"Yes, we're finally sleeping together, can you believe it? I don't know you that well, but I feel I can confide in you." The words came tumbling out of Isabel before she could stop them. They all laughed at the absurdity of the comment. Isabel turned to Christopher and smiled her brightest and mouthed, "Fuck you," before disappearing into the room.

"Kinky," Maxx replied as an afterthought, distracted by the swirl of attention surrounding him.

Isabel had forgotten how incensed Christopher could make her. In the past, they'd worked it out by physically attacking each other under the guise of play. All that wrestling, boxing, and snowball fighting helped to blow off steam from the tension between them. Now that they were sleeping together that energy had changed. She questioned whether the recent tenderness between them was the most honest part of their connection. Maybe their true intimacy existed only in the fights they'd had.

After an hour of unbearable small talk with dozens of acquaintances, Isabel went in search of her date. She found him sloppily draped over one of the many statuesque models festooned in TrippWear. Christopher had had too much to drink and the model was clearly growing impatient with her ward.

"Christopher, I'd like to leave now, please."

The model rolled her eyes and lip-synced an exaggerated thank-you to Isabel, pushing Christopher toward her. "Go to Mama, sweetheart."

Christopher didn't resist as Isabel led him outside. "Let's get you into a cab and home to bed," she said. "You're a mess." His condition had drained her of her anger.

Christopher hung on to Isabel for dear life. He seemed to

have lost the animosity he'd had for her earlier in the evening and had now given way to sadness. "What are you going to do with me?" he begged.

"I'm going to take you home."

"No, no, no," he interrupted. "I mean later, after, you know, after that . . ." and he pointed sloppily to her belly.

"Christopher, you're drunk. We're not having this conversation right now."

Christopher went from slurry and sloppy to rigid and precise. He stood up straight and his sudden sobriety startled her. "I'm drunk, but I'm not unconscious, Isabel. Answer the question."

"No, Chris, I'm not getting into it right now. And if you're feeling well enough, then I'm just going to go home to my apartment. You're a big boy, you can take care of yourself."

"It's awfully convenient to just run away, isn't it?" The man standing with her on the sidewalk resembled nothing of the person she'd known all these years. This new vulnerability made her feel dizzy. The earlier comment about the dress made sense to her now. He was angry with her—angry about the certainty that he would soon be abandoned. Isabel took his hand, which he left limp but didn't pull away.

"Come on," she said softly. "Let's go back uptown."

They let the argument drop and didn't speak at all in the cab on the way to Christopher's apartment. The city buzzed with the millions of lives and dramas being acted out on every corner, in every apartment along the twenty-minute trip three miles uptown. For a moment, their particular unfolding drama welcomingly receded in the context of the huge city.

They remained silent as they solemnly undressed in the

darkness and crawled into bed, where Christopher slept spooned against Isabel's backside through the night. Isabel awoke just before dawn and headed back to her apartment. She left Christopher snoring loudly, curled into a fetal position at the edge of his bed.

WHEN ISABEL ARRIVED at the office that morning, she was greeted by one of her direct reports, Ruth Anders, an ad rep.

"We need to talk," Ruth said.

"Everything okay?"

"I just had a strange meeting with Larry. He asked if I would want to take over the Prada account starting now." Ruth was practically in tears.

"What did you tell him?"

"I told him that it was your biggest account and that I doubted you would want to give it up. I said I'd be happy to manage it while you were out on maternity leave. Then he said something that made no sense whatsoever . . . something about how that was a long way away and anything could change by then. What's going on?"

Isabel's mind raced with paranoia. The whole thing made her feel sick. "He's trying to push me out. Ruth, don't worry, take care of yourself. If he wants you to take over the account, do it. I'll figure it out. Thank you for coming to me. It means a lot."

Behind closed doors of her office, Isabel called Sam.

"The Turtle just handed over Prada to Ruth," she said as soon as he picked up the phone.

"That slimy bastard."

"What should I do?"

"Don't do anything, Is. We'll let him hang himself. What's the worst-case scenario? You don't work for that douchebag anymore? Just make a note of your conversation with Ruth and put it someplace safe. And if you haven't already, make a note of what he said to you months ago about hiring pregnant women. Try to re-create the moment and trace the date. It might be useful. Don't sweat it, sweetheart. He needs you more than you need him."

Whenever Isabel sought Sam's counsel, she felt well protected. His ego never stood in the way of giving dependable advice and she admired his ability to keep the situation focused on what it actually was, rather than what it meant to him. She never felt that Sam had an alternate agenda. Hanging up the phone, she thought about the man she had left in bed that morning. Christopher's agenda was unpredictable even in the best of circumstances. In moments like these, Isabel felt certain of the downright stupidity of sleeping with Christopher. The affair wasn't worth the risk of hurting Sam, but somehow she couldn't put Sam and Christopher into the same equation.

Isabel tried not to let the news of the Prada account affect her, but she was so furious and tense she began to feel tightness around her belly. Determined not to let the Turtle influence one moment of her son's prenatal life, she breathed deeply in, out, in, out, until she loosened up and finally relaxed. Even as she sought to calm it, the pressure she'd felt excited her: it was the first sign of what labor might be like, the force of her abdominal muscles against the baby and the wave of power she had inside her.

CHAPTER TWELVE

Beth

THE SECOND NOTE arrived on Halloween.

This one had arrived by mail, postmarked in a plain white oversized envelope, among dozens of pieces of more benign communications. Sacha hurried into Beth's office to hand it over to her boss. It featured positions from the Kama Sutra with an image of Dr. Crane vulgarly insinuated into the illustrations. The RHM model's image had been torn from sample pages of magazine ads, photocopied to reduce it to size, and glued sloppily into place. Dr. Crane's lovely face had been obliterated with the same fluorescent orange ink. The sender had written "Karma Suture" across the bottom of the page. Philistine or maniac? Likely both. Most disturbing, the ads with Dr. Crane had not yet been printed or released to the public. Somehow, the sender either had access to the RHM offices or knew someone who was supplying them. Either way, the note convinced Beth that RHM had a stalker whose intentions—while not clear—certainly meant harm. This was no black humor.

Over the course of the following ten days, Beth received two more missives. Addressed to Beth in the same orange pen used to violate the images, each note incorporated a cultural reference, though not thematically consistent, except for the degradation of RHM. Not that Beth was looking for someone with a thesis—she just wished there were clues besides the orange pen.

The third was from an 1850 illustration of Lady Macbeth with Beth's head superimposed on the image and "Lady Beth-Mack" written below it. It would have been funny, except that it wasn't. The image was repeated, but in this version Lady BethMack's head had been removed from her body and pasted next to it. Beth wasn't easily intimidated, but the stalker had her attention.

Beth called him the Orange Pen Stalker or Special OPS for short. Not wanting to take any chances that the sender wasn't going to take these arcane threats any further, Beth hired a private detective.

The letters from Special OPS marked the end of a relatively eventless fall.

AFTER THE TRIP to Italy, Paul's health maintained a slow but steady decline. He hadn't been rehospitalized, but a persistent cough now plagued him and extreme fatigue forced him to slow down at work. The thought of Paul spending a few days a week in bed simply to rest told Beth more about the state of his constitution than anything else. She and Jessie saw him for dinner at least once a week now. Although the signs weren't dramatic, Beth sensed the asymptotic nature of Paul's future days. The question of how closely she'd allow Jessie to witness her father's death remained. One thing was for certain: she wanted Jessie to have as much time as possible with her father before she couldn't anymore.

Beth tried not to conflate the double threats of Paul's steady decline and the latest dispatches from Special OPS, but she felt besieged by the weight of each. In an effort to release some of the tension she felt, Beth booked an after-work massage at a spa near the office. She'd often promise herself the gift of regular appointments, but they always got canceled in service to something else demanding her attention. Desperate for some relief, she pulled herself away from work and walked the ten blocks to the discreet and simple day spa.

Beth felt her body begin to unwind the moment she stepped off the city street and into the calm of the spa space. Barely audible Indian sitar music played in the background, and incense filled the air with the scent of jasmine. The attendant handed Beth a robe and slippers and showed her to a massage room. After consulting with the masseuse about what kind of work she wanted done, Beth slipped under the sheet covers and tried to relax into the moment.

As the masseuse kneaded Beth's body, she felt tears rise from her core and a sob emerged as a hiccup as she tried to stifle it. The therapist intercepted Beth's resistance, saying, "Let it go, Beth. Just let it go." This simple directive released a torrent of tears and, with it, the tide of sorrow that had been waiting to breach the levee around Beth's heart.

The deeper the therapist worked, the more freely Beth's tears fell. Crying never came easily to her, but these tears, spurred by sadness and anxiety, also came with a kind of joy. Beth remembered a card she'd received from Isabel soon after she'd shared the news of Paul's HIV status with her. In it,

Isabel had written: "Remember, my beloved friend, there is no love without sorrow, no grace without pain."

Beth smiled through her tears now as she recalled the beautiful wisdom of her friend.

Amen, sister.

THE FOURTH LETTER from Special OPS arrived unceremoniously in the mail less than a week after the last. This one featured lines from a poem by Louise Labé (properly credited, it would turn out) written inside a comic speech balloon pointing to the mouth of a woman crudely drawn with Special OPS's signature pen. She was being kissed by one man and screwed by another. Xs crossed out her eyes. There was no reference at all to RHM in this one, except that it was addressed generally to "The Ladies of RHM."

Conflicted about whether she should warn the staff at RHM, Beth vacillated between full disclosure and total silence. On the one hand, Beth thought it might be best that they knew to keep their eyes and ears open for any potential threat. On the other, telling them just might freak them out unnecessarily if this was all just an extended, perverse joke. She decided to keep quiet for now, or at least until she had more information about the latest French missive. Beth couldn't read French, so she called Maggie.

"Do you have Georgette's phone number?" Beth asked, fully aware that she could have called Isabel, who could have translated the poem, if not know its source. But calling Georgette would be more interesting. Something had shifted during the roundtable discussion. Maggie walked in hating Georgette but left singing her praises. Beth suspected something was up between the two wives of John Harting. Never one to miss an opportunity, Beth opted for a conversation with Georgette.

Maggie caught Beth off guard when she responded instantly with Georgette's number off the top of her head, then added, "But she's back in Paris until next week. You can try her at the hotel she stays in when she's there. Wait, I'll get you the number . . . Why do you want to speak with Georgette?" Maggie didn't have the usual contempt in her voice when she spoke of anything having to do with Georgette Fontaine. Beth was intrigued.

"She's a French scholar, right? Special OPS sent another note. This one includes a French poem. I want more than a translation. I'm hoping Georgette can give me some context or help me interpret the message this prick is trying to send."

Maggie gave her the hotel's number. Beth dialed it and reached Georgette in her room on the first try. "Hi, Georgette, Beth Mack. Maggie gave me your number. I hope you don't mind me bothering you." Beth didn't really care one way or another if she was bothering Georgette.

"Not at all. What can I do for you?" Georgette was formal but friendly.

"RHM has been receiving notes from some guy who seems to have a bone to pick. No, actually, he seems demented . . ."

"Yes, Maggie has told me. It all sounds horrid . . ."

So Maggie and Georgette chat? This gets better and better, thought Beth.

"This last one is in French and I thought you might be able to translate it for me or, better yet, find some clue about what this fucker is after. It's short—can I read it to you?"

"Of course."

Beth stumbled through the first few lines of the poem:

> *Baise m'encor, rebaise-moi et baise;*
> *Donne m'en un de tes plus savoureux,*
> *Donne m'en un de tes plus amoureux . . .*

"Ah! That's a famous sixteenth-century poem," Georgette said without hesitation. "It's by Louise Labé."

"What does it mean? I know *baiser* means 'to kiss,' right?" Beth ventured.

"*Alors, oui et non. Baiser* used to mean 'kiss' but now means, colloquially, 'fuck' or, worse, 'rape,'" Georgette explained. "When the poem was written, the meaning could go either way and the author was being provocative by making a play on the word. Given the era it was written in, and the fact that the author was a woman, well, you can imagine the negative attention it brought. I can't believe this guy—whoever he is—would understand this nuance. But who knows? Maybe your stalker is a scholar."

"So basically this guy is saying he doesn't know if he wants to kiss us, fuck us, or kill us?"

"I don't know what he means by it, but he definitely has interesting taste in poetry."

RHM WAS GEARING up for a busy Christmas season. Beth's phone never stopped ringing. The store enjoyed record-breaking daily sales and the final quarter promised to end way ahead of the year before. The strong business kept Beth distracted from thoughts about Special OPS. After the Louise Labé poem, he had gone quiet and Beth was hoping she'd seen the last of the madman's hate notes. The private detective she'd hired had little to go on, but she kept him on retainer for extra security. By the time Thanksgiving rolled around, she started to see the whole thing as just another whack job getting off on trying to scare the shit out of some women.

Beth worked late a few nights a week during the hectic holiday season. Not wanting to miss dinner with Jessie, Hanna brought her to the neighborhood so they could all duck out for a quick meal together before Beth returned to the office for a few hours.

On Black Friday, RHM enjoyed the biggest sales day in its history. The offices upstairs were closed for the holiday weekend, and Beth took advantage of the empty space to work with no interruption. As was their custom, Hanna, Beth, and Jessie got a bite to eat in the neighborhood. As they said good-bye in front of the store, Beth felt a sudden unease. The man Maggie had pointed out to her over the summer—"Blue Eyes"—walked past them, a bit too close for comfort. Beth pulled Jessie close to her as he walked by to prevent him from colliding with her daughter. His action felt erratic, even though he seemed to move with intention. He looked steadily at Beth with his cool blues as he passed them.

Shaken, Beth wouldn't let Jessie and Hanna leave until he was a block away. She put them in a taxi and went back upstairs. In the dark and quiet office, the only light streamed from her office.

When she walked through her door, Beth was startled to see a potted poinsettia plant sitting in the middle of her desk that hadn't been there when she'd left for dinner. Skewered on a metal stake thrust into the dirt was a small note that read "Happy Black Friday," written in angry black crayon on RHM letterhead. Beth felt afraid for the first time; this epistle-writing fuckwad was getting way too close for comfort. Heart pounding in her ears, she left the office immediately and headed home, angry with herself for being frightened away by a maniacal bully.

Beth met with the private detective on Saturday at the offices. She wanted him to examine the scene. Since no crime had been committed (yet), the police weren't interested. It was small comfort that the private detective and building security team were on point. Beth was beginning to feel that she and her staff were vulnerable to this crazy man infatuated with his own sick joke.

On Monday morning, Beth called a staff meeting. The poinsettia incident shocked her with the harasser's new boldness. Beth wanted everyone to be aware of the lunatic in their midst.

RHM staff members took the news lightly, seasoned by the violent reactions from the protestors over the summer. Some of them spoke up about individual reprimands they'd received from people once their connection with RHM became apparent. One employee from the design department told how she'd been spat upon by an elderly woman as she was leaving the offices. Another in the marketing department said she'd received glares on the subway when she carried an RHM canvas tote.

After their meeting, Beth could feel a buzzy energy of solidarity among the employees. The following day, her publicity manager created buttons that read: RED HOT MAMA. FUCKING DEAL WITH IT. Everyone wore them proudly. They would not be deterred.

SHARING THE BURDEN lightened Beth's mood. The week wore on, and sales grew each day as Christmas shoppers flooded the store. No more gifts or letters showed up, and Beth again hoped that they'd seen the last of the bogeyman.

Late in the day on Friday, exactly one week after the poinsettia plant had been left on her desk, Beth was sitting in her office when she looked up and saw a man she didn't recognize walk past her office. There was something odd in his cadence, in the way he walked without moving his arms.

Beth got up to see who it was, but by the time she crossed the threshold to her office door, she didn't see him in either direction. Beth shook off her growing paranoia and returned to her desk. He could easily be a visitor of one of the employees or a freelancer, she told herself. The company had grown to the point where she couldn't know every single person coming into and out of the office. Still, her radar for signs of the stalker was on high alert. She tried to concentrate on the spreadsheet in front of her but found herself distracted by the man with stiff arms.

Beth sat back in her chair and took a few deep breaths. The man wouldn't leave her mind, so she rose to walk around the offices just to see what was what. Before she could cross the room, she saw the man again through the glass wall of her office, now standing by Sacha's desk. She called out, "Excuse me, can I help you with something?"

His back to her, she saw the man stop for a moment before dropping something onto Sacha's desk. He turned around to face her and Beth felt a jolt of nausea as she recognized the man Maggie called Blue Eyes. Her eyes fell to the orange pen in his shirt pocket. Beth inhaled sharply as she walked backward to her desk and picked up the phone to dial security. Her eyes locked with Special Ops's bright blues and she immediately wished the man dead even as her defiant stare dared him to come closer.

Then he smiled and winked at her, which threw her off her guard. The man was at once unnerving and compelling—just as Maggie had described him. When security picked up, she described the man to them as calmly as she could, making no effort to keep her voice low. Beth was angry now and had to stop herself from confronting him—*to do what?* She had no way of knowing whether his plans involved more than just harassment of the sordid letter sort. She could just see the next day's *Post* headline: "MacBeth Mack Attack." The thought made her laugh aloud, which inadvertently startled Special OPS who hadn't yet moved. He turned and fled toward the stairwell.

Special OPS was nabbed just as he opened the door to the lobby. The detective had already identified the signature in orange pen on the sign-in list and was standing by when Beth called down to security. The stalker was calm and expressionless; he offered no explanation. Police sirens wailed as they approached RHM.

AS IT TURNED out, Special OPS had a past record of harassment. A printing house deliveryman, he had been assigned to deliver packages to and from Beth's company over the summer. No one in the building had thought to question his continued presence into the fall. This solved the mystery of how he had had access to Dr. Crane's image before it was published and explained the hand deliveries. His unwelcome attentions constituted his third offense. The only common thread to his misdemeanors was the use of colored pens and that his targets were always women. The man, clearly deranged, could be held only for one day. He was slapped with a restraining order to keep him away from RHM, but until something truly gruesome happened, he was free to carry on with his serial harassment. He'd find another job, another set of circumstances. Eventually someone or something would capture his attention and he would figure out another way to satisfy his jones for his peculiar power trip. *What would it take to stop a person like him?* Beth wondered.

Beth was relieved that RHM would be freed from his eccentric threats, but she felt queasy with the certainty that another group of women would bear the burden of his deranged attention. It reminded her of the duplicity she felt when she agreed to keep Paul's secret.

AFTER THEY HAD finally divorced, Paul had continued to see women without sharing with them his HIV status. He had promised her he was practicing safe sex. Beth was doubtful. Was it her responsibility to expose him to protect the others who might be infected by his denial? Or was it his private personal health information to manage? How would she feel if her own daughter were of age? Beth was tormented by these questions and lost many nights' sleep over it. If Paul were to infect someone, Beth knew she would feel responsible.

She remembered meeting Paul and a girlfriend, Katie, for lunch one day. They had been Rollerblading and Paul sent Katie off to buy herself a pair of shoes with his credit card. When she disappeared into the store, he pulled off his blades to show Beth the lesions on his shins and feet. Paul had taken to sharing the horrors of the disease with Beth because he needed a witness. Helen would burst into tears whenever he brought it up, so he relied on Beth, the person he had hurt most, to share in the progression of the disease. Beth was appalled, but not by the purple splotches on his skin.

"Does Katie know about any of this?" Beth asked.

"About what?" Paul replied, his face a mask of innocence.

"About what these are and why you have them?" Beth's tone grew angry quickly.

"I told her that I have shingles. She doesn't need to know any more than that."

She looked at him in disbelief, but it was clear he believed every word he said. "Paul, you have to tell her. It isn't fair."

He stared hard at Beth, as if willing the conversation away. "I am not putting her in any danger," he promised.

Katie was a twenty-two-years-young woman from Akron, Ohio. She'd been living in New York City for six months and likely knew little or nothing of the ravages of the AIDS epidemic. *This is how tragedy strikes*, Beth thought. "Paul, promise me that you will tell her. Don't play God."

She left Paul standing on the sidewalk, socks pulled down to his ankles, Rollerblades in hand. She couldn't stand to face Katie as she walked out of the store, bright-faced and unsuspecting. Beth didn't trust herself not to blurt out the awful truth. She couldn't help but hate herself for not sticking around to do just that.

CHAPTER THIRTEEN

Anna

ANNA BEGAN THE first day of the rest of her life on the Monday before Halloween. The day started out at 6:00 A.M.—no differently from any other day. But instead of blow-drying her hair and dressing up, she slipped into her favorite pair of Jason's gray Champion sweatpants and a faded, threadbare red pearl button sweater—a garment she should have relegated to furniture polishing years ago. She pulled her unwashed hair into a ponytail and wore her glasses instead of contact lenses. Oscar, tipped off by his mother's lack of effort in her appearance, was beaming.

"You're staying home with me today? You're not going to work and Jenny's not coming?" The boys loved their nanny but rejected her quickly in favor of their mother.

"She's coming this afternoon. I'm yours and Henry's for the entire morning and every morning for the next couple of months. Does that make you happy?"

She and Jason had decided to keep Jenny on a part-time basis. She would come at 1:00 P.M. and stay until 6:00 P.M. four days a week. The new plan was to spend weekends out in Montauk, leaving Thursday evening and returning Monday morning. The schedule was downright languorous.

Oscar nodded chin to chest. "Come on, Mama, let's play. What do you want to play?"

"How about we make a train track with your Brio set?"

"No, I don't want to do that."

"Want to set up Build 'n Bash Construction?"

"No, not really."

"Want to play stickers?"

"No, we can do that when Henry is asleep so he doesn't use all of them." This implied, of course, that Oscar had no intention of taking a nap while his mother was around and couldn't wait to get his little brother out of the way so he could have her all to himself.

Anna knew that Oscar knew exactly what he wanted to do, but he also knew it was something she probably didn't approve of. This routine of zeroing in on doing what he wanted by exhausting all other possibilities was a brilliant tactic. He did it every weekend, so Anna wasn't surprised that he had leveraged the same strategy on a Monday. By the time it was decided what game they were going to play, Anna was usually so fed up with the conversation that she'd agree to anything just to get him to stop asking.

Oscar's eyes were darting back and forth from the kitchen counter, where a pink plastic bottle sat in the corner, to his mother. The action was supposed to tip her off. She wasn't getting it. Oscar, by now exasperated that Anna wasn't reading his mind, said, "I want to blow bubbles!"

Anna hated the mess the bubbles made, especially when

Henry got involved. They invariably spilled the entire bottle and Anna would spend half an hour mopping up the viscous slop.

Henry, upon hearing "bubbles," went into a frenzy. He ran to his mother's legs and began blowing through his lips. He cried, "Bop! Bop!" meaning he wanted her to blow the bubbles so he could pop them.

"Ugh," Anna said, and sighed. "Okay, guys, bubbles it is. Since it's raining outside, let's stay in the kitchen so we don't make too much of a mess . . ."

By the time one o'clock came, Anna had already mopped the bubble slop, scrubbed the floor clean after a dropped container of paint, and given Henry two baths—one to clean off the paint striped across his face, hair, and ears and one to clean the mess of an exploded diaper. Oscar, whenever Anna was tending to Henry, insisted on standing directly under her so he got elbowed and kicked. He had burst into tears three different times.

Day one and Anna wanted to scream.

Jason kept to himself in his office downstairs, coming up once to help during a particularly loud moment when the two boys were howling simultaneously.

Once Jenny came, Anna was able to put on a pair of jeans and boots and head out to do the shopping for dinner. Oscar insisted on going with her, which turned a half-hour errand into a ninety-minute exercise. She loved his company, so she didn't mind; besides, she had to remind herself, she really didn't have any schedule to adhere to, and it was to spend more time with the boys that she took the sabbatical in the first place. Anna tried to relax into the new agenda of no real agenda.

HALLOWEEN CAME WITH more fanfare every year, and Anna was happy to have a mission for her first Tuesday at home. While she normally didn't acknowledge the holiday, this year Oscar was determined to make the most of it. Dressed as Bob the Builder, he used a plastic toolbox to hold his candy and referred to his little brother as Pilchard the Cat. Henry accepted his fate as long as he also got to wear a yellow hard hat like his big brother.

Anna's heart broke a little watching Henry/Pilchard dutifully trying to keep up with Oscar/Bob as they negotiated the high front stoops of each row house in their tree-lined Brooklyn neighborhood. Unable to climb quickly enough, Oscar was often on his way down before Henry made it up to the door. Refusing his mother's help—Henry did have the more independent spirit of the two—he wound up whining at Oscar with frustration because he couldn't keep up with his big brother. As a gesture of his rage, he threw his hard hat over the locked wrought-iron gate leading to a ground-floor apartment, far enough away that Anna was unable to retrieve it. This, of course, made him cry harder, losing his pacifier in the process. Anna frantically searched her pockets for another as Henry screamed, "Ra-ra! Ra-ra!"—his baby-speak for the pacifier. Then, beneath the racket of her youngest, she noticed the unusual silence of her older son.

She looked around to find him seated on the bottom stair, surrounded by dozens of candy wrappers, everything from mini chocolate bars to gummy bears. He'd systematically tasted nearly every goody in his toolbox. Where his face wasn't smeared with chocolate, his skin was pallid. Anna knew what was about to happen next.

Still holding a sobbing Henry, now dangling under her arm like an oversized football, she ran down the stairs to Oscar and whipped him up with her other arm to deposit him curbside. Almost on cue, he vomited up every last bit of chocolate and partially chewed gummy bear all over the tire of a parked car. Better that, Anna consoled herself, than someone's front stoop.

Within forty minutes from setting out, their trick-or-treating ended, sticky and smelly and ready for a bath.

None of this was anything new to Anna. But now Monday through Friday looked a lot like Saturday and Sunday. She'd wished for a life of weekends and now she had it.

With Anna at home, Jason spent more time on his own work, which seemed fair enough, though it wasn't part of the scenario Anna had envisioned. Still, they managed to sneak out for a movie or a coffee when Jenny tended to Oscar and Henry in the afternoons and spent the occasional indulgent afternoon in bed when Jenny could coerce the boys out of the house for a few hours. In the beginning, Oscar didn't make it easy. While he'd become accustomed to Anna being gone all day at work, now that she was home, he wanted to monopolize her time. After a few weeks the family settled into a new routine.

Anna felt she should have predicted it, but she was still surprised to find that her days weren't any less taxing than when she'd gone to work every day. Now, however, she didn't feel like she accomplished half as much. Where before she'd been at meetings with the staff of RHM, she was now folding laundry and picking up the boys' Matchbox cars. Instead of eating at Da Tommaso with Beth, she was sharing a box of macaroni and cheese or a peanut butter sandwich with the kids. Instead of staring at a screen of e-mails, she was watching construction truck videos—what she called "truckie porn"—three times a day.

She called her sister. "Is, I am not living the dream. What is wrong with me?"

"Why, what's happening?" Isabel asked.

"All I do is laundry, clean up after the boys, and watch road-building videos and Thomas the Tank Engine. I want to poke my eyes out!"

"Ha! I guess toddlers are pretty tedious? Maybe you're bored . . . Can you at least work some in the afternoons?"

"No! I told Beth I was going to disconnect, and she had Eric step into my role. But I'm not sure that disconnecting was the best idea after all." She paused, then continued: "Oh, God, I can't believe I'm saying this, but yes! *I. Am. Bored!*

"Am I crazy?" Anna asked, feeling absolutely crazy.

"Nah, you're just a twenty-first-century woman . . . Okay, big sis, gotta go to a meeting. Talk later."

Not to be deterred by a disastrous Halloween, and a little at a loss about what to do with herself, Anna decided she'd make her mother proud and plan a big Thanksgiving family dinner. Bobby and his wife flew in from California. She invited Beth and Jessie to join them as well. Surely preparations for a holiday dinner for twelve would occupy the part of her brain that needed to feel productive.

The festive occasion was almost derailed when the boys caught a twenty-four-hour stomach flu just days before Thanksgiving. Added to the disaster of Halloween, it felt like an inauspicious start to a new life. Anna willed herself to not take any of it as a bad omen.

The preparations were not to be in vain, however. Thursday arrived, and by some miracle, they were all there, worse for wear and wine by the end of the day, but together nonetheless.

Isabel barely moved from the couch the entire day—doctor's orders—and Sam lovingly attended to her every need. Isabel had a dreamy quality about her. With only six weeks before her due date, Anna guessed she was in silent preparation for what was to inevitably come.

When Sam wasn't by her side, Jessie and Isabel played cards together. The seven-year-old tended to her immobile friend with a wisdom far beyond most her age. Isabel, being the youngest of three siblings, was also the youngest in spirit. There were moments when she and the remarkably grown-up Jessie seemed more like peers. It struck Anna that most children and adults were really not that different from each other outside of the responsibility adults shoulder.

In Anna's never-ending efforts to stem the chaos and detritus of a houseful of people, she made several trips to empty the garbage into the backyard bins. On more than one occasion she witnessed Bobby and Beth engaged in the intimate repartee they always fell back into whenever they saw each other. Their brief love affair ended when they met and married their respective mates. Anna smiled at them kindly and raised an eyebrow to suggest she was paying no mind at all to their conversation, when in fact she was tickled by the unusual friendship they'd weaved over the years. She knew their romance would never reignite, but the connection remained a nostalgic tether to a simpler time in their lives. When she returned to the living room, she caught Isabel's attention and nodded her head to the back of the house.

"Looks like some heavy reminiscing is going on back there . . ."

"Oh?" Isabel craned her neck to take a look but couldn't see past the kitchen. "Maybe I have to get up to pee right about now. Here, Jess, help me up."

Anna was in motion all day and did her best to dismiss her mother's entreaties for her to relax.

"Anna, let Jason bring out the garbage. Take a break."

"Mom, stop hovering. I'm fine, really."

"That's what you always say, Anna. Who are you trying to convince?"

Instead of responding to her mother's familiar harangue, Anna watched as Isabel wobbled toward the kitchen. Her sister stood in the doorway watching Bobby and Beth for a moment before turning gingerly and heading into the bathroom. Anna felt an old pang of love for Isabel, the kind she'd felt when they were children, when she could hardly contain the full heart she had for her adorable little sister. She'd teased Isabel at times, subtle reminders of her seniority. When Anna thought about it now, she wondered what lasting effect those insinuations might have had. The youngest Ducci seemed to have escaped with a fierce determinism that Anna lacked for herself. Isabel had a sense of entitlement Anna could never claim, and there were times when Anna felt fury toward her—not so much for what Isabel could do, but for what Anna felt she couldn't do herself.

A detective friend of Anna's had told her once that Thanksgiving was the one holiday police officers would trade for a week's worth of duty time. When Anna asked why, he simply stated, "Families, alcohol, and knives don't mix well."

But their dinner was wonderfully uneventful. Detective wisdom be damned. Anna thought how tales of disastrous family gatherings were drama meant to fill a void. In Anna's experience, these gatherings were, for the most part, a bit boring. Maybe that was a good thing, she realized now.

As Anna surveyed her tryptophan-drugged family, she wondered if it was in these "boring" life moments where meaning resided. Time to pause in the ordinariness that a fulfilled life can bring. And if that were the case, then every moment need not be filled with drive and accomplishment. *Shouldn't that come as a relief?* she asked. From then on, Anna promised herself to try to welcome the calm she often called "boredom" and appreciate the love those moments could reveal.

BY THE TIME Thanksgiving had come and gone, just one month into her sabbatical, Anna was still confused about how she wanted to live her life. Her momentary Thanksgiving epiphany helped, but putting it into practice proved harder than she thought it would be.

Since the boys were born, she'd desperately wanted to spend daytime hours with her family. That dream turned into reality lacked the swell of satisfaction she'd thought she'd feel. Going to work every day and being pulled in seven directions at once, she'd felt justified in her complaints about needing to be everywhere for everyone all at once. With less calling for her attention now, she had expected to feel more relaxed. Instead, she was frustrated with herself for the lack of resolve she had about finally being at home with the family.

What was worse, Oscar and Henry seemed to sense her

ambivalence. When they cried out at night, it was for Jason, not Anna. When they needed something fixed like a broken truck or their Thomas the Tank engine ran out of batteries, they ran to their father. Although Jason spent less time with the boys than she did, he gave them undivided and unconflicted attention. Anna did not. As much as she tried to reverse the tendency, she'd often attempt to accomplish something else during their time together. The boys didn't understand enough to complain about it. Instead, they responded by being either overly needy with her or dismissive. Anna began to feel perennially disappointed with herself for not being productive enough or attentive enough, creating a cycle of benign regret that caused Anna a new kind of discomfort.

Jason had worked out a much more satisfying behavior pattern with his sons, no doubt a result of the ease with which he approached his day. It was the flip side of what Anna had always chided men for—their ability to do only one thing at a time. Anna hadn't understood until now that this kind of singular focus could be something to admire, not scorn. The ability to give someone or something your full attention was a more harmonious way to live. Multitasking was a bullshit, no-win scenario.

CHAPTER FOURTEEN

Maggie

AFTER THEIR WEEKEND trip to the shore, Maggie noticed that John was spending more days away—trips alone on his motorcycle—to Bear Mountain, out to Far Rockaway. Between Maggie's preoccupation with taking care of the three kids and keeping up with the demands of a busy season at RHM, there were days when she didn't speak with John even when he was around.

"Hey, are you mad at me about something?" he asked her on one of these days.

"No, why are you asking?" Maggie answered as she helped Lily and Jules build a tent out of sheets across the dining room table and chairs. The kids squealed as they crawled on their knees through the makeshift fort and Maggie laughed with them.

"You, um, you haven't said a word to me all day," John said more matter-of-factly than she thought he felt. She did feel badly for him. It was true: she was shutting him out.

"No, everything is fine," she lied. "Hey, maybe you can

help Justine with her homework tonight. I know she's been struggling with science class."

"She didn't tell me that." John was hurt.

"You should try talking to her more. You might learn some things."

John got up from the couch and left the room.

They never again discussed the prospect of another child, as if the issue had just vaporized when, in fact, the opposite was happening. Maggie was already six weeks along. She didn't want to share the news with John and refused to think about the ethical consequences of not doing so. She did want to extricate herself from her marriage, but time was running short—she would need to address the fact that this child was coming. She needed a plan.

"LET'S FACE IT," Maggie said to Beth the next day as they headed up to the office after the roundtable taping, "men are a luxury, one I can live without."

"You have one major problem, Maggs. You're married to one."

"Maybe I can just send him back," Maggie answered blithely. The women laughed hard as they walked into the building.

But the idea, said in jest, started to take hold in her mind.

Why not send him back to Georgette? she thought later that night. *What if she's my salvation, not my nemesis? When it comes down to it, Georgette isn't the problem, John is.*

And on an impulse she decided to test-drive the idea.

After Maggie put Lily to sleep, and Jules and Justine sat at the dining room table doing their homework, she plopped herself down on the couch next to John.

"I saw Georgette today. She looked great."

"What do you mean, you saw Georgette?"

"She was at the taping today. Surprise guest. She was actually terrific for the roundtable. I have to say I saw a side to her I liked very much . . . Anyway, didn't she call the kids?"

"Uh, yeah, she did, but they didn't tell me that she was back from Paris."

"She's only in town for two days. She's going to see them tomorrow. We talked for a bit after the taping and made plans."

Her calm clearly unnerved John. "Maggie, what are you talking about? You meet Georgette in person for the first time and now you two are making plans?"

"You know, John," Maggie said, bolder by the second. "I'm not quite sure why your marriage didn't make it. From what I can tell, you two are very well suited to each other."

"Have you gone mad?"

"No, just making an observation." She patted John on the knee and stood up from the couch and stretched her arms above her head. "I'm beat and going to bed. Good night."

Maggie could tell by John's stunned silence that she had hit some kind of nerve. *This might actually work*, she told herself optimistically as she prepared for bed.

As she brushed her teeth, she recalled reading a book years before by Susan Maushart called *Wifework*, in which the author said she'd had more time for herself as the single mother of three children under five than she'd had when she was married to their father. Maggie was feeling more resolved by the hour.

When she arrived at Georgette's the following evening to take Jules and Justine back to Jersey City, the family was just finishing up dinner. Georgette told the kids to gather their things.

"Would you like some coffee? It's decaf," Georgette offered Maggie. John's ex was guarded but friendly, which calmed Maggie's nerves a bit. "I put butter in mine. Would you like the same?"

"Yeah, sure, why not?" Maggie said with a smile.

Buttered coffee seemed a bit weird, but *whatever works*, Maggie told herself.

Now that Maggie was resolved to orchestrate the reconciliation of John and Georgette, she wanted to get them back together before she had to deal with the recognizable fact of her second child.

John's two wives sat down together at the family table. Maggie's eyes settled on Georgette's. She blinked hard and said, "Something you said yesterday at the roundtable made me think that you would, or could, forgive John for what he did. Is that really true, or am I reading you all wrong?"

Georgette stared intently at Maggie, who fought hard not to look away.

"No, you're not wrong. I would forgive John if he had the guts to ask for my forgiveness . . . and then begged me to take him back." Georgette flashed a *take that* smile at Maggie.

"Well, now that you mentioned it . . . I did want to talk with you about something."

Georgette raised her eyebrows and nodded.

"What if I offered to help you get him back?" Maggie said, surprising herself at how this came with no preamble. "I know this sounds crazy, but I mean it."

"You've grown tired of your lover, Maggie?" Georgette's stare bore right through Maggie, making her shift back in her seat.

"That's not it at all," Maggie scrambled. But what was "it"?

"Then what could 'it' possibly be?" Georgette uncannily echoed Maggie's thoughts, seeming as puzzled as she was annoyed.

"Georgette, listen, it occurred to me yesterday during the roundtable that you and John were together for such a long time for a reason. What you write about is true, and we—John and I—should have been over just as quickly as we started. I don't quite know how to explain it . . . He seems lost being married to me. Please don't take this the wrong way, but I don't need him and I think maybe . . . you do." Maggie swallowed those last words, aware she was treading on insult.

"I mean, 'need' sounds all wrong . . . but you make John shine and I think I dull him . . . Oh, for God's sake, am I making any sense?"

"No. Not really." Georgette's face was tight now.

"Listen, Georgette. I'm sorry to have caused you so much heartbreak, but if you want John back, I think he feels the same way." Maggie was on shaky ground again; she had no idea what John wanted. "And maybe I can help you get him back." Maggie cringed even hearing her words as Georgette might have heard them, but she meant them with all her heart.

Georgette's eyes softened for a moment, then narrowed again. "Why would I trust you of all people, Maggie?"

"You shouldn't, not after what happened. Still, you have to ask what motives I would have under these circumstances to hurt you further." Maggie took a deep breath. She was light-headed with emotion and the stakes of the conversation, but also with excitement at the prospect of her absurd plan actually working.

"Maybe you're a sociopath—how would I know?" Georgette's sparring sounded almost flirtatious to Maggie, but also angry. Still, underneath it something glacial was melting.

"If you thought that, you wouldn't have trusted me with your children," Maggie challenged.

"Ha!" Georgette said without mirth. "Yes, you have a point there. It's true, I don't imagine you are a sociopath . . . but you are selfish and perhaps a little bit cruel."

Maggie cringed, then straightened her shoulders. She had to acknowledge truth where it was due. "Okay, I'll take that. But I also thought I was saving John from an unhappy marriage."

"How could you know anything about my marriage to John?" Georgette pressed. "All marriages are unhappy at times—of course they are. But that seems like quite the neat little excuse to justify your affair with my husband."

"Maybe you're right, Georgette. I don't really know myself anymore." Maggie grew quiet for a minute before carefully proceeding. "Listen," Maggie let out a tension-filled breath. "I won't insult you with a litany of mea culpas. Just please believe that I am truly sorry for the inexcusable disregard I had for you and your feelings in my affair with John. Oh, God, that sounds lame . . . Please just think about it, and call me from Paris if you want to continue the conversation."

Maggie called out to the kids and bustled them out the door before Georgette could say another word.

GEORGETTE CALLED A week after she flew back to Paris. "What makes you think this is possible?" Georgette demanded without preamble.

As far as Maggie knew, this kind of reversal was unprecedented. She played out the details of the scenario in her head, and it all seemed to make so much practical sense to her, she couldn't believe she hadn't heard about more people doing this. Or maybe there were husbands and wives everywhere negotiating reconciliation after a played-out affair behind closed doors. Of course there were.

"Because I have completely checked out and John knows it. I can't make him feel the way you can. We bring out the worst in each other. Frankly, Georgette, I can't imagine why he wouldn't want to be with you. He seems lost to me."

"And what about you, Maggie? What's in this for you?"

"I'm not sure how I feel about having a man—any man—in my life right now. I just don't know that I want that."

"*Tant pis pour toi.*" Georgette's sarcasm skewered Maggie, who knew she deserved Georgette's rancor and was more than willing to suffer it, especially if it meant she could push her plan into action.

"What about Lily?"

"Lily will be fine."

Maggie didn't want to be disparaging about John, especially as she was trying to get him back with Georgette, but he took so little interest in his daughter that she wasn't so sure Lily would even notice he was gone. As for the new baby, Maggie wanted to get things under way before anyone knew about it. Maybe John didn't ever need to know. After all, only Maggie could be certain who the father was. Wasn't that the one card women always held? The one thing men had been fighting to take away from women since the beginning of time? Moral ramifications be damned, Maggie was keeping her little secret to herself. At least for the time being.

BUZZING WITH CONFIDENCE that her plan would work, she was momentarily thrown off by Beth's disturbing news about Special OPS. It wasn't until Beth had received the third letter that she confided in Maggie about the lunatic sending threatening messages to RHM.

"I don't get it. Why do you call him Special OPS?"

"Here, look at this," Beth said as she thrust into Maggie's hand the picture he had made of her, scrawled with the incriminating orange pen. "I call him the Orange Pen Stalker, Special OPS for short."

"Geez, this is wacko . . ." Maggie suddenly turned white and her hand holding the letter began to shake.

"What, Maggie? You look like you just saw a ghost." Beth grabbed her elbow.

"Remember Blue Eyes? That day I spilled the ice cream on my new blouse? I pointed him out to you later that day . . . ? Well, he had an orange-capped pen in his pocket. Don't ask me why I noticed it, but I did. Could it be the same guy?"

"Fuck! No, it's got to be a coincidence, don't you think?" Beth asked.

"Oh, *God*! Have I been masturbating to a sociopath?!"

"Oh, Maggie, you haven't . . ." Beth roared with laughter for a moment before cutting herself short and catching her breath.

"This isn't really funny at all, is it? Anyway, I hired a private detective to help us catch the bastard. It's getting a little scary. I'll let you know what we find out."

"Why do we automatically assume that the sender is male?" Maggie asked.

Beth just raised her eyebrows at Maggie with a *can you really be serious?* look.

"Of course it's a man . . ." Maggie knew it to be true. She also knew in her heart that it was Blue Eyes. He happened to be around a bit too much for comfort.

MAGGIE KNEW HER plan was off to a good start when she saw a brochure announcing a Paris conference on Italian films in December on the dining room table. Was John hoping she'd see it? Unlike her, he wasn't that calculating. No matter, Georgette was in France until the end of the year. It would be a perfect way for the Hartings to spend Christmas.

Maggie couldn't have dreamed up a better opportunity. She called Georgette.

"There's a conference in December at the International Film School of Paris focusing on Italian films of the mid-twentieth century. I'll buy John tickets as an early Christmas present . . . What do you think?"

"How do you know he'll want to come?" Georgette asked.

"He will. And he can take Jules and Justine with him so you guys can have a family holiday. I'll tell him that I'm going to take Lily to Disney World in December, or somewhere else equally awful that he would rather die than go to. This will be the perfect out for him," Maggie said.

"Maggie, you are truly evil." Georgette laughed as she said it. "Yes, it would be perfect for our family to spend the holidays together. Let's do it."

Maggie turned her attention to John next. "You should go. It sounds like a perfect opportunity for you. You could even take Jules and Justine with you to spend the holiday in Paris. I'm sure they would love to see their mother. Lily and I will be fine." Maggie tried not to sound overly enthusiastic.

AS JOHN'S TWO wives conspired to get him to Paris, Maggie did everything she could to conceal the fact of her pregnancy, wearing loose-fitting dresses that covered her swollen breasts and bloated belly. It wouldn't be long before she popped, though she was lucky that she hadn't gained much weight yet. It was Lily who first commented on her mother's bulge.

"Mommy, what's that?" she asked as she pointed her tiny forefinger into her mother's abdomen.

"What, Lil?"

"That, big belly."

Maggie was astonished that Lily could see the barely perceptible change in her size. It had gone unnoticed by John.

"Oh, Mommy's just been eating too much ice cream."

"Too much ice cream?" asked Lily, and she laughed, too young to make the connection between ice cream and its potential side effect.

When John came back from Paris, she'd have to tell him something. With any luck, he'd have already fallen for Georgette all over again.

She honestly couldn't see how John wouldn't fall back in love with her. Over the course of her conversations with Georgette, Maggie had been completely seduced by John's ex. Most surprising was Georgette's openness about the book she was writing, since it essentially attacked John and Maggie's lustful disregard for the sanctity of marriage.

She'd read somewhere that Georgette had said, "Men and women can never be friends, only lovers," which struck Maggie as absurd. As they organized John's trip to Paris, Maggie asked Georgette about it.

"So, do you really think men and women can't be friends? I read that once and I'm not sure I buy it."

"I would say that, like the animals we are, we always regard each other as potential mates whether we are aware of it or not." Georgette paused. "I don't mean that all women and men will jump in the sack together, but the possibility and the imperative is always there."

Maggie breathed out hard. "God, that sounds so exhausting!"

Maggie wanted to offer Georgette something, a way to help her know that she understood. "Listen, I know I am the 'other woman' to you, but there have been 'other women' in my life as well." Maggie shook her head as if to shake off the awkwardness of what she was trying to say. "What I mean to say is that I never felt anger toward the other woman, only toward the man who betrayed us both. Really, I guess I wound up feeling betrayed by the situation. Don't get me wrong, I don't blame John—"

"I hope you wouldn't be that stupid considering you're trying to get us back together . . ." Georgette interrupted.

"Ha! Oh, I'm just bumbling here . . ." Maggie continued.

"What I really want to say is that I hope you can eventually come to see me as a woman who loved the same man you did. I don't expect you to, but I can hope for it. If you said I didn't deserve your respect, I would accept that."

"Okay if I get back to you on that one?" Georgette replied. From her tone, Maggie could tell she was only half teasing.

MAGGIE BEGAN TO imagine life with just her and Lily and the new baby. She could sell the loft in Jersey City and scale back to a small two-bedroom apartment in Manhattan. She imagined a simpler existence and felt she was on the verge of owning her life again.

By the end of November, two things were certain: John was going to Paris in December, where Georgette would welcome him with open arms. And Blue Eyes was indeed the feared serial pen pal. She felt purged and ready for a white Christmas.

The capture of Hollander Frye, the birth name of Blue Eyes, aka Special OPS, was a relief to all. Maggie had received a frantic call from Beth just moments after his arrest.

"We got him, Maggie, and he's your guy."

"Dark hair, husky-dog blue eyes, enormous nose? . . . Hey, wait, he was never my guy!"

"He was here, Maggie, in our offices. I wonder if he knew you worked here. This is all too weird . . ."

"That's it, Beth. I'm retiring from the life. I'm going to go and have this baby and live happily and manless ever after."

A week earlier Beth had asked Maggie, "Are you pregnant again? Your collarbones have disappeared." A clue only a woman would pick up on.

Now Beth said, "And what do you plan to do with your husband?"

"Oh, him." Maggie shrugged. "He's going to Paris for the holidays."

CHAPTER FIFTEEN

Isabel

LEAVING CHRISTOPHER THE morning after the fashion party, Isabel didn't see him for a few weeks. She knew that she'd exorcised some right of passage at Sam's expense, and she now realized that it had been at Christopher's expense as well. As Isabel began to shift away from him that night, she gave way to a different kind of need, one that relied heavily on the trust she put in Sam.

Isabel and Christopher spoke without subtext for the first time when they finally met up for dinner three weeks after their last entanglement. Isabel moved gingerly now; the horizontal growth of her belly made it look like another limb. She sat uncomfortably in the bent hardwood chair in the restaurant.

"Did I scare you the night of Maxx Tripp's party?" Christopher asked plainly.

Isabel's eyes met his directly for the first time that night. "It worried me that I couldn't read you. I think you were trying to tell me that your heart was a little broken. Is that right?" Isabel couldn't believe that after years of bouncing off Christopher's force field of inscrutability, she had finally reached his heart only now to break it.

"Yes, it is." His wore a stoic expression.

The two sat for a long time without talking. Isabel kept shifting her weight from one side of her buttocks to the other to try to relieve the numbness in her legs.

"Why are you fidgeting?" Christopher finally asked.

"It's this chair, it's killing me."

"Do you want to leave? We can try someplace else or just go to my apartment and order something."

"I'd actually prefer to go to your apartment, though I'm not up for sex. Does that matter to you tonight?" Isabel's voice was tired, even to her own ears, her breath short from the pressure against her diaphragm made worse from sitting up. "I'd rather we just had some time to talk."

Back in the comfort of Christopher's apartment, the lovers lay side by side on the bed, facing each other with their heads resting on puffy pillows. Christopher gave Isabel a long cushion to support the weight of her belly.

"Are you having regrets about these last few months?" Isabel asked him.

"No. I don't know. I don't think so," Christopher said as he swept his hair out of his eyes. "I don't entirely trust myself, though," he admitted. "I only pursue things I have to wage battle for." He smiled weakly at this bit of unimpressive self-knowledge. "If you weren't with Sam and having a child, would my heart be breaking like it is now? I can't say. I guess I'll never know."

"I'm not sure it matters," Isabel told him, but then clarified by adding, "Not about whether your heart is broken, but whether it would be or not if I weren't with Sam. We've been on a wobbly course since we met—this is just one more phase along the way. If it's any solace at all, my heart was broken over you for years." She realized at that very moment that she'd never admitted so much to him before.

"How did you recover?" Christopher seemed not a little disappointed that she had.

"Oh, I went to see a man about a heart . . ." Isabel teased.

"No, really. What changed?"

"I was lonely in love, Chris, and that started to wear on me. Being in love takes two. Unrequited love started to feel like an exercise in loneliness."

"Where was I?"

"Someplace else. I don't really know."

"Strange affair, this is," he huffed, and rolled over onto his back.

Isabel did the same. The lovers stared at the ceiling quietly for a long time. Chris reached over and touched Isabel's hair and Isabel held his hand there.

Isabel could see now that finally connecting with Christopher sexually had cemented her commitment to motherhood and creating a family. She was about to say as much to him, then paused, wondering if it was too cruel. She didn't think he'd see it that way. Wasn't that the pull of Christopher over all these years? His impenetrability? Conventional ground rules and emotional responses never applied when it came to him. And yet . . .

Instead, she told him, "I do still love you, Chris. But it's a kind of love that has no model. Romantic, but not entirely of the heart. Physical, without transcending that physicality. Does that make sense?"

"Mostly. But how? Why?"

Christopher's curiosity opened the door wider for Isabel to enter with honesty. She paused for a minute to give verbal structure to what she'd been feeling.

"Without the consummation of our relationship, you would have been the personification of all the futures not chosen," she explained. "I used to love you in a way that confused me. And now I feel that I can love you without wondering if we should be together, because I don't think we should, not in the traditional sense. But I hope we are tethered forever in friendship. I know I risked that by sleeping with you."

"I can't promise you friendship, Isabel," he said. "I'm not sure what that would look like after you and Sam and Junior are one. I seriously doubt there will be room enough for me."

"Then my heart will break again," Isabel told him.

A WEEK LATER, on the Wednesday before Thanksgiving, Christopher and Isabel spent the afternoon together with plans to watch the blowing up of the Macy's Thanksgiving Day Parade balloons along Seventy-Second Street that night. Sam, much to his consternation, had to spend the entire Thanksgiving holiday working.

Isabel had witnessed the inimitable folly that is the inflation of two-story-sized balloons only once before when she was in her twenties, but she'd been with Beth and they'd had too many margaritas to remember much of it. Christopher, reluctant at first, succumbed to Isabel's enthusiasm. They planned dinner at his apartment, strategically located above Seventy-Second Street, from where they could witness the festivities while avoiding the crowds and the cold.

They had fallen asleep after an early dinner. She awoke to Christopher lightly kissing her cheek, trying to awaken her. It was a lazy evening inside, already dark, but they could hear the activity from the street below. "We should get up now, they've started blowing up Underdog," he told her, but made no motion to raise himself from her side.

At the mention of Underdog, Isabel leapt up from the bed, trying to pull Christopher with her. She realized instantly that it wasn't the wisest of moves. Her breath sharpened and she gasped from the concentration of pain on her right side. Christopher held her shoulders to prevent her from falling over as she clutched the sides of her belly. The muscles grew taut and she could see what looked like the form of the baby. She had just entered her thirty-fourth week, too early for the baby to come.

"What's happening?" Christopher asked, terrified. "Did I hurt you?"

Isabel tried to breathe deeply. "No, just let me walk around for a minute." She paced the apartment and waited for what felt like the mother of all cramps to subside. It disappeared completely and she sat down to catch her breath. The sudden onset of pain had left her spacy.

Christopher came out of the bedroom looking pale. "What can I do to help?"

"Please bring me the phone," Isabel said, composed. Poor Christopher looked unnerved. He brought her the phone and sat next to her on the couch, nibbling at his fingers in anxiety. Isabel dialed Beth's cell phone. As she did so she made a plan for each next small step. If she couldn't get Beth, she would call Anna next.

Beth's voice mail picked up.

"Hi, Beth, it's me. How do I know whether I'm having Braxton Hicks or if I'm in preterm labor? I just got a fuck of a contraction. It took my breath away. Call me. I'm at Christopher's . . ."

Christopher's shoulders slumped forward as he continued biting his thumb. He looked undone, another first. Isabel reached over to comfort him. "Don't worry, I'm going to have this baby one way or another." They sat silently on the couch in the charcoal dusk of evening, the mood inside strikingly somber compared with the ruckus outside.

As Isabel stood up she was struck again with another contraction. "Damn, this hurts, and I think it's just practice." She made her way to the bathroom before vomiting suddenly and violently. "This doesn't seem right," she said aloud to herself as she doubled over from pain and nausea. "Christopher!" she called out, "I think I need to get to the hospital."

Christopher grabbed their coats and guided Isabel toward the elevator.

Standing curbside outside his apartment building, he tried to hail a taxi, but the crowds made it difficult to navigate. He moved to the middle of the street as one barreled down Central Park West, daring it to mow him down. When the car stopped, he yelled, "My wife is in labor, please take us to the hospital." To which the driver replied, "Get out of the way, asshole" before speeding away.

Isabel was considering taking a bus across town when a taxi pulled up to the curb even though its off-duty light was on. The driver leaned out the window and said, "Looks like you could use a ride somewhere. Am I right?"

"Yes, thank you so much for stopping." She called out to Christopher and pointed to the car before sliding into the seat.

"You okay? What hospital?" the driver asked.

"I'll be fine. Lenox Hill, please, Seventy-Seventh and Lex."

"You don't look fine. I've been through this four times and it looks to me like you're about to have that baby."

Christopher jumped into the car from the traffic side. He had a wild look about him, and for the first time in their unusual friendship, Isabel felt sorry for him. His arm's-length emotional access in the past had fooled her into thinking she'd be absolved from taking care of his heart. Isabel struggled with what to say to him now, and coming up short, she just wanted him gone.

"Chris, maybe you should go back home."

"Don't be ridiculous. I'm going with you." He was breathing heavily.

"Listen to me . . . Just call Beth and ask her to meet me at Lenox Hill. I'd call but I'm a little out of breath." Isabel held on to the strap and braced herself for another contraction. She prayed she wouldn't vomit in the car. It would be unfair payback to the driver for such a good deed.

"Please, sir, pull over if you can. I'm about to be sick." Isabel got the door open in time to spew on the street.

The driver handed Christopher a handkerchief. "Here, give this to your wife."

"She's not my wife!" Christopher shouted. As soon as the

words came tumbling out of him, he grabbed Isabel's hand and looked at her to apologize. She just smiled and pressed his hand to her face.

"I think this might be the end of our affair," she told him before gagging into the handkerchief again.

They pulled up to the hospital just as Isabel was getting hit with another contraction, the strongest yet. The worse the pain got, the more focused Isabel felt. Her only desire was to be alone; the pain so basic it seemed to stem from some atavistic urge to hide behind a bush and give birth where other animals wouldn't find her.

Christopher regained his poise. He paid the driver and said, "Hey, thanks, buddy. Sorry about the outburst."

"No problem, man. Take care of your woman there, whoever she is."

They reached the maternity ward safely, though Isabel couldn't recall how she'd gotten there. Before she knew it, she was hooked up to an IV and a baby monitor.

"Are you the father?" an intern asked Christopher.

"No, I'm a friend."

"Is the father available?" the intern persisted.

"I don't know." Christopher sounded uncomfortable again.

Isabel had wondered when, if ever, Christopher and Sam would collide. She had hoped that if they had to, it wouldn't be in a way that would threaten Sam, jeopardize her friendship with Chris, or compromise herself. It was a lot to ask for.

She'd been careful about her time with Christopher, never once being careless or nonchalant about their behavior in public, fully aware how any hint of it would break Sam's heart. It felt to Isabel that their affair, though it never felt quite right to call it that, existed in a vacuum. That could remain true as long as Sam didn't know and as long as she and Christopher never took it further than she intended. She was confident of the latter. She prayed now she would be able to keep it a private connection.

She pulled out her cell phone to call Sam.

"Excuse me, ma'am, you can't use a cell phone in the hospital ward," a nurse told her.

"I have to call my husband."

"Sorry." She nodded her head toward Christopher. "He can call from downstairs."

Isabel weighed the options. She could have Christopher call Anna to ask her to call Sam, but that would involve Anna in a deception she wouldn't welcome. Involving anyone else seemed unfair. Beth was an exception, partly because her unequivocal disapproval exempted her from being a coconspirator. Disapproval had never crossed the line toward judgment between them—it was one of the things that kept their friendship intact over the many years of sticky predicaments. But Beth would have called by now if she'd gotten Isabel's earlier message. As brutal as it was for her husband to receive such a call from her lover, at this point she was out of options. Isabel handed the phone to Christopher.

"Please, take this and go downstairs and call Sam. Tell him what's going on."

Christopher looked at her with a *you can't be serious* expression.

Isabel told him, "Just do it, Chris!"

She tried to imagine what the conversation between her husband and lover would be like. Could she trust Christopher to be kind and reliably vague? That she couldn't answer that question with certainty reminded her of Christopher's pull and push over her.

While Christopher was calling her husband, Isabel's doctor gave her medication to stop the contractions. The drug made her legs shake uncontrollably and her breathing shallow. Isabel remained stoically calm. When Christopher returned to Isabel's room, he said, "Sam is getting on the next flight out. He'll be here as soon as he can."

Moments later, Beth burst into the room, pushing past Christopher and the nurses. "Sorry, sweetheart! I was at Mount Sinai visiting Paul and didn't have the cell on, they don't let you use them inside the hospital . . ."

"I know. Chris just had to call Sam from outside."

Beth took in a sharp breath, and Isabel shook her head at her own audacity.

Beth muttered, "Jesus, Is . . . ," then, louder, "You go into preterm labor the same night Paul is readmitted to the hospital. What is with this day?"

"Oh, God, Beth, I am so sorry."

"It wouldn't be so bad if his family weren't bent on trying to play matchmaker with his boyfriend and sister as he lays dying under their clueless watch. And speaking of clueless"—Beth nodded toward Christopher, who had just left the room—"if I wasn't so crazed right now, I'd ask you a hundred questions about what you were doing with Christopher that put you into labor." Beth gave Isabel a stern look, one a mother might give a child who's stolen another's toy. "Is Sam on the way? Are you guys okay?"

"We're fine. This has nothing to do with Sam, though there's probably no one in the world who would believe that besides you—on a day you're feeling generous—and maybe Anna." Isabel shuddered uncontrollably as a side effect of the drugs, but her voice remained remarkably steady and she kept her focus on Beth and the situation at hand. "Sam doesn't know and never needs to know. If he suspects anything, he won't ask. He's too smart to want to suffer . . ." Isabel had a major contraction just at that moment and leaned over the bed to vomit into a pan.

"I'd throw up too if I were you. That's an awful lot of bullshit to swallow," Beth said.

As Isabel pulled her head up from the pan she felt fine again. It amazed her that in between contractions and vomiting, she felt that she could get up and walk away.

"Yeah, well, I guess you're right . . . Anyway, go to Paul. Sam will be here later tonight. Chris can stay with me until then. Anna is at her in-laws', and while I'm sure she'd love an excuse to leave, I don't want to put her into a panic. I'll call her tomorrow."

Beth kissed Isabel on the lips and squeezed her still-trembling leg. "If anyone can handle this mess, it's you. Good luck. I'll check up on you later. Love you."

Isabel fell asleep for what felt like a few minutes, not realizing that one of the many tubes hooked up contained something to help her relax. When she woke up, the buzz of the hospital seemed to have subsided and it took her several minutes to figure out that she was now in a private room. She didn't recall asking for one—Christopher must have arranged it—but she was grateful for the quiet. Christopher was curled up on a chair next to the bed, looking tense even in sleep. She turned away from him, toward the door, and fell into a dazed half slumber.

A FEW HOURS before dawn, Isabel felt Sam quietly enter the room. Weak with fatigue, she cried out in relief when she saw him. Christopher sensed his entrance as well and awoke with a start. He stood up abruptly from his chair. The two men stood face-to-face for a brief moment before Christopher moved out of the way so Sam could stand next to Isabel. He kissed his wife on the lips and put his hand on her stomach. "You guys okay?"

"Looks like it." Isabel smiled groggily at her husband. "I'm glad you're here. Sorry for the scare."

Sam turned to Christopher and swallowed hard as if to squelch any suspicions he might have had about the fact that he was there with Isabel. He graciously managed a half smile as he held out his hand and said, "Thank you for taking care of Isabel."

Christopher nodded as he shook Sam's hand. He turned and quietly slipped out the door.

Intervention stopped the contractions soon enough and Isabel hadn't yet begun to dilate, so after hydrating her and monitoring her overnight, the doctor sent her home with the command that she stay on bed rest for the next two weeks. He told her he wanted to keep the baby from being born before thirty-six weeks, at which time the baby's lungs would be fully and safely functional.

She and Sam made it to Anna's for Thanksgiving dinner, where Isabel never left the couch except to eat and use the bathroom.

Once home, Isabel considered how bed rest would affect her work. Unable to make sales calls or attend meetings, she feared what the Turtle might do to sabotage her. If the baby came in two weeks, she would be out of the office four weeks earlier than originally planned.

"Oh, the Turtle is going to love this," Isabel said to herself. Ruth had been giving her updates about her boss's maneuvers. He didn't bother speaking much to Isabel anymore, which Isabel knew was his passive-aggressive attempt to make her feel dispensable. According to Ruth, he'd been cozying up to her strongest clients. Isabel fought her instinct to call him at home on Thanksgiving weekend to let him know she wouldn't be back to work, but she didn't want to sound defensive. She'd wait until Monday and considered even showing up at the office to speak with him in person.

"Absolutely not," Anna said when Isabel told her over Thanksgiving dinner that she planned to make an appearance at the office after the weekend. "The doctor said bed rest, Is, and he meant it. Why would you jeopardize the health of your baby for that schmuck?" The entire family agreed.

"She's not going in, don't worry. I'll be home to make sure that doesn't happen," Sam said.

"I don't have a good feeling about this, Sam," Isabel protested. "Is there some way he can use this against me?"

"Sweetheart, no. He can't. But if he tries, we'll sue his ass. Doesn't he have a kid of his own?"

"Yes, but when his kid was having emergency surgery just days after being born, he came into the office to show his fucking devotion."

"Forget it. He's not your problem, baby. You rest."

For two weeks, she did little but eat and sleep. She kept up with work e-mails and calls from the apartment. Sam arranged to work by video conference from his New York office so he could be close by in case Isabel went into labor again. When she reached the thirty-six-week mark they visited the doctor. He told her that their baby was out of danger and that Isabel could return to normal activity.

After the doctor's appointment, Sam and Isabel walked home through Central Park. Other than Thanksgiving dinner, she hadn't been out of the apartment for the past two weeks, and in that time her world had shifted from impermanence to something grounded and solid. The imminent birth of her son and the presence of her husband anchored Isabel to a different set of priorities, priorities that didn't put her first, and she welcomed the shift away from solipsism to something bigger.

It was a soft but sunless December day, much milder than it looked from inside. The park, cozy and protective, muffled the sounds from the city streets. Although the city was festive with holiday shoppers and revelers, the park was empty, and for a few blissful moments she imagined Central Park was theirs alone. When they reached Fifty-Ninth Street, they hailed a cab in front of the Plaza Hotel and headed home. Isabel followed Sam into their bedroom, where they made love slowly and carefully.

For the first time in a long time, she felt that they were family. Sex between her and Sam was a gift shared, one of love, between husband and wife, father and mother. With Christopher, over the past months, she had been selfish and reveled in her own satisfaction. She and Sam, on the other hand, had made a life together, and everything they did together became something stronger than her will or her ego. Her time with Christopher helped her to relinquish the individual claim she'd held on her life. It was a relief and a blessing.

ISABEL DECIDED SHE would go back to work until the baby was born. The Christmas season kept work blessedly quiet. She was able to clean up a few loose ends she'd left behind when she'd gone on bed rest. Sam and Isabel both thought it would be fine for Sam to go back to Chicago for a few days, since signs were that the baby had decided to go the distance after all. So on Thursday evening, just four days before the New Year, Sam headed to the airport again, and Isabel made plans to have dinner with Anna in Brooklyn. Just as she was about to hail a cab, she was hit with a small contraction. Even as the pain waned, Isabel found herself in a highly concentrated state. She called Anna to say she wasn't up for dinner and didn't offer more. The outside world receded and she had that same animal directive she'd felt the first time she went into labor, that urge to go to a safe place and wait alone as her body prepared itself.

Isabel made it to her apartment in a state of suspended consciousness similar to what she'd experienced four weeks before, with no recollection of how she'd gotten there. She lay down in the dark bedroom.

"I should call someone," she said aloud, but she didn't want to move.

The contractions came in waves. She timed them: twelve minutes apart. Plenty of time, she thought, to rest a bit. Isabel would pick up the phone when she had to, but until then she simply wanted quiet and solitude. She closed her eyes and breathed through the otherworldly feeling of her coming labor.

ISABEL CAME TO when her water broke. With a renewed sense of urgency, she called the doctor, who told her to meet him at the hospital right away. She left a message on Sam's cell phone—he was already in flight. She called Anna next. Jason had run out for a few hours and Anna was home with the children, so she wasn't able to meet her. Isabel promised to keep her posted. Beth was next. She called a neighbor to come by to stay with Jessie, then hopped in a taxi to meet Isabel at the apartment. By the time Beth arrived, Isabel had packed a small bag and held a towel by her side.

Beth held the door to the taxi she had waiting outside. "Your chariot, my hussy."

"Seriously, Beth?" Isabel huffed.

"Okay, seriously. How are you doing?" Beth asked as she held Isabel's hand.

"I'm fine. This all seems anticlimactic after all these months of pregnancy."

"Oh, this calm feeling you're having is all just practice," Beth assured her. "Pregnancy and birth are a cinch compared to knowing that you can't protect your child every moment of the day from the second he's born. So enjoy the next few hours. This is as peaceful as it gets."

It was one of those times when Isabel appreciated Beth the most. Words that might have seemed harsh to others were the perfect antidote to Isabel's anxiety about giving birth. The pain came and it grew and Isabel welcomed it as good pain, the kind that meant something wonderful was on the other end, as opposed to something broken or gone. By the time they got to the hospital, Isabel had already dilated to six centimeters.

Beth had disappeared to track down Sam using Isabel's cell, and by the time she got back, Isabel was already set up in a delivery room.

"I just spoke with Sam," Beth told Isabel, who vomited into a bedpan with each wave of nausea. "Geez, Is, you don't make it easy on yourself . . ."

"That's helpful . . . What did he say?"

"He never left O'Hare and he's on the next flight back. I'd say hang on for him, but I don't think that's happening." Beth raised her eyebrow. "The doctor said you're getting close to ready . . ."

Isabel felt her face fall. Sam had waited for this moment and she wanted to share it with him. She was ready now for her singular and independent life to become part of a family of three.

Beth voiced her friend's regret aloud: "I'm sorry Sam isn't here to see your little guy come into the world, but I get to be here with you, best friend. We'll get you through this together . . ."

"Were you sick when you were delivering Jessie?" Isabel managed between breaths.

"No, I actually thought it was kind of fun. Frankly, I was so relieved that Jessie and I weren't HIV positive, I thought it was all gravy."

Isabel wasn't having any fun because she continued vomiting with each contraction. Beth held the bedpan for her and fed her ice chips during lulls from the pain. "You know, Is, you can do this the easy way and get an epidural."

"I know, but I want to try to do this without drugs. I don't want to miss any of it. If it gets too bad, I'll let you know."

Isabel breathed into another contraction. Beth winced and actually said "ouch" aloud. Isabel had the wherewithal to laugh. It helped that Beth had been there before her.

When the pain grew to the point where it threatened to drown her in its intensity, Isabel asked for the anesthesiologist. First, her ob-gyn checked her out. "Too late," he said. "You're already at ten centimeters. Time to push."

Beth let Isabel squeeze her hand, and breathed with her friend through the pushes. Isabel grimaced and sweated but didn't once complain. After fifty minutes of pushing, the baby's head crowned, only to disappear again into the birth canal. Beth watched as the doctor sliced open Isabel's perineum, not to Isabel's knowledge, this last insult minor compared with the rest of the physical trauma of bearing her child.

At last the baby burst out from Isabel's womb. Amniotic fluid and blood sprayed the room, a scene to make Sam Peckinpah proud. The doctor caught the baby in midair. Beth cut the umbilical cord and cried with her happy, spent friend.

"You've done it, Is," Beth said, delighted. "Another man in the world, created by a woman. And no one can say it's otherwise."

The sound of her son's cry, one that she would come to feel as much as hear, was beautiful, dissonant music to her ears. His eyes were too swollen to open and his nose looked broken. Not more than one minute old and he already looked as if he'd been in a fight.

"He may not be pretty, but he's mine," Isabel said when the doctor held him up for her to see. Love wasn't quite what she felt at that moment—rather she felt an uncharacteristic shyness in meeting her newborn son. Now that he had separated from her own body, she would get to know him on his terms. The power of that helpless, bloody creature held before her was undeniable and humbling.

Isabel wanted to maintain a sense of whatever it was she felt at the moment. She would recall it as peace, this visceral knowledge and unqualified acceptance of the irreversible shift away from life as she had lived it.

Sam arrived just as the nurse was bringing Samuel Jr. to Isabel for his first feeding. The infant had been cleaned up and swaddled in a white cotton blanket with blue and pink stripes. Sam Sr. walked gingerly across the room as if to protect the silence there. He instinctively held out his hands toward Isabel to accept the alien bundle and choked up as he gazed into the face of their newborn child.

Sam held him confidently, reverently, as he put his nose and mouth against the baby's head and breathed in the scent of new life. Isabel pushed aside her dressing gown to expose a nipple as Sam placed their son against Isabel's breast. Sammy took to the task like he was born to it, and Isabel smiled in wonder at her body's response to perhaps the second most basic act in nature. This simple act of nursing her son brought her grace. She'd never known it before.

CHAPTER SIXTEEN

Beth

WHEN SAM ARRIVED at the hospital, Beth went downstairs to get some coffee and to call home to tell Jessie the news of baby Sammy's arrival. Realizing that she was no longer needed, she took the elevator back up to Isabel's room to tell her she'd be back later that day. Isabel was sound asleep, her newborn son beside her in a small trolley crib. Sam stood at the foot of the bed gazing at his wife and child. Beth stood silently next to him and he put an arm around her shoulders. Sam turned to give her a full hug and she saw he was crying through his smile.

"You would have been proud of her, Sam. She handled it like a warrior," Beth whispered.

"I have no doubt," Sam said, holding the embrace. "Thank you for being here with her." Sam kissed the top of Beth's head.

The moment held the weight of their shared love for Isabel. "She's lucky to have us both," Beth said, not entirely with humor.

No sooner had she witnessed the birth of her friend's baby than she received the message she'd been dreading for a long time. Paul had slipped into another coma, caused by another respiratory failure, and there was little hope that he would awake from it this time.

Beth rushed off to meet Helen at a coffee shop near the hospital where Paul lay dying.

"You can't see him, Beth. Mom is up there," Helen warned as Beth sat down in the booth across from her.

"She can't stay there forever. I'll wait until she leaves. Will you call me? I want to bring him a card Jessie made. I know he's not conscious but I promised her. Besides, I need to see him too."

Beth didn't want to upset Helen any more than she was already, but Beth had long grown sick of the family's paranoia perpetuating the myth that she was responsible for Paul's demise. "I am going to see him before he dies, Helen. I think he would want that."

"He would . . . he does," Helen said. "Just please, wait until I give you the all clear so that you and Mom don't cross paths."

Helen left the coffee shop and headed to the hospital. Just thirty minutes later, Beth received her text: "You have an hour with him."

Paul's private room had flowers spilling from the windowsill and a crowded corner table, above which floated red Mylar balloon hearts gathered with silver string. The only sounds were the hiss of the respirator and the subtle beep of the heart monitor. Nurses quietly padded in and out, but there was no one else around. Beth wondered what kind of warning Helen had issued to clear the family for her visit. She thought of the scene from *The Godfather* when Michael visits his father in the hospital after he's been shot in a failed assassination attempt. The room is left unguarded and Michael realizes his father's enemies are about to try again. The nurse, believing Michael is disturbing his father, tries to get him to leave the room. He tells her: *"You know my father? Men are coming here to kill him. Now help me. Please."*

Now Beth recast the famous scene, changing the dialogue for Paul's unconscious benefit: "You know my son? His ex-wife is coming here to help him. Kill her. Please." She giggled at her silly joke and thought she saw the slightest smirk on Paul's otherwise expressionless face.

Beth felt a sense of calm resignation as she sat next to Paul on the bed. She knew it was the last time that she would see him alive.

"Oh, Paul. I am so sorry you are going to die. You know, I would have loved you from the beginning just as much as an openly gay man. I hope you can know that in your heart before you disappear from your sorrowful life on earth and into the next." She squeezed Paul's hand as she said this, hoping for some sign of acknowledgment, but there was nothing.

She pulled out Jessie's card.

"This is from Jessie. I promised her I would share it with you . . . On the cover is a colored pencil drawing of a bearded man in a flowing robe with a brown dog by his side." Beth turned the card toward Paul to show it to him, although his eyes were now forever shut to the world outside.

"Inside the card," she told him, "Jessie wrote in purple pencil: 'Pop, I knew a boy who believed in God, but he didn't believe in dingoes. I hope where you're going you will find both God and dingoes.'" Beth laughed aloud as she read Jessie's message. She hadn't seen the card before Jessie had stapled it closed.

Jessie was referring to a funny little refrain the three of

them had shared, based on something a boy told her in first grade. She'd come home from school one day and told Beth over dinner: "I met a boy today who said he believed in God but he didn't believe in dingoes." Such a bizarre notion, they had turned it into a little ditty the three of them sang together: *I knew a boy . . . who believed in God . . . but he didn't believe . . . in dingoes!*

"Did I ever tell you Jessie's other God story?" Beth said now as she held Paul's hand. "She and five of her classmates were discussing God and Santa over lunch one day close to the holidays. One of the kids asked the question 'Do you believe in God or Santa?' As they went around the table each kid responded. When Jessie told the story, she said, 'Every single one of them said they believed in God, but not one of them believed in Santa.' So I asked her, 'What did you say?' And Jessie said, 'I told them that I believed in Santa, but not in God.'

"Clearly, Paul, you imbued your daughter with a curiosity about the mysteries of the divine and a sense of humor to go along with it. Well done." Beth knew Paul would be proud of their daughter's fearlessness in expressing a contrary view. He would appreciate the various symbols of faith as well, uncertain as he was at times about his own.

Beth sat silently with Paul for the rest of the hour. She finally arose and slipped the card Jessie had made for him under his pillow. On the back of the folded paper Jessie had drawn a picture of the three of them sitting by the Portofino wharf in the rain.

Beth kissed Paul one last time before turning to leave. "I've loved you all along, Paul. And while I've had a hard time completely forgiving you, I've never stopped trying." She squeezed his leg gently in a quiet and final good-bye.

Beth left Paul's room and traveled across town to visit Isabel, at home now with Sammy Jr. She needed to witness a new life, one safe from the specter of death, at least for now. It would give her the ballast she needed to go home to Jessie and tell her about Paul. As she rode the subway downtown, she debated whether it was wise to let Jessie see him one last time. Her daughter seemed so grown-up, even though she'd only just turned eight, and Beth had to remind herself that she was still a little girl. By the time she got home that evening, she'd decided that it would be best for Jessie to remember him as she last saw him, rather than comatose in a sterile hospital room with tubes protruding from his body. The situation with Paul's family didn't make it any easier. Jessie didn't need any part of that insanity.

Helen called Beth the next day to give her an update. Her voice sounded lighter than it had in years to Beth. "Mom saw the card Jessie made. It caused quite a stir in the hospital room."

"How so?" Beth asked, amused. She hadn't even considered the discovery of the card, only that it should be with Paul until the very end.

"Standard Mom. She said it was proof of your godlessness—she really couldn't wrap her head around God and dingoes! She finally landed on 'God will get her for this!' What was that about anyway?"

Beth explained the card to Helen, who found the story hilarious. "I think your visit gave Paul a moment of strength. When I saw him later last night, he was breathing easier than he had in days. He did always love you, you know that, right?"

Helen then offered news of the previous night's escapades at Paul's bedside. Apparently Raymond had come by and the family had played matchmaker again with him and Helen. Helen thought it apt that they couldn't quite put together who Raymond was, in spite of his openness about being gay and his intimacy with Paul. They simply chose to ignore the fact and carried on about what a cute couple Raymond and Helen would make. All this while Paul lay dying beside them. The absurdity of it all certainly made the whole thing easier for Beth to take.

The following few days felt like a holding pattern between life and death. Paul remained in critical but stable condition. His lung capacity deteriorated every day.

On New Year's Day, just minutes after the ball dropped in Times Square, Paul Marchand succumbed to respiratory failure with Raymond sleeping next to him in the hospital bed. *In the end, as it should be*, thought Beth, and with her thoughts, she took solace from this last image of Paul, dying next to the only other person who accepted him fully in spite of his ambiguity.

Beth and Jessie cried together at the news and then wrote an appropriately silly and sweet rhyming eulogy in honor of his passing. Jessie asked her mother if she could read it at the funeral, and Beth didn't have the heart to tell her that the family would most likely not welcome it. When Beth called to find out the arrangements for the service the following day, the final blow came from Helen.

"Mom doesn't want you and Jessie to come to the funeral. She's afraid of what you might say or do."

Beth filled with anger, which displaced the sadness that had been welling. "You've got to be fucking kidding me, Helen! She would deny his daughter, *her granddaughter*, a final good-bye? I'm sorry, but that's just not going to happen." She was yelling so loud she knew others in the office could hear her.

"It would undo her, Beth, to have you there. You can't come," Helen said.

"I don't give a flying fuck. I am going to his funeral, Helen. Just warn her that I *will* be there with Jessie."

Beth slammed the phone down and let out an anguished cry as her heart began to race with rage and her mind with fantasies of vindication. The past nine years of controlling her anger and her fears, of protecting Paul and his secrets, of wearing a scarlet letter as a mask for his denial, came tumbling out in a fury of tears and garbled ranting.

Maggie, in the office for the day, ran into Beth's office.

"My God, Beth, what's happened?" Maggie asked. "Are you okay? Is Jessie okay?"

Pacing with heavy and fast steps around her office, Beth circled her desk several times, hands in her hair as if to pull it out. On the final circumlocution, she swung her chair into the wall. She was breathing hard.

"Helen just told me that Paul's mother *dis*invited me and Jessie to Paul's funeral," and with this, she collapsed on the floor and sat there, back pressed against her desk. Maggie sat across from her, grabbed her hands and waited. Beth's breathing slowed after a minute or two.

"Do you know why I'm so upset?" Beth finally said, her voice now steady. "It's not that Paul is dead, or that his family has disinvited me from the funeral . . ." Beth paused to choose her words carefully. "I just wish that they would know me now for the person in Paul's life who gave him the most, not the one who took it away."

"You know it, Beth. That's what matters," Maggie said, as Beth squeezed back tears of rage. She paused for a few moments before asking, "So what are you going to do?"

"I don't know . . ." Beth shook her head hard. "I told Helen I was going no matter what. But is that the right thing to do? And what about Jessie? She needs to be able to say good-bye to her father."

"Maybe you can go without them knowing," Maggie suggested. "I mean, not incognito, clearly." At this Beth began to choke out hysterical laughter. When she'd finished Maggie added, "If the church is big enough, maybe you can sit in the back and leave early?"

"So I have to sneak into my ex-husband's funeral with our daughter? How fucked-up is that?! I'm sorry, I'm not angry with you . . ."

"I know you're not."

Beth regained her composure. "Listen, Maggie, I'm all right now. Thanks for coming to the rescue."

Maggie grabbed Beth's hands and kissed them. "You are one amazing woman."

PAUL'S FUNERAL TOOK place at Saint Ignatius Loyola on Park Avenue and Eighty-Fourth Street. Beth and Jessie showed up late. They stayed to the back of the church, in a corner where they wouldn't be noticed. Seated next to Paul's mother was Jeannie, the necessary girlfriend in mourning. As in life, Paul's death was veiled in lies.

Raymond sat in the back of the church as well and gave a tearful hug to Beth and Jessie when they arrived. Sam and Isabel came with the baby and sat next to them. It was important to Beth that she and Jessie attend Paul's funeral, but not important enough to ignore a grieving mother's wishes. If nothing else, Beth wanted to respect the unfathomable tragedy of Mrs. Marchand having lost her son. All the lies in the world would not make it one bit less painful.

Since speaking with Maggie, Beth had been turning her anger over in her head. Now, perched on the church pew, she realized it didn't matter if Paul's family recognized what she meant to Paul or vice versa. Their relationship had nothing to do with them. She didn't even fully understand it, so how could anyone else? Now he was dead, and it was over anyway. Why would his family think any differently about her at this point? And what did it matter? For the first time since Paul had passed, Beth fully relaxed, relieved to have come to an understanding with herself. She sat back in the pew and closed her eyes, opening them again only when she felt Jessie grab her hand. They smiled sadly at each other, but no tears came.

Jessie whispered, "Mom, I'm praying to God and dingoes for Paul."

CHAPTER SEVENTEEN

Anna

ANNA HELD A laundry basket in one arm and Henry in the other. Oscar trailed behind her, holding on to her sweatpants. In an attempt to get chores done and include the boys, everything took three times as long as it needed to.

"Okay, guys, let's dump the clean clothes over here on the couch and you can help me fold them!" she said, trying to sound more enthusiastic than she felt. Before she had unburdened herself of the clean clothes and the boys, she stepped on a yellow Lego piece, bruising the arch of her foot.

"Goddamn it!" she yelled between clenched teeth as she dropped the laundry basket and the clothes spilled onto the floor.

"Why is this place such a mess all the time?" she asked no one, but accusing all. At her harsh tone Oscar began to cry, and Henry, not knowing what was going on, imitated his big brother with his own whining. Hopping on one foot, her two sons clinging to her and crying, Anna screamed at Jason, who sat at the kitchen table eating a bowl of granola and reading the latest issue of *Wallpaper*.

"Can you do something to help me out here, please? Take the boys and do something useful?" She turned her frustration on Jason more and more now that she was home. His self-exemption from the morning's drama made her hate him at that moment. How could he remain so calm when three-quarters of the family was melting down before his very eyes?

"You do it to yourself, you know," Jason said without even looking up from the pages of the magazine.

Anna flashed him a look of enraged confusion. "What's that supposed to mean?"

"Let the housekeeper do the laundry," Jason calmly explained. "Why do you insist on doing it yourself? And with the boys in tow? They were fine not helping with the laundry when you were at work every day."

Anna plopped down on the couch and rubbed her injured foot. Then she grabbed her boys and hugged them to apologize for her outburst.

"You're right. I have no idea what I'm doing . . ." Anna capitulated, speaking more to herself than to Jason. Because that's how she felt now, all the time. She wanted to work, she wanted to spend time with her boys, but not knowing how to navigate between the two, she couldn't even say for sure what she wanted. While being with the boys could be intensely satisfying—*the good kind of boring!*—she couldn't reconcile how mind-numbing toddler-play was after the first twenty minutes.

She and Jason had considered putting Oscar in preschool, but Anna didn't want to confuse him with a message that now that she was home, he had to leave. She tried a few playgroups around the neighborhood but soon became fed up with the conversations with the other mothers. They were all stay-at-home moms—what she'd thought she wanted to be—but she didn't connect with any of them. Anna was beginning to feel that her frustration was chronic.

The birth of Sammy gave Anna a new mission. Her reinvented life was supposed to be all about avoiding missions and learning to enjoy an unstructured day. Instead, Anna ran into the city three times a week to lend a hand to Isabel, despite the fact she had never once asked for help. It occurred to Anna more than once that she was fleeing her own household to feel useful somewhere else, but she felt if she parted with her new source of autonomous purpose she would go mad. With Jenny there part-time, Anna had so much more time on her hands, and yet she filled every minute either tending to the household or, now that she had a nephew, helping Isabel. She wasn't unhappy with any of the ways in which she spent her time; it's just that she seemed incapable of organizing her days short of chaos no matter the actual obligation.

THE THIRD WEEK into the New Year, Anna received an urgent message from Eric at RHM. They'd had a phone meeting once a week since Anna's sabbatical started, but it was mostly to assure Eric that he was doing fine in her place. She'd prepped him well before taking leave and found him so efficient that she'd begun to wonder if she had effectively been replaced.

Anna felt not a little pleased to hear the urgency in his voice. When she was working, those messages caused dread. Now, she couldn't wait to get Eric on the phone. She called him back immediately.

"Eric, what's going on?"

"We got a call from our manufacturer in Brazil. He said the matter was urgent but he refuses to speak with me about it. He said he needed to speak to you," Eric explained. "When I told him you were out, he asked if he could speak with Beth but then said he'd rather speak with you instead. Sorry to bother you, but I didn't know what else to do."

"Give me his number. I'll call him." Anna's voice felt stronger than it had in a year. Just having a professional task in front of her gave her a jolt of energy. She waited until Jenny arrived before calling the supplier back.

Anna learned that a flood had destroyed the textile plant from where RHM procured much of its fabric. It wouldn't have been so bad if the advance orders for the company's most lucrative line didn't completely depend on the availability of the fabric manufactured at this specific site. The flood event required shifting operations to another plant while the original was being repaired. There would be a lag in deliveries unless decisions could be made posthaste. Anna knew they needed someone on the ground there immediately. If she decided not to go, this was the moment to step away completely and hand over the reins to Eric and Beth.

After hanging up the phone, Anna grabbed her coat and bag and slipped out of the apartment. She headed across the river into Manhattan to catch the Lexington subway line north. She barely knew where she was heading, but her body pushed in the direction of the Upper East Side. Her mind raced—was it a betrayal to her children if she returned to work full-time, or was it an inevitable result of the last few months at home?

The Metropolitan Museum of Art's Sackler Wing, which housed the Temple of Dendur, had always been one of the places in which Anna could think most clearly. With its reflecting pool and sloping windowed wall looking out on Central Park, it provided an oasis of calm in the otherwise overly stimulating city. Over the years, the room had become a reliable respite from the noise on the street and in her head. Her last visit to the museum did little for her peace of mind, but she was in a decidedly different place now, even if unsure where that was exactly.

Anna climbed the grand marble stairway and entered through the main hallway. She climbed again to the center hall as she wound her way to the Sackler Wing. It had been years since she'd visited this part of the museum, yet her body followed some homing directive. She found a bench in the corner of the vast room. The echo off the marble reminded her of church, but the secular nature of the space allowed her mind its own expanse not bogged down in dogma. She listened to the click of the visitors' footsteps on the floor and watched the light stream in from the three-story windows.

ANNA HAD NEVER fully understood the exhortation to "live in the present." She'd turn to what needed to be accomplished in the immediate or far future and prided herself on her planning—no wonder she was never satisfied in the moment, she began to realize. Her manic efficiency was more mania than efficiency and it basically sucked for everyone.

Anna considered how her childhood of witnessing subordination to a husband made her feel like she needed to do and be everything as a result. But now she saw her way wound up being a different version of her perceived fates of her mother and aunts and grandmothers. In many ways, it was worse. Instead of expecting her husband to shoulder his part, she expected nothing. The self-imposed burden of each and every labor—from earning the money and controlling the household finances to planning the children's meals for the week, scheduling their doctor's appointments, and countless other domestic tasks—made her resentful. Jason was a ready and willing helpful partner, but she took on more than necessary out of a perverse, ill-conceived sense of empowerment. Anna had swung the pendulum too far in the other direction: walnuts alone were not all they were cracked up to be.

As Anna watched the movements of the other visitors in the great room without really seeing any of them, she tried to visualize a new kind of life, a life where she could hold the conflicts of work and family simultaneously, without tipping the scales unhappily in one direction or another. Her ambition had been tainted with the realities of the sacrifices it demanded.

Ambition was no longer a necessary part of the equation. She'd already succeeded. She worked at a company whose value systems very much reflected her own and she'd helped it get there successfully. As a devoted mother and wife to a true partner, she valued the personal part of her life more than anything else. Anna needed to accept that as fact. Her lifelong fight to define herself outside of the family dynamic into which she was born was made futile now that she found herself at the center of her own little family, one of her own creation. Those old laws held power over her only so long as she allowed them to. Why was she fighting unconditional love?

Anna sighed now with the relief of feeling for the first time like she had nothing to prove, not in her life as a mother nor as a professional. Her own mother's words had finally wormed their way into her emotional consciousness. She knew with certainty that placing blame for the miscarriage was just another deflection, a lie meant to take the place of surrendering control of something she could not let go.

Sitting in the temple, she gradually began to see the flood in Brazil as her chance at renewal. Maybe this was the opportunity Anna needed to help her make the transition to a viable way of life. She could work out some creative ways of getting the job done. Since the next few months of work would entail some traveling, maybe she could make some of the trips with the family in tow. Jenny could travel with them if necessary. She could do much of the work at home as well. Surely Beth would be open to some kind of arrangement. Her job at RHM entailed finding creative solutions to make the business work within its means. Why wasn't she applying these same skills to her own life? She had been so fierce about compartmentalizing her work life and her home life, but what if she no longer split one from the other? That was an Old World way of living. It may have worked for men like her father, but she was dividing herself in the process. The time had come for a new way of making it all possible.

The light filtering through the massive museum windows had shifted from ambient winter daylight to the soft gray hue of the coming evening. Anna felt peaceful and rose with welcome determination to tackle what lay before her. She stretched her arms toward the vaulted ceiling and then headed home to discuss the news of the day with Jason.

PART FOUR

SUMMER

CHAPTER EIGHTEEN

Isabel, Beth, Anna, and Maggie

"ICE-COLD MARTINIS ON the way, ladies!"

"Make mine hot and dirty!" Beth hollered to Maggie from the living room.

"Same for me!" Anna chimed in.

"Only dirty for me. I don't know how hot pepper gets metabolized in mother's milk and I'm not sure I want to find out," Isabel said with a frown. "Although, I do have plenty of the expressed milk in the fridge for the occasion . . . On second thought, make mine a hot and dirty one too!"

"Are you sure? Or are you just taking the opportunity to say that aloud?" Maggie asked with a smirk.

Maggie expertly mixed up a pitcher of vodka martinis while her two-month-old daughter slept soundly in the bouncy chair perched on the kitchen table. Isabel, seated on the small couch in the kitchen with a pillow on her lap, nursed her almost eight-month-old son, anticipating the first sip of a martini since before she became pregnant. Anna and Beth played hide-and-seek with Jessie, Lily, and the boys, generating shrieks of surprise and delight that drowned out the Dixie Chicks playing over the house speakers.

Over a year after the protests at RHM, the roundtable on motherhood was to be aired on national television. For the occasion, the participants had gathered for a weekend at the Ducci bungalow in Montauk. The magazine format show would debut on Sunday morning, and the women had decided to make a little holiday of it. Children included, no husbands. Anna and Isabel arrived on Thursday night to prepare the house to accommodate four adults and six children varying in age from newbie to eight years old. By Friday evening, the old cedar-shingled house was bursting with activity.

"I thought Georgette was coming. I was looking forward to hearing her version of the reconciliation with John," Isabel said to Maggie, trying to provoke some lively storytelling. "And I was dying to ask her if it's true that sex is better with an ex."

"Oh, that . . ." Maggie smiled as she answered Isabel and rolled her eyes at the thought of what had actually transpired to get John and Georgette back together. "It was a bit hairy, but it all worked out in the end. I'll tell you when we have time for a saga. Georgette was going to join us with Jules and Justine, but they all spent the summer in France and they aren't coming back until next week."

"Is John excited about Evvy?" Isabel asked Maggie, referring to the tiny creature blessedly asleep in her chair.

"'Excited' isn't what I would call it, no," Maggie said, laughing. "But he was a sport about the whole thing—and he didn't have to be. It's not like I gave him a say in the matter one way or another."

"We can be selfish bitches, can't we?" Isabel said with more bravura than she intended. Beth, of course, didn't miss a thing.

"What's this about selfish bitches?" Beth asked, eyebrow raised, as she ran breathless into the kitchen to collect her martini. "Man, the kids are wearing me out! I need a drink, stat!"

Maggie iced four martini glasses and coated each with vermouth before pouring in the vodka and festively garnishing the cocktails with dark purple kalamata olives. She ceremoniously set the first in front of Isabel and handed the others over to Beth and to Anna, who held Henry on her lap.

"Did you ever hear about the All-Girl Martini Club?" Maggie asked. "I knew the kick-ass woman who started it a while back. They met once a month, each time at a different bar, and the group gained such notoriety that men started trying to crash it. The women had to wait until an hour before they met to find out the locale to prevent leakage of their whereabouts."

"Oh, yeah, I remember reading something about them," Beth chimed in. "I guess it's hard for men to imagine anything being any fun without them."

Isabel held up her glass and said, "To the All-Girl Martini Club. I hope they're still at it!" With that, Isabel took her first sip, eyes closed in reverent delight. "Maggie, you are a magician!"

MAGGIE'S IDEA FOR a weekly show on the real lives of women today, entitled *The End of Men?*, had been green-lighted after the cable network viewed the rough cut of the first roundtable. She had produced five additional segments, which were scheduled to run throughout July. Depending on the success of the initial six episodes, the network had a second season in mind.

While Maggie was still consulting at RHM, she now focused most of her work on producing. She'd hired an associate who was able to handle the day-to-day work for the company, and Maggie remained in touch with Beth on a weekly basis.

Beth's mini empire was growing exponentially. As a result of her generous employee policies, healthy profit margins, and aggressive ad campaigns (not to mention the press generated by them), she had been profiled as one of the most influential businesswomen of the new millennium. In spite of the many heated voices against it, the company provided a desperately desired product to the millions of pregnant women around the country. And while the ads had stirred up controversy, as more women (and men, for that matter) learned about RHM, the overall consensus applauded their message. Pregnancy was sexy. Mothers were powerful. Beth couldn't have been happier.

After Paul's death, Beth's attorney had come to her to reveal that the angel investor had been her ex-husband. He must have known that Beth would never have accepted his participation, so he'd set himself up as a silent partner, leaving his shares to Jessie upon his death.

Anna had dealt swiftly and effectively in the wake of the flood that destroyed the inventory at RHM's textile supplier. She'd made holidays of the trips abroad, taking the family with her while also getting the company back on track. She'd also set up the launch of a toy division and was working to expand into other children's and childcare products. Anna had cut her workweek to four days, with three days in the office and one working at home. Delegation, she'd finally accepted, was a working mother's friend. Fridays Anna devoted entirely to her boys. The new routine addressed everything Anna wanted out of her life. More time with the family, and a rewarding work life that supported her family but didn't suck up all of her energy in the process.

Isabel's work life had become more contentious and her suspicions about job security had been well-founded. The Turtle fired her from *Pink* just two months after she returned to work from maternity leave, and she was suing the company for discrimination. She'd been warned that initiating the lawsuit would make her untouchable as far as other jobs were concerned, but she saw the warning as an attempt to intimidate her from causing problems for *Pink*. With support and advice from Sam and friends, she'd decided to risk her future appeal as an employee to make a point. She wondered how many women kept their mouths shut, afraid of the repercussions of speaking out and, unlike her, unable to afford the alternative. Sam's colleagues enthusiastically took on the case, determined to set a precedent and make some noise. Maggie ensured the lawsuit got plenty of press attention.

When RHM was approached by a major media company about launching a magazine, Isabel enthusiastically accepted the position of publisher. The much-anticipated launch issue was scheduled for the following winter.

ISABEL WAS ONLY two sips into the delicious martini when Sammy began to cry. Isabel took him upstairs to quieter quarters, balancing her martini in her left hand—she'd dreamed of this martini since she'd learned she was pregnant a year and a half ago and couldn't bear to abandon it now.

Isabel walked her infant around attempting to rock him to

sleep. Her martini sat on the dresser top, sweat forming around the glass. A warm August night, the martini quickly lost its crisp coldness. Isabel, determined to enjoy the drink, held her baby to her breast with her right arm as she sat on the floor with her legs crossed in front of her. She deftly lifted the martini with her left hand and brought the glass to her lips. Her baby suckled contentedly, and Isabel considered for a moment the absurd symmetry between mother's milk and a vodka martini. The thought made her laugh aloud, which only started Sammy crying again. That beautiful martini would have to wait, but not without one last sip before Isabel pulled herself up and paced the room, singing songs she'd made up for her little boy.

Half an hour passed and Isabel still had no luck consoling her discontented child. She wanted to cry herself. All she wanted was to join the group of laughing women downstairs. Tom Jones played at full volume from below, and the loud group sing-along to "Delilah" sounded ridiculously awesome.

"My, my, *my* . . . Delilah! Why, why, *why* . . . Delilah? . . ."

Still, as much as Isabel wanted to join her friends, she basked in feeling essential to her infant, that this small sacrifice would be one barely perceptible glitch in a lifelong effort to shield her baby from the discomfort life would inevitably bring.

But as Sammy continued crying relentlessly, she felt her contentment slipping away. Just as she was about to tear up, Maggie quietly knocked on the door. "Hi," she whispered, "you guys okay?"

"Poor little guy can't seem to get comfortable. I've nursed him and rocked him and he still won't fall asleep."

Maggie gently reached for him. "Take a break. Let me hold him."

Isabel hesitated before handing over her hoarse-from-wailing baby. Maggie cuddled him and spoke to him, and although it was not his own mother's voice, Sammy was calmed by it. He let his body relax and fell fast asleep in all of five minutes.

"How did you do that?" Isabel asked, dumbfounded, grateful, and hurt.

"He just wore himself out and my timing was good. No magic here." Maggie's calm comforted Isabel as well. "Sometimes any change can stop the crying cycle. Lily would do the same thing with me. John would finally take over after hours of my struggling and she would fall asleep in three minutes. Used to piss me off until I realized that it has nothing to do with technique and more to do with timing and a change in motion, sound, or voice. It really is that frustratingly simple."

Isabel welcomed the relief and wisdom of an experienced mother and reached for her room-temp martini. She was dying to drink the damn thing, even if it now tasted like warm metal.

The sip of the martini encouraged Isabel to change the subject to adult issues. "So, you and Georgette seem to be pals. How's that working out?"

"You know, I've grown to really like her. And best of all, she and John seem to be really happy together," Maggie said, smiling, before she grew serious. "I've realized I judged her without knowing anything about her. She had to make choices—partly because of the havoc I brought to her life. They may have been different choices from what I'd have made, but who am I to judge? I've made some pretty excellent messes myself. She's a good mother and a better partner for John.

"As for John, well, I'm sure her struggles with him were not dissimilar to my own, but she was more demanding, so it got

John off his ass. It all seems to have worked out fairly." Maggie sounded centered and assured. Isabel admired how she'd worked her way out of a messy situation to a place of resolution.

"What about that article she wrote and the smear campaign—how'd you get over that?" Isabel had always wanted to ask this of Maggie but never wanted to fess up to having read it.

Maggie smiled. "That was about her, not me. She didn't know me then. And I have to admit, she did have some fair points . . ."

The two women laughed quietly as they put Sammy down in his crib. Before they reached the bottom of the stairs, Maggie's own infant daughter woke for a feeding.

"You go ahead, I'll try to make it back down after I nurse Evvy," Maggie whispered. "There's a pitcher of cold martinis in the freezer. Dump out that tepid one and pour yourself another."

Sleep-deprived and exhausted, Isabel couldn't imagine having two children at that moment—Maggie seemed nothing short of an angel. With Sammy down for the night, Isabel gamely took Maggie's advice and got herself another drink before joining the others dancing in the living room.

. . .

ISABEL WAS THE first to wake on Sunday morning. Sammy rarely slept past six and usually awoke famished. She nursed and changed him before inhaling a bagel with lox, cream cheese, and a slice of tomato. Isabel couldn't get used to how hungry she was now. Since Sammy didn't take well to a bottle, Isabel nursed him all day long, which was an invitation to eat four thousand calories a day. She'd lost all the weight from pregnancy and then some—getting her waist back but also keeping her larger-by-far breasts. She thought nursing was terribly underrated.

By seven thirty, she and Sammy were already out the door and heading down to the beach. Shortly thereafter, Anna arrived with the boys, pulling their big beach wagon full of front loaders and backhoes, dump trucks and shovels. By eight thirty, Sammy fell asleep on Isabel's chest and Anna's boys were nowhere near ready to go home.

"We're never going to make it back by nine o'clock to see the show," Isabel whispered to her sister. She was lying on her back with the morning sun warming her face. She had no intention of moving. "Do you think Maggie will be upset?"

"Maggie will understand," Anna said. "Besides, she's probably taping it. We can watch it later."

Back at the house, Jessie had awoken with a craving for waffles, so Beth had taken her and Lily into town, leaving a note for Maggie, who was passed out with Evvy. Beth turned the television on to the channel airing the show before leaving the house, hoping Maggie might wake to it.

The twenty-minute wait for a table at the local diner meant they'd never make it back in time. At a few minutes to nine, Beth called Maggie's cell to remind her to record the show. The call flipped to voice mail right away. Surely Maggie was still asleep, after waking every two hours over the course of the night with Evvy.

For the rest of the morning, the blue light of the television flickered against the walls of the empty room, and at nine the discussion on motherhood, taped nine months before, filled the quiet house.

ACKNOWLEDGMENTS

I am grateful to so many who helped to bring *The End of Men* into the world. My thanks to . . .

Kim Witherspoon and Alexis Hurley at Inkwell, whose never-say-die attitude is a lesson for us all.

Rebecca Miller, whose wonderful film, *Maggie's Plan*, breathed new life into this novel.

Erin Wicks, who kicked my ass in the best of ways. I wrote this book for women like her, and I am honored to say that her influence is all over it.

Amy Baker, publisher of Perennial and her killer team, Mary Sasso and Paul Florez.

Leslie Cohen and SallyAnne McCartin, publicists *extraordinaires*.

Dori Carlson, Suzette Lam, and Leydiana Rodriguez for tending to the necessary details that turn a manuscript into a book; and to Adalis Martinez for the inspired cover.

Michael Morrison and Jonathan Burnham, awesome boss-men of Harper, who welcomed this novel into our publishing home.

Mike Magers, for the gift of his photography and friendship.

Bob Levine and Kim Schefler, for reliable counsel on all things big and small.

Kassie Evashevski, who helps me every day in every way. Her spirit and friendship imbue this book from start to finish.

Colin Dickerman, for encouraging me to not burn these pages and more.

Kristina Rinaldi, Chris Padgett, Allison Warren, Victoria Comella, Ann Patty, Joe Dolce, Roger Trilling, early readers and *la famiglia*, all.

Joel Rose, whose love, encouragement, and long-suffering patience give me faith in myself when I lose sight of it.

Celine and Chloe, who humble me with their grace and love.

Rocco and Gio, who grant me the courage to try to live and write as honestly as I am able (and who insisted I keep the original title). They teach me more than they can know.

ABOUT THE AUTHOR

Karen Rinaldi is the publisher of Harper Wave, an imprint she founded in 2012, and a senior vice president at Harper-Collins Publishers. While she has worked in the publishing industry for more than two decades as a publisher, editor, and content creator, this is her first time in the role of novelist. *The End of Men* inspired the 2016 film *Maggie's Plan*. Karen's non-fiction work has appeared on Oprah.com, in the *New York Times*, and *Prevention* magazine, among others. She and her family split their time between New York, New Jersey, and (whenever possible) Costa Rica.

About the author

About the book

Read on

Insights,
Interviews
& More . . .

What Is a Man For?

A version of this piece originally appeared in the New York Times's *Modern Love column on July 1, 2016. Used with permission.*

By the time I was thirty-three, I had already been married and divorced twice. There were no regrets. I loved each man I married and carry with me great affection for them still, even though the end of each union came with its own pain.

My first marriage fell apart when my husband's struggle with his sexual identity manifested itself in lies that eroded my trust and ultimately ended his life.

It was the early days of the AIDS epidemic. When he discovered he was HIV positive, he lied to me about his secret life with anonymous men and blamed his infection on my previous boyfriend.

He admitted the truth only after we received the good news that I had tested negative. I was tested every six months for the next two years and lived with the terror that I would seroconvert. We divorced, but he asked me to be the keeper of his tortured secret, and we remained close until the day he died, just before his thirty-third birthday.

I married my second husband after only one date. I had been so wrong about my first, I wondered: What would happen if I married someone I didn't know?

I was testing the universe.

He was handsome, strong, accomplished, and funny. But after a few years of dating backward (we married without knowing each other and spent the next three years becoming familiar and intimate), I realized I couldn't live with him. He was possessive, and my need for freedom didn't make for a secure marriage. He referred to me as "my wife" even when speaking to my own father.

Besides the two marriages, I cohabitated with two other men and dated others. A serial monogamist, I found that at every turn I was constrained by issues of, well, maleness. There was a kind of inherent dominance that tipped the balance of power away from me, and I often felt I was playing a role.

Money was often a factor in these early relationships, and eventually I came to believe in these unassailable truths:

1. If the man made more money, then you were doing things his way.
2. If he was broke, he resented your ability to support him.
3. If there was economic parity, he made sure you knew who was really the boss.

Once, when I was breaking up with a long-term boyfriend, my therapist asked me why I was anxious. "Is it because you are afraid you will be alone?" he asked.

"No," I told him. "It's the opposite. I am afraid we'll break up and there will be another right behind him."

My mother tried to figure it out as well. "Why have you had so many failed relationships?" she asked.

"You see them as failed," I told her. "I see them as successful, but finite."

It was the finite part that felt most right. At the time, she had been married to my father for sixty years, which some may call successful. While I love my parents dearly and respect their endurance, I didn't want to repeat their dynamic.

She had a lifelong fear that he would cheat on her. He ▶

What Is a Man For? *(continued)*

monitored all of her spending. He had a social life outside of the house, but she didn't do anything without him. Their marriage was based on an age-old patriarchy, and they didn't see anything wrong with it. I did not wish to live my life similarly.

Once my second husband moved out, I was resolute about never getting married again. I bought myself a coveted band of gold with sapphires from my favorite jeweler that I put on my left ring finger and wear it to this day.

I cherished living in my Greenwich Village apartment alone; lovers could come and go as I pleased. There were no schedules or egos to contend with. I was happy. Resolved only to having children, I needed a plan.

I was already supporting myself. I figured I would manage as well with a child, so the idea of being provided for was moot. Besides, I preferred having my own money and, therefore, my own agency.

The notion of protection was not only outdated and unnecessary, but it was an idea that had failed more than it had succeeded, both historically—men have never really been able to protect women from other men—and personally. As far as procreation, I needed a second gamete and I would be on my way to motherhood.

I called a friend and asked, "What's a man for, really? If not to provide, protect, or procreate, why do we need them? Face it, it's the end of men."

She laughed and admitted it was

a confusing time. After many long conversations with her, I decided to conceive with a willing gay friend and committed to being a single parent. The only questions he and I had to decide on were: To baste or not to baste? Or do it the old-fashioned way?

Because life does not work according to plan, I then fell in love—most inconveniently—with a man who was married and had a family. We had grown close as confidants. As a friend, he told me about the problems in his marriage and difficulties in his career as a writer. I told him of my frustration with coupledom and my plans to parent alone.

His marriage was initially a welcome barrier to the possibility of a romantic relationship. Once we became lovers, he told me he didn't want me to have a child with my gay friend. Instead, he wanted me to have a child with him and share our lives together. An affair I had blithely entered into had just turned messy and emotionally wrought.

That shouldn't have come as a surprise: What affair isn't messy and emotionally wrought? But it shattered my sense of certitude about what I wanted. I had finally shaken the binds of convention that I had been raised to accept. Now this.

My father interjected this time and asked, "Why do you make your life so complicated?"

I objected only to the word "make." I wasn't trying to complicate things; ▶

What Is a Man For? *(continued)*

I was trying to simplify them by figuring out something essential that eluded me. What did I need a man for?

Clearly I kept coming back around to that strong pull, one I couldn't reason away. Was it an atavistic urge? An evolutionary imperative? I didn't buy that.

Still, my attraction to men and my desire for a deeper connection with a partner was as unavoidable as my need to breathe. I loved living life by following my own compass, and yet somehow this had entangled me in a monogamous relationship again, one with major consequences.

I still had doubts that women and men could live together in anything approaching harmony. We had a long way to go to become equals, both in the world and in the home.

And the historical and political implications were personal for me. I was certain of three things: I didn't want a husband, I did want a child, and I wasn't sure how it all stacked up.

Twenty years and two children later, I am still with that same man. I don't need him, but I want him in my life. He doesn't protect me from others, only from my worst instincts. And as far as procreating, well, we did it the old-fashioned way and that will never get old. When I made him promise never to propose marriage, he said, "Okay . . ."

Ironically, six or seven years into our relationship, our accountant persuaded us to head to city hall. Marrying allowed us to capture the tax benefits that marriage confers.

My husband and I still don't know the year and date of our civil ceremony without consulting our marriage certificate—wherever that is. We have shared the joys of raising our two sons and his two daughters with balance and grace—except, of course, when we have failed to find either balance or grace. But we have muddled through.

I go to work every day and he stays home to write. He does laundry and cooks during the week. I do the same on the weekends. He takes care of our home. I pay the bills.

He is comfortable in his masculinity and doesn't need to remind me of who is boss, because in our relationship there isn't one. Our lives are shared at every level, and I realize now what a man is for.

He is a true partner. He is a lover and a friend. He is the father of my children and the only one in the world who cares about the minutiae of their lives like I do.

What could be better than that? 〜

The Story Behind
The End of Men

The seeds of this novel were sown fifteen years ago on the infertile grounds of the New Jersey Transit bus system. On the two-and-a-half-hour commute to a job I loved as an editor, my mind would often wander to consider the life I had designed for myself: fulfilled professional, mother of two young sons, partnered with a man I loved. *The End of Men* came from the stories I wrote on that commute as a way of honoring my many friends who were living similar, hectic lives. We were pushing at the boundaries of accomplishment—breadwinners and mothers, living life according to our own rules—with all of the conflict that portends. Yet I didn't see any of our stories represented in the media.

Isabel, Anna, Beth, and Maggie became composites of all of the remarkable and complex women I knew and loved. Their stories became a draft of a novel, and then . . . I put the manuscript in the drawer. But my characters continued to live fully in my mind. I would often take the novel out and tinker with it—to spend time on the page with these women—but the demands of my life pushed writing to the backseat of more immediate demands.

More than a decade later, my friend, director Rebecca Miller and I were watching our sons at fencing lessons. Rebecca was looking for material for a new film. I told her the story of a woman named Maggie, who decides to give her husband back to his first wife—a plotline from *The End of Men.* "What is that?" Rebecca asked. "I love it! I want it to be my next movie."

More than four years later, in May 2016, Rebecca's wonderful film *Maggie's Plan* released into theaters, and my novel was pulled out of the drawer. Now, after nearly thirty years of being a publisher and an editor, I find myself on the other side of the desk, humbled and schooled by the very profession on which I have built my career. And I am thoroughly enjoying the process!

A decade and a half ago, I was trying to get to something essential about being a woman in today's world. And while the ground keeps shifting—for the better, I think (and thank goodness!)—I hope to add a voice to the sometimes insane, often wonderful, and equally challenging lives of the women, both real and fictional, I hold so dearly. ∽

The Day I Was Stronger Than I Ever Thought Possible

*Excerpt courtesy of Oprah.com.
Used with permission.*

My best wave ever wasn't particularly elegant. It wasn't the biggest I'd ever made, and it certainly wasn't the fastest. It was a soft little peeler I surfed alongside my fifteen-year-old son, Rocco, one blessed July morning. It had been five months since I'd been in the water.

At the start of that same year, I had been diagnosed with cancer. My doctors had found an aggressive, invasive tumor in my left breast. Three lumpectomies over the course of the next two months resulted in questionable margins. We decided to treat the cancer systemically with chemotherapy before dealing with the localized DCIS (ductal carcinoma in situ) cells stubbornly residing in my breast.

When I was about to enter my sixth and final round of chemo, we found a second tumor. Between the double threats of the residual DCIS and the appearance of the new tumor, my doctors and I decided to do a mastectomy right away. We will never know if the second tumor was missed in the original diagnosis or if it broke through the chemo—though I prefer to believe the former, as the latter does not bode well for my future.

In either case, the treatment I'd endured was determined ineffectual, so I would have to undergo another protocol of chemo—different drugs, more aggressive—once I recovered from the mastectomy. I had a two-week respite between the end of the first failed protocol and the mastectomy plus subsequent chemo—enough time to get in at least one surf session before being land-bound for another four or five months.

Not much had gone right all year, but on that beautiful New Jersey July day with perfect, light offshore winds grooming small swell lines of thigh-high wave faces, the universe would conspire to make everything right again, if only momentarily. Rocco and I paddled out through the green Atlantic water together. He stroked easily through gutless white water and was sitting on his board in the lineup (just beyond where the waves break) a minute or two later. I struggled: arms powerless, heart pounding, lungs heavy. *My goodness,* I thought, *this year has kicked my ass.* I couldn't do it. Choking back a sob, I turned my sleek white nine-foot-three Jim Phillips single-fin board around to head back to shore. My inner voice nagged, *There is no way you can do this.* As I reached shallow water near the shoreline, I suddenly saw myself as my son might have seen me from the lineup. I looked defeated.

Instead of hiking my board out of the water, I swung it back around to face the small crashing waves. I put my head down (which you never do in the ocean, but even holding my head up took energy I didn't have) and paddled with every bit of juice left in my body. I pushed through past the break. When I paddled up to Rocco, heaving from the effort, he just smiled at me and said, "You made it," before deftly turning and paddling into a wave.

I have to admit: I am blessed with an incredibly generous teenager who doesn't mind surfing with his middle-aged mother. We started when Rocco was four and I was forty. In the beginning, we both stayed on the inside, where we would get pushed by the white water to shore. I would position and push him into waves until he was strong enough to propel himself. When I began to paddle out to catch a few open faces, I would keep watch over him in the white water from beyond the break. When he was very young, he would cry out in fear for my safety ▸

if I stayed out too long, or if the current pulled me too far north or south beyond his sight line.

Then one day, when he was thirteen, I was taken completely by surprise to find Rocco in the lineup. He'd never been past the break before, and it terrified me that he'd gotten there without my knowledge of his effort. I'd thought he'd gone back to shore already. "How the hell did you get out here?" I asked when he paddled up beside me. "I thought you went in!"

"It took me half an hour, but I made it." He was very proud, and so was I. From that day forward, we paddled out together.

This summer, the tide has now turned. I watch him duck-dive and paddle through enormous breaking waves, and drop into bombs I do everything to avoid. When the waves get too heavy for me, I will surf on the inside, while he heads for the horizon in hopes of catching a big one. It still takes every ounce of faith to not panic when he disappears into the swell, or with the pull of the drifting current.

On the day that I caught the best wave of my life, Rocco's smile as I approached the lineup gave me more confidence than he can possibly understand.

One wave was all I needed.

After bobbing in the surf with my boy for a half hour, a sweet little swell line came my way. I swung my board around to face shore, and saw Rocco to my left. It was his wave; he was closer to the peak. Surfing etiquette dictates that you cede to the person in best position. If it had been anyone else, I would have given the surfer the right of way, but I put etiquette aside in favor of sharing a wave with my son, hoping I wouldn't kook out and blow it for him. I paddled harder than seemed necessary to catch the waist-high bump and caught the energy of the wave, which lifted and pushed me forward as I popped up, turned, and glided along in perfect trim. The wave was slow and forgiving, the ocean uncharacteristically merciful. Rocco slid just twenty feet ahead of me. The two of us rode along until the wave unfolded onto the shore. He kicked out the back of the wave while I tumbled off the board into the white water.

Breathless from the beauty of that moment—and from the physical effort—I wept as I headed back out to the lineup. I didn't catch another wave during that session, and it was more than four months before I ventured back into the ocean.

In my treatment, the worst was yet to come. While recovering from the mastectomy that would compromise the entire left side of my torso, I endured another two months of brutal chemotherapy—a protocol unaffectionately known as the "red devil." When I was too sick to work, or too tired to move, I would close my eyes and ride that one wave with Rocco over and over again. I ride it still, each time I visit the doctor or paddle out, trying to find peace in the mystery of where the next wave will take me. ∾